13.00

More praise for Charles Baxter's *A Relative Stranger*

"Baxter orchestrates the details of mundane day-to-day reality into surprising patterns of grace and revelation. . . . We finish the book with the satisfaction of having been immersed in a beautifully rendered and fully imagined world."

—Michiko Kakutani, *New York Times*

"Charles Baxter just gets better and better."   —Ann Beattie

"Without question, Charles Baxter is among our best contemporary writers, always graceful, always dramatic in the very highest sense, and *A Relative Stranger* will make his literary star shine all the brighter. These stories are powerful, heartfelt, and beautifully told. Superlatives are insufficient. Here is literature. Here is art."

—Tim O'Brien

"*A Relative Stranger* is an extraordinary demonstration of Charles Baxter's virtuosity as a writer. This is art that is profoundly disruptive, completely original and *necessary*, and as such it is both valuable and beautiful."   —Richard Bausch

"[*A Relative Stranger*] gives another boost to [Charles Baxter's] reputation as one of the best and brightest practitioners of the short story. . . . A major book."   —*Choice*

"He can break your heart with the smallest turn of his precise unflinching prose."   —Paul Auster

"Like William Trevor and Raymond Carver, Baxter has the special gift of capturing the shadow of genuine significance as it flits across the face of the ordinary."   —Ted Solotaroff, *The Nation*

"Thirteen stories, many set in the Midwest, by an author with perfect fictional pitch."

—*Boston Globe* (New and Recommended)

"The magnificence of this collection . . . refreshes a reader with its quiet and ultimately uplifting insistence that strangers can lend a hand and do make a difference."   —*Washington Post Book World*

"Baxter writes so well that these stories, like some miracle literary supersolvent, silently slip through your skin. . . . Charles Baxter touches you with uncanny precision. That kind of talent is hard to find in America."   —*Tallahassee Democrat*

BY CHARLES BAXTER

FICTION

The Feast of Love

Believers

Shadow Play

A Relative Stranger

First Light

Through the Safety Net

Harmony of the World

POETRY

Imaginary Paintings

ESSAYS

Burning Down the House

A Relative Stranger

STORIES

Charles Baxter

W. W. Norton & Company

New York / London

The text of this book is composed in 12/13.5 Bembo,
with the display set in Garamond No. 3.
Composition and manufacturing by the Haddon Craftsmen, Inc.
Book and ornament design by Margaret M. Wagner.

First published as a Norton paperback 2001

Library of Congress Cataloging-in-Publication Data
Baxter, Charles, 1947–
A relative stranger : stories / Charles Baxter.
p.   cm.
I. Title.
PS3552.A8543R4   1990
813'.54—dc20   89-49371

ISBN 0-393-02867-4
ISBN 0-393-32220-3 pbk.

W. W. Norton & Company, Inc.
500 Fifth Avenue, New York, N.Y. 10110
www.wwnorton.com

W. W. Norton & Company Ltd.
Castle House, 75/76 Wells Street, London W1T 3QT

1 2 3 4 5 6 7 8 9 0

FOR DANIEL

Contents

Fenstad's Mother
3

Westland
19

Prowlers
43

A Relative Stranger
61

Shelter
79

Snow
99

Silent Movie
113

The Old Fascist in Retirement
119

THREE PARABOLIC TALES

1 / Lake Stephen
135

2 / Scissors
145

3 / Scheherazade
155

/ /

The Disappeared
161

Saul and Patsy Are Pregnant
191

Acknowledgments

The stories in this collection appeared in the following magazines and anthologies: The Atlantic, *"Fenstad's Mother"*; Denver Quarterly, *"The Old Fascist in Retirement"*; The Georgia Review, *"Shelter"*; Grand Street, *"Prowlers"*; Harper's, *"Scheherazade"*; Indiana Review, *"A Relative Stranger" (published as "How I Found My Brother")*; The Iowa Review, *"Saul and Patsy Are Pregnant"*; Michigan Quarterly Review, *"The Disappeared"*; The New Yorker, *"Snow"*; The Paris Review, *"Westland"*; PEN Syndicated Fiction, *"Lake Stephen"*; Story, *"Scissors."*

"Fenstad's Mother" appeared in Best American Short Stories 1989; *"A Relative Stranger"* appeared in Best American Short Stories 1987; *"Westland"* appeared in Pushcart Prize XIV; *"Shelter"* appeared in Louder Than Words: 22 Writers Donate Stories to Benefit Share Our Strength's Fight Against Hunger, Homelessness, and Illiteracy.

"Silent Movie" calls upon several lines from "Tulips" in Ariel *by Sylvia Plath (Harper & Row, 1966).*

"Fenstad's Mother" is in memory of Helen Baxter. "The Disappeared" is for Alvin Greenberg. "Westland" is for Janet Kauffman.

A RELATIVE
STRANGER

Fenstad's Mother

ON SUNDAY morning after communion Fenstad drove across town to visit his mother. Behind the wheel, he exhaled with his hand flat in front of his mouth to determine if the wine on his breath could be detected. He didn't think so. Fenstad's mother was a lifelong social progressive who was amused by her son's churchgoing, and, wine or no wine, she could guess where he had been. She had spent her life in the company of rebels and deviationists, and she recognized all their styles.

Passing a frozen pond in the city park, Fenstad slowed down to watch the skaters, many of whom he knew by name and skating style. From a distance they were dots of color ready for flight, frictionless. To express grief on skates seemed almost impossible, and Fenstad liked that. He parked his car on a residential block and took out his skates from the back seat, where he kept them all winter. With his fingertips he touched the wooden blade guards, thinking of the time. He checked his watch; he had fifteen minutes.

Out on the ice, still wearing his churchy Sunday-morning suit, tie, and overcoat, but now

3

circling the outside edge of the pond with his bare hands in his overcoat pockets, Fenstad admired the overcast sky and luxuriated in the brittle cold. He was active and alert in winter but felt sleepy throughout the summer. He passed a little girl in a pink jacket, pushing a tiny chair over the ice. He waved to his friend Ann, an off-duty cop, practicing her twirls. He waved to other friends. Without exception they waved back. As usual, he was impressed by the way skates improved human character.

Twenty minutes later, in the doorway of her apartment, his mother said, "Your cheeks are red." She glanced down at his trousers, damp with melted snow. "You've been skating." She kissed him on the cheek and turned to walk into her living room. "Skating after church? Isn't that some sort of doctrinal error?"

"It's just happiness," Fenstad said. Quickly he checked her apartment for any signs of memory loss or depression. He found none and immediately felt relief. The apartment smelled of soap and Lysol, the signs of an old woman who wouldn't tolerate nonsense. Out on her coffee table, as usual, were the letters she was writing to her congressman and to political dictators around the globe. Fenstad's mother pleaded for enlightened behavior and berated the dictators for their bad political habits.

She grasped the arm of the sofa and let herself down slowly. Only then did she smile. "How's your soul, Harry?" she asked. "What's the news?"

He smiled back and smoothed his hair. Martin Luther King's eyes locked into his from the framed picture on the wall opposite him. In the picture King was shaking hands with Fenstad's mother, the two of them surrounded by smiling faces. "My soul's okay, Ma," he said. "It's a hard project. I'm always working on it." He reached down for a chocolate-chunk cookie from a box on top of the television. "Who brought you these?"

"Your daughter Sharon. She came to see me on Friday." Fenstad's mother tilted her head at him. "You *want* to be a good person, but she's the real article. Goodness comes to her without any effort at all. She says you have a new girlfriend. A pharmacist this time. Susan, is it?" Fenstad nodded. "Harry, why does your generation always have to find the right person? Why can't you learn to live with the wrong person? Sooner or later everyone's wrong. Love isn't the most important thing, Harry, far from it. Why can't you see that? I still don't comprehend why you couldn't live with Eleanor." Eleanor was Fenstad's ex-wife. They had been divorced for a decade, but Fenstad's mother hoped for a reconciliation.

"Come on, Ma," Fenstad said. "Over and done with, gone and gone." He took another cookie.

"You live with somebody so that you're living with *somebody,* and then you go out and do the work of the world. I don't understand all this pickiness about lovers. In a pinch anybody'll do, Harry, believe me."

On the side table was a picture of her late husband, Fenstad's mild, middle-of-the-road father. Fenstad glanced at the picture and let the silence hang between them before asking, "How are you, Ma?"

"I'm all right." She leaned back in the sofa, whose springs made a strange, almost human groan. "I want to get out. I spend too much time in this place in January. You should expand my horizons. Take me somewhere."

"Come to my composition class," Fenstad said. "I'll pick you up at dinnertime on Tuesday. Eat early."

"They'll notice me," she said, squinting. "I'm too old."

"I'll introduce you," her son said. "You'll fit right in."

FENSTAD wrote brochures in the publicity department of a computer company during the day, and taught an extension English-composition class at the downtown campus of the state university two nights a week. He didn't need the money; he taught the class because he liked teaching strangers and because he enjoyed the sense of hope that classrooms held for him. This hopefulness and didacticism he had picked up from his mother.

On Tuesday night she was standing at the door of the retirement apartment building, dressed in a dark blue overcoat—her best. Her stylishness was belied slightly by a pair of old fuzzy red earmuffs. Inside the car Fenstad noticed that she had put on perfume, unusual for her. Leaning back, she gazed out contentedly at the nighttime lights.

"Who's in this group of students?" she asked. "Working-class people, I hope. Those are the ones you should be teaching. Anything else is just a career."

"Oh, they work, all right." He looked at his mother and saw, as they passed under a streetlight, a combination of sadness and delicacy in her face. Her usual mask of tough optimism seemed to be deserting her. He braked at a red light and said, "I have a hairdresser and a garage mechanic and a housewife, a Mrs. Nelson, and three guys who're sanitation workers. Plenty of others. One guy you'll really like is a young black man with glasses who sits in the back row and reads *Workers' Vanguard* and Bakunin during class. He's brilliant. I don't know why he didn't test out of this class. His name's York Follette, and he's—"

"I want to meet him," she said quickly. She scowled at the moonlit snow. "A man with ideas. People like that have gone out of my life." She looked over at her son. "What I hate about being my age is how *nice* everyone tries to be. I was never nice, but now everybody is pelting me with sugar cubes." She opened her window an inch and let the cold air blow over her, ruffling her stiff gray hair.

WHEN they arrived at the school, snow had started to fall, and at the other end of the parking lot a police car's flashing light beamed long crimson rays through the dense flakes. Fenstad's mother walked deliberately toward the door, shaking her head mistrustfully at the building and the police. Approaching the steps, she took her son's hand. "I liked the columns on the old buildings," she said, "the old university buildings, I mean. I liked

Greek Revival better than this Modernist-bunker stuff." Inside, she blinked in the light at the smooth, waxed linoleum floors and cement-block walls. She held up her hand to shade her eyes. Fenstad took her elbow to guide her over the snow melting in puddles in the entryway. "I never asked you what you're teaching tonight."

"Logic," Fenstad said.

"Ah." She smiled and nodded. "Dialectics!"

"Not quite. Just logic."

She shrugged. She was looking at the clumps of students standing in the glare of the hallway, drinking coffee from paper cups and smoking cigarettes in the general conversational din. She wasn't used to such noise: she stopped in the middle of the corridor underneath a wall clock and stared happily in no particular direction. With her eyes shut she breathed in the close air, smelling of wet overcoats and smoke, and Fenstad remembered how much his mother had always liked smoke-filled rooms, where ideas fought each other, and where some of those ideas died.

"Come on," he said, taking her hand again. Inside Fenstad's classroom six people sat in the angular postures of pre-boredom. York Follette was already in the back row, his copy of *Workers' Vanguard* shielding his face. Fenstad's mother headed straight for him and sat down in the desk next to his. Fenstad saw them shake hands, and in two minutes they were talking in low, rushed murmurs. He saw York Follette laugh quietly and nod. What was it that blacks saw and appreciated in his mother? They had always liked her—written to her, called her, checked up on her—and Fenstad wondered if they recognized something in his mother that he himself had never been able to see.

At seven thirty-five most of the students had arrived and were talking to each other vigorously, as if they didn't want Fenstad to start and thought they could delay him. He stared at them, and when they wouldn't quiet down, he made himself rigid and said, "Good evening. We have a guest tonight." Immediately the class grew silent. He held his arm out straight, indicating with a flick of his hand the old woman in the back row. "My mother," he said. "Clara Fenstad." For the first time all semester his students appeared to be paying attention: they turned around collectively and looked at Fenstad's mother, who smiled and waved. A few of the students began to applaud; others joined in. The applause was quiet but apparently genuine. Fenstad's mother brought herself slowly to her feet and made a suggestion of a bow. Two of the students sitting in front of her turned around and began to talk to her. At the front of the class Fenstad started his lecture on logic, but his mother wouldn't quiet down. This was a class for adults. They were free to do as they liked.

Lowering his head and facing the blackboard, Fenstad reviewed problems in logic, following point by point the outline set down by the textbook: *post hoc* fallacies, false authorities, begging the question, circular reasoning, *ad hominem* arguments, all the rest. Explaining these problems, his back turned, he heard sighs of boredom, boldly expressed. Occasionally he glanced at the back of the room. His mother was watching him carefully, and her face was expressing all the complexity of dismay. Dismay radiated from her. Her disappointment wasn't personal, because his mother didn't think that people as individuals were at fault for what they did. As usual, her disappointed hope was located in history and in the way people agreed with already existing histories.

She was angry with him for collaborating with grammar. She would call it unconsciously installed authority. Then she would find other names for it.

"All right," he said loudly, trying to make eye contact with someone in the room besides his mother, "let's try some examples. Can anyone tell me what, if anything, is wrong with the following sentence? 'I, like most people, have a unique problem.' "

The three sanitation workers, in the third row, began to laugh. Fenstad caught himself glowering and singled out the middle one.

"Yes, it is funny, isn't it?"

The man in the middle smirked and looked at the floor. "I was just thinking of my unique problem."

"Right," Fenstad said. "But what's wrong with saying, 'I, like most people, have a unique problem'?"

"Solving it?" This was Mrs. Nelson, who sat by the window so that she could gaze at the tree outside, lit by a streetlight. All through class she looked at the tree as if it were a lover.

"Solving what?"

"Solving the problem you have. What is the problem?"

"That's actually not what I'm getting at," Fenstad said. "Although it's a good *related* point. I'm asking what might be wrong logically with that sentence."

"It depends," Harold Ronson said. He worked in a service station and sometimes came to class wearing his work shirt with his name tag, HAROLD, stitched into it. "It depends on what your problem is. You haven't told us your problem."

"No," Fenstad said, "my problem is *not* the problem." He thought of Alice in Wonderland and felt, physically, as if he himself were getting small. "Let's try this again. What might be wrong with saying that most people have a unique problem?"

"You shouldn't be so critical," Timothy Melville said. "You should look on the bright side, if possible."

"What?"

"He's right," Mrs. Nelson said. "Most people have unique problems, but many people do their best to help themselves, such as taking night classes or working at meditation."

"No doubt that's true," Fenstad said. "But why can't most people have a unique problem?"

"Oh, I disagree," Mrs. Nelson said, still looking at her tree. Fenstad glanced at it and saw that it was crested with snow. It *was* beautiful. No wonder she looked at it. "I believe that most people do have unique problems. They just shouldn't talk about them all the time."

"Can anyone," Fenstad asked, looking at the back wall and hoping to see something there that was not wall, "can anyone give me an example of a unique problem?"

"Divorce," Barb Kjellerud said. She sat near the door and knitted during class. She answered questions without looking up. "Divorce is unique."

"No, it isn't!" Fenstad said, failing in the crucial moment to control his voice. He and his mother exchanged glances. In his mother's face for a split second was the history of her compassionate, ambivalent attention to him. "Divorce is not unique." He waited to calm himself. "It's everywhere. Now try again. Give me a unique problem."

Silence. "This is a trick question," Arlene Hubbly said. "I'm sure it's a trick question."

"Not necessarily. Does anyone know what *unique* means?"

"One of a kind," York Follette said, gazing at Fenstad with dry amusement. Sometimes he took pity on Fenstad and helped him out of jams. Fenstad's mother smiled and nodded.

"Right," Fenstad crowed, racing toward the blackboard as if he were about to write something. "So let's try again. Give me a unique problem."

"You give *us* a unique problem," one of the sanitation workers said. Fenstad didn't know whether he'd been given a statement or a command. He decided to treat it as a command.

"All right," he said. He stopped and looked down at his shoes. Maybe it *was* a trick question. He thought for ten seconds. Problem after problem presented itself to him. He thought of poverty, of the assaults on the earth, of the awful complexities of love. "I can't think of one," Fenstad said. His hands went into his pockets.

"That's because problems aren't personal," Fenstad's mother said from the back of the room. "They're collective." She waited while several students in the class sat up and nodded. "And people must work together on their solutions." She talked for another two minutes, taking the subject out of logic and putting it neatly in politics, where she knew it belonged.

THE SNOW had stopped by the time the class was over. Fenstad took his mother's arm and escorted her to the car. After letting her down on the passenger side and starting the engine, he began to clear the front windshield. He didn't have a scraper and had forgotten his gloves, so he was using his bare hands. When he brushed the snow away on his mother's side, she looked out at him, surprised, a terribly aged Sleeping Beauty awakened against her will.

Once the car had warmed up, she was in a gruff mood and repositioned herself under the seat belt while making quiet but aggressive remarks. The sight of the new snow didn't seem to calm her. "Logic," she said at last. "That wasn't logic. Those are just rhetorical tactics. It's filler and drudgery."

"I don't want to discuss it now."

"All right. I'm sorry. Let's talk about something more pleasant."

They rode together in silence. Then she began to shake her head. "Don't take me home," she said. "I want to have a spot of tea somewhere before I go back. A nice place where they serve tea, all right?"

He parked outside an all-night restaurant with huge front plate-glass windows; it was called Country Bob's. He held his mother's elbow from the car to the door. At the door, looking back to make sure that he had turned off his headlights, he saw his tracks and his mother's in the snow. His were separate footprints, but hers formed two long lines.

Inside, at the table, she sipped her tea and gazed at her son for a long time. "Thanks for the adventure, Harry. I do appreciate it. What're you doing in class next week? Oh, I remember. How-to papers. That should be interesting."

"Want to come?"

"Very much. I'll keep quiet next time, if you want me to."

Fenstad shook his head. "It's okay. It's fun having you along. You can say whatever you want. The students loved you. I knew you'd be a sensation, and you were. They'd probably rather have you teaching the class than me."

He noticed that his mother was watching something going on behind him, and Fenstad turned around in the booth so that he could see what it was. At first all he saw was a woman, a young woman with long hair wet from snow and hanging in clumps, talking in the aisle to two young men, both of whom were nodding at her. Then she moved on to the next table. She spoke softly. Fenstad couldn't hear her words, but he saw the solitary customer to whom she was speaking shake his head once, keeping his eyes down. Then the woman saw Fenstad and his mother. In a moment she was standing in front of them.

She wore two green plaid flannel shirts and a thin torn jacket. Like Fenstad, she wore no gloves. Her jeans were patched, and she gave off a strong smell, something like hay, Fenstad thought, mixed with tar and sweat. He looked down at her feet and saw that she was wearing penny loafers with no socks. Coins, old pennies, were in both shoes; the leather was wet and cracked. He looked in the woman's face. Under a hat that seemed to collapse on either side of her head, the woman's face was thin and chalk-white except for the fatigue lines under her eyes. The eyes themselves were bright blue, beautiful, and crazy. To Fenstad, she looked desperate, percolating slightly with insanity, and he was about to say so to his mother when the woman bent down toward him and said, "Mister, can you spare any money?"

Involuntarily, Fenstad looked toward the kitchen, hoping that the manager would spot this person and take her away. When he looked back again, his mother was taking her blue coat off, wriggling in the booth to free her arms from the sleeves. Stopping and starting again, she appeared to be stuck inside the coat; then she lifted herself up, trying to stand, and with a quick, quiet groan slipped the coat off. She reached down and folded the coat over and held it toward the woman. "Here," she said. "Here's my coat. Take it before my son stops me."

"Mother, you can't." Fenstad reached forward to grab the coat, but his mother pulled it away from him.

When Fenstad looked back at the woman, her mouth was open, showing several gray teeth. Her hands were outstretched, and he understood, after a moment, that this was a posture of refusal, a gesture saying no, and that the woman wasn't used to it and did it awkwardly. Fenstad's mother was standing and trying to push the coat toward the woman, not toward her hands but lower, at waist level, and she was saying, "Here, here, here, here." The sound, like a human birdcall, frightened Fenstad, and he stood up quickly, reached for his wallet, and removed the first two bills he could find, two twenties. He grabbed the woman's chapped, ungloved left hand.

"Take these," he said, putting the two bills in her icy palm, "for the love of God, and please go."

He was close to her face. Tonight he would pray for her. For a moment the woman's expression was vacant. His mother was still pushing the coat at her, and the woman was unsteadily bracing herself. The woman's mouth was open, and her stagnant-water breath washed over him. "I know you," she said. "You're my little baby cousin."

"Go away, please," Fenstad said. He pushed at her. She turned, clutching his money. He reached around to put his hands on his mother's shoulders. "Ma," he said, "she's gone now. Mother, sit down. I gave her money for a coat." His mother fell down on her side of the booth, and her blue coat rolled over on the bench beside her, showing the label and the shiny inner lining. When he looked up, the woman who had been begging had disappeared, though he could still smell her odor, an essence of wretchedness.

"Excuse me, Harry," his mother said. "I have to go to the bathroom."

She rose and walked toward the front of the restaurant, turned a corner, and was out of sight. Fenstad sat and tried to collect himself. When the waiter came, a boy with an earring and red hair in a flattop, Fenstad just shook his head and said, "More tea." He realized that his mother hadn't taken off her earmuffs, and the image of his mother in the ladies' room with her earmuffs on gave him a fit of uneasiness. After getting up from the booth and following the path that his mother had taken, he stood outside the ladies'-room door and, when no one came in or out, he knocked. He waited for a decent interval. Still hearing no answer, he opened the door.

His mother was standing with her arms down on either side of the first sink. She was holding herself there, her eyes following the hot water as it poured from the tap around the bright porcelain sink down into the drain, and she looked furious. Fenstad touched her and she snapped toward him.

"Your logic!" she said.

He opened the door for her and helped her back to the booth. The second cup of tea had been served, and Fenstad's mother sipped it in silence. They did not converse. When she had finished, she said, "All right. I do feel better now. Let's go."

At the curb in front of her apartment building he leaned forward and kissed her on the cheek. "Pick me up next Tuesday," she said. "I want to go back to that class." He nodded. He watched as she made her way past the security guard at the front desk; then he put his car into drive and started home.

That night he skated in the dark for an hour with his friend, Susan, the pharmacist. She was an excellent skater; they had met on the ice. She kept late hours and, like Fenstad, enjoyed skating at night. She listened attentively to his story about his mother and the woman in the restaurant. To his great relief she recommended no course of action. She listened. She didn't believe in giving advice, even when asked.

THE FOLLOWING TUESDAY, Fenstad's mother was again in the back row next to York Follette. One of the fluorescent lights overhead was flickering, which gave the room, Fenstad thought, a sinister quality, like a debtors' prison or a refuge for the homeless. He'd been thinking about such people for the entire week. For seven days now he had caught whiffs of the woman's breath in the air, and one morning, Friday, he thought he caught a touch of the rotten-celery smell on his own breath, after a particularly difficult sales meeting.

Tonight was how-to night. The students were expected to stand at the front of the class and read their papers, instructing their peers and answering questions if necessary. Starting off, and reading her paper in a frightened monotone, Mrs. Nelson told the class how to bake a cheese soufflé. Arlene Hubbly's paper was about mushroom hunting. Fenstad was put off by the introduction. "The advantage to mushrooms," Arlene Hubbly read, "is that they are delicious. The disadvantage to mushrooms is that they can make you sick, even die." But then she explained how to recognize the common shaggymane by its cylindrical cap and dark tufts; she drew a model on the board. She warned the class against the *Clitocybe illudens,* the Jack-o'-Lantern. "Never eat a mushroom like this one or *any* mushroom that glows in the dark. Take heed!" she said, fixing her gaze on the class. Fenstad saw his mother taking rapid notes. Harold Ronson, the mechanic, reading his own prose painfully and slowly, told the class how to get rust spots out of their automobiles. Again Fenstad noticed his mother taking notes. York Follette told the class about the proper procedures for laying down attic insulation and how to know when enough was enough, so that a homeowner wouldn't be robbed blind, as he put it, by the salesmen, in whose ranks he had once counted himself.

Barb Kjellerud had brought along a cassette player, and told the class that her hobby was ballroom dancing; she would instruct them in the basic waltz. She pushed the play button on the tape machine, and "Tales from the Vienna Woods" came booming out. To the accompaniment of the music she read her paper, illustrating, as she went, how the steps were to be performed. She danced alone in front of them, doing so with flair. Her blond hair swayed as she danced, Fenstad noticed. She looked a bit like a contestant in a beauty contest who had too much personality to win. She explained to the men the necessity of leading. Someone had to lead, she said, and tradition had given this responsibility to the male. Fenstad heard his mother snicker.

When Barb Kjellerud asked for volunteers, Fenstad's mother raised her hand. She said she knew how to waltz and would help out. At the front of the class she made a counterclockwise motion with her hand, and for the next minute, sitting at the back of the room, Fenstad watched his mother and one of the sanitation workers waltzing under the flickering fluorescent lights.

"WHAT a wonderful class," Fenstad's mother said on the way home. "I hope you're paying attention to what they tell you."

Fenstad nodded. "Tea?" he asked.

She shook her head. "Where're you going after you drop me off?"

"Skating," he said. "I usually go skating. I have a date."

"With the pharmacist? In the dark?"

"We both like it, Ma." As he drove, he made an all-purpose gesture. "The moon and the stars," he said simply.

When he left her off, he felt unsettled. He considered, as a point of courtesy, staying with her a few minutes, but by the time he had this idea he was already away from the building and was headed down the street.

HE AND SUSAN were out on the ice together, skating in large circles, when Susan pointed to a solitary figure sitting on a park bench near the lake's edge. The sky had cleared; the moon gave everything a cold, fine-edged clarity. When Fenstad followed the line of Susan's finger, he saw at once that the figure on the bench was his mother. He realized it simply because of the way she sat there, drawn into herself, attentive even in the winter dark. He skated through the uncleared snow over the ice until he was standing close enough to speak to her. "Mother," he said, "what are you doing here?"

She was bundled up, a thick woolen cap drawn over her head, and two scarves covering much of her face. He could see little other than the two lenses of her glasses facing him in the dark. "I wanted to see you two," she told him. "I thought you'd look happy, and you did. I like to watch happiness. I always have."

"How can you see us? We're so far away."

"That's how I saw you."

This made no sense to him, so he asked, "How'd you get here?"

"I took a cab. That part was easy."

"Aren't you freezing?"

"I don't know. I don't know if I'm freezing or not."

He and Susan took her back to her apartment as soon as they could get their boots on. In the car Mrs. Fenstad insisted on asking Susan what kind of safety procedures were used to ensure that drugs weren't smuggled out of pharmacies and sold illegally, but she didn't appear to listen to the answer, and by the time they reached her building, she seemed to be falling asleep. They helped her up to her apartment. Susan thought that they should give her a warm bath before putting her into bed, and, together, they did. She did not protest. She didn't even seem to notice them as they guided her in and out of the bathtub.

Fenstad feared that his mother would catch some lung infection, and it turned out to be bronchitis, which kept her in her apartment for the first three weeks of February, until her cough went down. Fenstad came by every other day to see how she was, and one Tuesday, after work, he went up to her floor and heard piano music: an old recording, which sounded much-played, of the brightest and fastest jazz piano he had ever heard—music of superhuman brilliance. He swung open the door to her apartment and saw York Follette sitting near his mother's bed. On the bedside table was a small tape player, from which the music poured into the room.

Fenstad's mother was leaning back against the pillow, smiling, her eyes closed.

Follette turned toward Fenstad. He had been talking softly. He motioned toward the tape machine and said, "Art Tatum. It's a cut called 'Battery Bounce.' Your mother's never heard it."

"Jazz, Harry," Fenstad's mother said, her eyes still closed, not needing to see her son. "York is explaining to me about Art Tatum and jazz. Next week he's going to try something more progressive on me." Now his mother opened her eyes. "Have you ever heard such music before, Harry?"

They were both looking at him. "No," he said, "I never heard anything like it."

"This is my unique problem, Harry." Fenstad's mother coughed and then waited to recover her breath. "I never heard enough jazz." She smiled. "What glimpses!" she said at last.

After she recovered, he often found her listening to the tape machine that York Follette had given her. She liked to hear the Oscar Peterson Trio as the sun set and the lights of evening came on. She now often mentioned glimpses. Back at home, every night, Fenstad spoke about his mother in his prayers of remembrance and thanksgiving, even though he knew she would disapprove.

Westland

SATURDAY morning at the zoo, facing the
lions' cage, overcast sky and a light breeze carrying the smell of peanuts and animal dung, the
peacocks making their stilted progress across the
sidewalks. I was standing in front of the gorge
separating the human viewers from the lions.
The lions weren't caged, exactly; they just
weren't free to go. One male and one female
were slumbering on fake rock ledges. Raw meat
was nearby. My hands were in my pockets and
I was waiting for a moment of energy so I could
leave and do my Saturday morning errands.
Then this girl, this teenager, appeared from behind me, hands in *her* pockets, and she stopped
a few feet away on my right. In an up-all-night
voice, she said, "What would you do if I shot
that lion?" She nodded her head: she meant the
male, the closer one.

"Shot it?"

"That's right."

"I don't know." Sometimes you have to
humor people, pretend as if they're talking about
something real. "Do you have a gun?"

"Of course I have a gun." She wore a protective blankness on her thin face. She was fixed on the lion. "I have it here in my pocket."

"I'd report you," I said. "I'd try to stop you. There are guards here. People don't shoot caged animals. You shouldn't even carry a concealed weapon, a girl your age."

"This is Detroit," she explained.

"I know it is," I said. "But people don't shoot caged lions in Detroit or anywhere else."

"It wouldn't be that bad," she said, nodding at the lions again. "You can tell from their faces how much they want to check out."

I said I didn't think so.

She turned to look at me. Her skin was so pale it seemed bleached, and she was wearing a vaudeville-length overcoat and a pair of hightop tennis shoes and jeans with slits at the knees. She looked like a fifteen-year-old bag lady. "It's because you're a disconnected person that you can't see it," she said. She shivered and reached into her pocket and pulled out a crumpled pack of cigarettes. "Lions are so human. Things get to them. They experience everything more than we do. They're romantic." She glanced at her crushed pack of cigarettes, and in a shivering motion she tossed it into the gorge. She swayed back and forth. "They want to kill and feast and feel," she said.

I looked at this girl's bleached skin, that candy-bar-and-cola complexion, and I said, "Are you all right?"

"I slept here last night," she said. She pointed vaguely behind her. "I was sleeping over there. Under those trees. Near the polar bears."

"Why'd you do that?"

"I wasn't alone *all* night." She was answering a question I hadn't asked. "This guy, he came in with me for a while to be nice and amorous but he couldn't see the point in staying. He split around midnight. He said it was righteous coming in here and being solid with the animal world, but he said you had to know when to stop. I told him I wouldn't defend him to his friends if he left, and he left, so as far as I'm concerned, he is over, he is zippo."

She was really shivering now, and she was huddling inside that long overcoat. I don't like to help strangers, but she needed help. "Are you hungry?" I asked. "You want a hamburger?"

"I'll eat it," she said, "but only if you buy it."

I took her to a fast-food restaurant and sat her down and brought her one of their famous giant cheeseburgers. She held it in her hands familiarly as she watched the cars passing on Woodward Avenue. I let my gaze follow hers, and when I looked back, half the cheeseburger was gone. She wasn't even chewing. She didn't look at the food. She ate like a soldier in a foxhole. What was left of her food she gripped in her skinny fingers decorated with flaking pink nail polish. She was pretty in a raw and sloppy way.

"You're looking at me."

"Yes, I am," I admitted.

"How come?"

"A person can look," I said.

"Maybe." Now she looked back. "Are you one of those creeps?"

"Which kind?"

"The kind of old man creep who picks up girls and drives them places, and, like, terrorizes them for days and then dumps them into fields."

"No," I said. "I'm not like that. And I'm not that old."

"Maybe it's the accent," she said. "You don't sound American."

"I was born in England," I told her, "but I've been in this country for thirty years. I'm an American citizen."

"You've got to be born in this country to sound American," she said, sucking at her chocolate shake through her straw. She was still gazing at the traffic. Looking at traffic seemed to restore her peace of mind. "I guess you're okay," she said distantly, "and I'm not worried anyhow, because, like I told you, I've got a gun."

"Oh yeah," I said.

"You're not a real American because you don't *believe!*" Then this child fumbled in her coat pocket and clunked down a small shiny handgun on the table, next to the plastic containers and the french fries. "So there," she said.

"Put it back," I told her. "Jesus, I hope the safety's on."

"I think so." She wiped her hand on a napkin and dropped the thing back into her pocket. "So tell me your name, Mr. Samaritan."

"Warren," I said. "My name's Warren. What's yours?"

"I'm Jaynee. What do you do, Warren? You must do something. You look like someone who does something."

I explained to her about governmental funding for social work and therapy, but her eyes glazed and she cut me off.

"Oh yeah," she said, chewing her french fries with her mouth open so that you could see inside if you wanted to. "One of those professional friends. I've seen people like you."

I drove her home. She admired the tape machine in the car and the carpeting on the floor. She gave me directions on how to get to her house in Westland, one of the suburbs. Detroit has four shopping centers at its cardinal points: Westland, Eastland, Southland, and Northland. A town grew up around Westland, a blue-collar area, and now Westland is the name of both the shopping center and the town.

She took me down fast-food alley and then through a series of right and left ninety-degree turns on streets with bungalows covered by aluminum siding. Few trees, not much green except the lawns, and the half-sun dropped onto those perpendicular lines with nothing to stop it or get in its way. The girl, Jaynee, picked at her knees and nodded, as if any one of the houses would do. The houses all looked exposed to me, with a straight shot at the elements out there on that flat grid.

I was going to drop her off at what she said was her driveway, but there was an old chrome-loaded Pontiac in the way, one of those vintage 1950s cars, its front end up on a hoist and some man working on his back on a rolling dolly underneath it. "That's him," the girl said. "You want to meet him?"

I parked the car and got out. The man pulled himself away from underneath the car and looked over at us. He stood up, wiping his hands on a rag, and scowled at his daughter. He wasn't going to look at me right away. I think he was checking Jaynee for signs of damage.

"What's this?" he asked. "What's this about, Jaynee?"

"This is about nothing," she said. "I spent the night in the zoo and this person found me and brought me home."

"At the zoo. Jesus Christ. At the zoo. Is that what happened?" He was asking me.

"That's where I saw her," I told him. "She looked pretty cold."

He dropped a screwdriver I hadn't noticed he was holding. He was standing there in his driveway next to the Pontiac, looking at his daughter and me and then at the sky. I'd had those moments, too, when nothing made any sense and I didn't know where my responsibilities lay. "Go inside," he told his daughter. "Take a shower. I'm not talking to you here on the driveway. I know that."

We both watched her go into the house. She looked like an overcoat with legs. I felt ashamed of myself for thinking of her that way, but there are some ideas you can't prevent.

We were both watching her, and the man said, "You can't go to the public library and find out how to raise a girl like that." He said something else, but an airplane passed so low above us that I couldn't hear him. We were about three miles from the airport. He ended his speech by saying, "I don't know who's right."

"I don't either."

"Earl Lampson." He held out his hand. I shook it and took away a feel of bone and grease and flesh. I could see a fading tattoo on his forearm of a rose run through with a sword.

"Warren Banks," I said. "I guess I'll have to be going."

"Wait a minute, Warren. Let me do two things. First, let me thank you for bringing my daughter home. Unhurt." I nodded to show I understood. "Second. A question. You got any kids?"

"Two," I said. "Both boys."

"Then you know about it. You know what a child can do to you. I was awake last night. I didn't know what had happened to her. I didn't know if she had planned it. That was the worst. She makes plans. Jesus Christ. The zoo. The lions?"

I nodded.

"She'll do anything. And it isn't an act with her." He looked up and down the street, as if he were waiting for something to appear, and I had the wild idea that I was going to see a float coming our way, with beauty queens on it, and little men dressed up in costumes.

I told him I had to leave. He shook his head.

"Stay a minute, Warren," he said. "Come into the backyard. I want to show you something."

He turned around and walked through the garage, past a pile of snow tires and two rusted-out bicycles. I followed him, thinking of my boys this morning at their Scout meeting, and of my wife, out shopping or maybe home by now and wondering vaguely where I was. I was supposed to be getting groceries. Here I was in this garage. She would look at the clock, do something else, then look back at the clock.

"Now how about this?" Earl pointed an index finger toward a wooden construction that stood in the middle of his yard, running from one side to another: a play structure, with monkey bars and a swing set, a high perch like a ship's crow's nest, a set of tunnels to crawl through and climb on, and a little rope bridge between two towers. I had never seen anything like it, so much human effort expended on a backyard toy, this huge contraption.

I whistled. "It must have taken you years."

"Eighteen months," he said. "And she hasn't played on it since she was twelve." He shook his head. "I bought the wood and put

it together piece by piece. She was only three years old when I
did it, weekends when I wasn't doing overtime at Ford's. She was
my assistant. She'd bring me nails. I told her to hold the hammer
when I wasn't using it, and she'd stand there, real serious, just
holding the hammer. Of course now she's too old for it. I have
the biggest backyard toy in Michigan and a daughter who goes
off to the zoo and spends the night there and that's her idea of
a good time."

A light rain had started to fall. "What are you going to do
with this thing?" I asked.

"Take it apart, I guess." He glanced at the sky. "Warren, you
want a beer?"

It was eleven o'clock in the morning. "Sure," I said.

WE SAT in silence on his cluttered back porch. We sipped our
beers and watched the rain fall over things in our line of sight.
Neither of us was saying much. It was better being there than
being at home, and my morning gloom was on its way out. It
wasn't lifting so much as converting into something else, as it
does when you're in someone else's house. I didn't want to move
as long as I felt that way.

I had been in the zoo that morning because I had been reading
the newspaper again, and this time I had read about a uranium
plant here in Michigan whose employees were spraying pasture-
land with a fertilizer recycled from radioactive wastes. They
called it treated raffinate. The paper said that in addition to trace
amounts of radium and radioactive thorium, this fertilizer spray
had at least eighteen poisonous heavy metals in it, including
molybdenum, arsenic, and lead. It had been sprayed out into the
pastures and was going into the food supply. I was supposed to
get up from the table and go out and get the groceries, but I had
gone to the zoo instead to stare at the animals. This had been
happening more often lately. I couldn't keep my mind on ordinary, daily things. I had come to believe that depression was the

realism of the future, and phobias a sign of sanity. I was supposed to know better, but I didn't.

I had felt crazy and helpless, but there, on Earl Lampson's porch, I was feeling a little better. Calm strangers sometimes have that effect on you.

Jaynee came out just then. She'd been in the shower, and I could see why some kid might want to spend a night in the zoo with her. She was in a T-shirt and jeans, and the hot water had perked her up. I stood and excused myself. I couldn't stand to see her just then, breaking my mood. Earl went to a standing position and shook my hand and said he appreciated what I had done for his daughter. I said it was nothing and started to leave when Earl, for no reason that I could see, suddenly said he'd be calling me during the week, if that was all right. I told him that I would be happy to hear from him.

Walking away from there, I decided, on the evidence so far, that Earl had a good heart and didn't know what to do with it, just as he didn't know what to do with that thing in his backyard. He just had it, and it was no use to him.

HE CALLED my office on Wednesday. I'd given him the number. There was something new in his voice, of someone wanting help. He repeated his daughter's line about how I was a professional friend, and I said, yes, sometimes that was what I was. He asked me if I ever worked with "bad kids"—that was his phrase—and I said that sometimes I did. Then he asked me if I'd help him take apart his daughter's play structure on the following Saturday. He said there'd be plenty of beer. I could see what he was after: a bit of free counseling, but since I hadn't prepared myself for his invitation, I didn't have a good defense ready. I looked around my office cubicle, and I saw myself in Earl's backyard, a screwdriver in one hand and a beer in the other. I said yes.

THE DAY I came over, it was a fair morning, for Michigan. This state is like Holland. Cold clammy mists mix with freezing rain in autumn, and hard rains in the spring are broken by tropical heat and tornadoes. It's attack weather. The sky covers you over with a metallic blue, watercolor wash over tinfoil. But this day was all right. I worked out there with Earl, pulling the wood apart with our crowbars and screwdrivers, and we had an audience, Jaynee and Earl's new woman. That was how she was introduced to me: Jody. She's the new woman. She didn't seem to have more than about eight or nine years on Jaynee, and she was nearsighted. She had those thick corrective lenses. But she was pretty in the details, and when she looked at Earl, the lenses enlarged those eyes, so that the love was large and naked and obvious.

I was pulling down a support bar for the north end of the structure and observing from time to time the neighboring backyards. My boys had gone off to a Scout meeting again, and my wife was busy, catching up on some office work. No one missed me. I was pulling at the wood, enjoying myself, talking to Earl and Jaynee and Jody about some of the techniques people in my profession use to resolve bad family quarrels; Jaynee and Jody were working at pulling down some of the wood, too. We already had two piles of scrap lumber.

I had heard a little of how Earl raised Jaynee. Her mother had taken off, the way they sometimes do, when Jaynee was three years old. He'd done the parental work. "You've been the dad, haven't you, Earl?" Jody said, bumping her hip at him. She sat down to watch a sparrow. Her hair was in a ponytail, one of those feminine brooms. "Earl doesn't know the first thing about being a woman, and he had to teach it all to Jaynee here." Jody pointed her cigarette at Jaynee. "Well, she learned it from somewhere. There's not much left she doesn't know."

"Where's the mystery?" Jaynee asked. She was pounding a hammer absentmindedly into a piece of wood lying flat on the ground. "It's easier being a woman than a girl. Men treat you better 'cause they want you."

Earl stopped turning his wrench. "Only if you don't go to the zoo anytime some punk asks you."

"That was once," she said.

Earl aimed himself at me. "I was strict with her. She knows about the laws I laid down. Fourteen laws. They're framed in her bedroom. Nobody in this country knows what it is to be decent anymore, but I'm trying. It sure to hell isn't easy."

Jody smiled at me. "Earl restrained himself until I came along." She laughed. Earl turned away, so I wouldn't see his face.

"I only spent the night in the zoo *once*," Jaynee repeated, as if no one had been listening. "And besides, I was protected."

"Protected," Earl repeated, staring at her.

"You know." Jaynee pointed her index finger at her father with her thumb in the air and the other fingers pulled back, and she made an explosive sound in her mouth.

"You took that?" her father said. "You took that to the zoo?"

Jaynee shrugged. At this particular moment, Earl turned to me. "Warren, did you see it?"

I assumed he meant the gun. I looked over toward him from the bolt I was unscrewing, and I nodded. I was so involved in the work of this job that I didn't want my peaceful laboring disturbed.

"You shouldn't have said that," Jody said to Jaynee. Earl had disappeared inside the house. "You know your father well enough by now to know that." Jody stood up and walked to the yard's back fence. "Your father thinks that women and guns are a terrible combination."

"He always said I should watch out for myself," Jaynee said, her back to us. She pulled a cookie out of her pocket and began to eat it.

"Not with a gun," Jody said.

"He showed me how to use it," the daughter said loudly. "I'm not ignorant about firearms." She didn't seem especially interested in the way the conversation was going.

"That was just information," Jody said. "It wasn't for you to

use." She was standing and waiting for Earl to reappear. I didn't do work like this, and I didn't hear conversations like this during the rest of the week, and so I was the only person still dismantling the play structure when Earl reappeared in the backyard with the revolver in his right hand. He had his shirt sleeve pulled back so anybody could see the tattoo of the rose run through with the saber on his forearm. Because I didn't know what he was going to do with that gun, I thought I had just better continue to work.

"The ninth law in your bedroom," Earl announced, "says you use violence only in self-defense." He stepped to the fence, then held his arm straight up into the air and fired once. That sound, that shattering, made me drop my wrench. It hit the ground with a clank, three inches from my right foot. Through all the back-yards of Westland I heard the blast echoing. The neighborhood dogs set up a barking chain; front and back doors slammed.

Earl was breathing hard and staring at his daughter. We were in a valley, I thought, of distinct silence. "That's all the bullets I own for that weapon," he said. He put the gun on the doorstep. Then he made his way over to where his daughter was sitting. There's a kind of walk, a little stiff, where you know every step has been thought about, every step is a decision. This was like that.

Jaynee was munching the last of her cookie. Her father grabbed her by the shoulders and began to shake her. It was like what you see in movies, someone waking up a sleepwalker. Back and forth her head tossed. "Never never never never never," he said. I started to laugh, but it was too crazed and despairing to be funny. He stopped. I could see he wanted to make a parental speech: his face was tightening up, his flesh stiff, but he didn't know how to start it, the right choice for the first word, and his daughter pushed him away and ran into the house. In that run, something happened to me, and I knew I had to get out of there.

I glanced at Jody, the new woman. She stood with her hands in her blue jeans. She looked bored. She had lived here all her life. What had just happened was a disturbance in the morning's activities. Meanwhile, Earl had picked up a board and was tentatively beating the ground with it. He was staring at the revolver on the steps. "I got to take that gun and throw it into Ford Lake," he said. "First thing I do this afternoon."

"Have to go, Earl," I said. Everything about me was getting just a little bit out of control, and I thought I had better get home.

"You're going?" Earl said, trying to concentrate on me for a moment. "You're going now? You're sure you don't want another beer?"

I said I was sure. The new woman, Jody, went over to Earl and whispered something to him. I couldn't see why, right now, out loud, she couldn't say what she wanted to say. Christ, we were all adults, after all.

"She wants you to take that .22 and throw it," Earl said. He went over to the steps, picked up the gun, and returned to where I was standing. He dropped it into my hand. The barrel was warm, and the whole apparatus smelled of cordite.

"Okay, Earl," I said. I held this heavy object in my hand, and I had the insane idea that my life was just beginning. "You have any particular preference about where I should dispose of it?"

He looked at me, his right eyebrow going up. This kind of diction he hadn't heard from me before. "Particular preference?" He laughed without smiling. "Last I heard," he said, "when you throw a gun out, it doesn't matter where it goes so long as it's gone."

"Gotcha," I said. I was going around to the front of the house. "Be in touch, right?"

Those two were back to themselves again, talking. They'd be interested in saying goodbye to me about two hours from now, when they would notice that I wasn't there.

In the story that would end here, I go out to Belle Isle in the city of Detroit and drop Earl's revolver off the Belle Isle Bridge at the exact moment when no one is looking. But this story has a way to go. That's not what I did. To start with, I drove around with that gun in my car, underneath the front seat, like half the

other residents of this area. I drove to work and at the end of
the day I drove home, a model bureaucrat, and each time I sat
in the car and turned on the ignition, I felt better than I should
have because that gun was on the floor. After about a week, the
only problem I had was not that the gun was there but that it
wasn't loaded. So I went to the ammo store—it's actually called
the Michigan Rod and Gun Club—about two miles away from
my house and bought some bullets for it. This was all very easy.
In fact, the various details were getting easier and easier. I hadn't
foreseen this. I've read Freud and Heinz Kohut and D. W.
Winnicott, and I can talk to you about psychotic breaks and
object-relations and fixation on oedipal grandiosity characterized
by the admixture of strong object cathexes and the implicitly
disguised presence of castration fears, and, by virtue of my being
able to talk about those conditions, I have had some trouble
getting into gear and moving when the occasion called for it. But
now, with the magic wand under the front seat, I was getting
ready for some kind of adventure.

Around the house my character was improving rather than
degenerating. Knowing my little secret, I was able to sit with
Gary, my younger son, as he practiced the piano, and I complimented him on the Czerny passages he had mastered, and I helped
him through the sections he hadn't learned. I was a fiery angel
of patience. With Sam, my older boy, I worked on a model train
layout. I cooked a few more dinners than I usually did: from
honey-mustard chicken, I went on to varieties of stuffed fish and
other dishes with sauces that I had only imagined. I was attentive
to Ann. The nature of our intimacies improved. We were whispering to each other again. We hadn't whispered in years.

I was frontloading a little fantasy. After all, I had tried intelligence. Intelligence was not working, not with me, not with the
world. So it was time to try the other thing.

My only interruption was that I was getting calls from Earl.
He called the house. He had the impression that I understood the
mind and could make his ideas feel better. I told him that nobody

could make his ideas feel better, ideas either feel good or not, but he didn't believe me.

"Do you mind me calling like this?" he asked. It was just before dinner. I was in the study, and the news was on. I pushed the MUTE button on the remote control. While Earl talked, I watched the silent coverage of mayhem.

"No, I don't mind."

"I shouldn't do this, I know, 'cause you get paid to listen, being a professional friend. But I have to ask your advice."

"Don't call me a professional friend. Earl, what's your question?" The pictures in front of me showed a boy being shot in the streets of Beirut.

"Well, I went into Jaynee's room to clean up. You know how teenage girls are. Messy and everything."

"Yes." More Beirut carnage, then back to Tom Brokaw.

"And I found her diary. How was I to know she had a diary? She never told me."

"They often don't, Earl. Was it locked?"

"What?"

"Locked. Sometimes diaries have locks."

"Well," Earl said, "this one didn't."

"Sounds as though you read it." Shots now on the TV of Ed Koch, the mayor, then shots of bag ladies in the streets of New York.

Earl was silent. I decided not to get ahead of him again. "I thought that maybe I shouldn't read it, but then I did."

"How much?"

"All of it," he said, "I read all of it."

I waited. He had called *me*. I hadn't called him. I watched the pictures of Gorbachev, then pictures of a girl whose face had been slashed by an ex-boyfriend. "It must be hard, reading your daughter's diary," I said. "And not *right,* if you see what I mean."

"Not the way you think." He took a deep breath. "I don't mind the talk about boys. She's growing up, and you can wish it won't happen, but it does. You know what I'm saying?"

"Yes, I do, Earl." A commercial now, for Toyotas.

"I don't even mind the sex, how she thinks about it. Hey, I was no priest myself when I was that age, and now the women, they want to have the freedom we had, so how am I going to stop it, and maybe why should I?"

"I see what you mean."

"She's very aggressive. *Very* aggressive. The things she does. You sort of wonder if you should believe it."

"Diaries are often fantasies. You probably shouldn't be reading your daughter's diary at all. It's *hers,* Earl. She's writing for herself, not for you."

"She writes about me, sometimes."

"You shouldn't read it, Earl."

Tom Brokaw again, and now pictures of a nuclear reactor, and shots of men in white outer-space protective suits with lead shielding, cleaning up some new mess. I felt my anger rising, as usual.

"I can't help reading it," Earl said. "A person starts prying, he can't stop."

"You shouldn't be reading it."

"You haven't heard what I'm about to say," Earl told me. "It's why I'm calling you. It's what she says."

"What's that?" I asked him.

"Not what I expected," he said. "She pities me."

"Well," I said. More shots of the nuclear reactor. I was getting an idea.

"Well is right." He took another breath. "First she says she loves me. That was shock number one. Then she says she feels sorry for me. That was shock number two. Because I work on the line at Ford's and I drink beer and I live in Westland. Where does she get off? That's what I'd like to know. She mentions the play structure. She feels *sorry* for me! My God, I always hated pity. I could never stand it. It weakens you. I never wanted anybody on earth pitying me, and now here's my punk daughter doing it."

"Earl, put that diary away."

"I hear you," he said. "By the way, what did you do with that gun?"

"Threw it off the Belle Isle Bridge," I said.

"Sure you did," he said. "Well, anyway, thanks for listening, Warren." Then he hung up. On the screen in front of me, Tom Brokaw was introducing the last news story of the evening.

MOST landscapes, no matter where you are, manage to keep something wild about them, but the land in southern Michigan along the Ohio border has always looked to me as if it had lost its self-respect some time ago. This goes beyond being tamed. This land has been beaten up. The industrial brass knuckles have been applied to wipe out the trees, and the corporate blackjack has stunned the soil, and what grows there—the grasses and brush and scrub pine—grows tentatively. The plant life looks scared and defeated, but all the other earthly powers are busily at work.

Such were my thoughts as I drove down to the nuclear reactor in Holbein, Michigan, on a clear Saturday morning in August, my loaded gun under my seat. I was in a merry mood. Recently activated madcap joy brayed and sang inside my head. I was speeding. My car was trembling because the front end was improperly aligned and I was doing about seventy-five. One false move on the steering wheel and I'd be permanently combined with a telephone pole. I had an eye out for the constables but knew I would not be arrested. A magic shield surrounded my car, and I was so invincible that Martians could not have stopped me.

Although this was therapy rather than political action, I was taking it very seriously, especially at the moment when my car rose over the humble crest of a humiliated grassy hill, and I saw the infernal dome and cooling towers of the Holbein reactor a mile or so behind a clutch of hills and trees ahead and to my left. The power company had surrounded all this land with high Cyclone fencing, crowned with barbed wire and that new kind of coiled lacerating razor wire they've invented. I slowed down to see the place better.

There wasn't much to see because they didn't want you to see anything; they'd built the reactor far back from the road, and in this one case they had let the trees grow (the usual demoralized silver maples and willows and jack pines) to hide the view. I drove past the main gate and noted that a sign outside the guards' office regretted that the company could not give tours because of the danger of sabotage. Right. I hadn't expected to get inside. A person doesn't always have to get inside.

About one mile down, the fence took a ninety-degree turn to the left, and a smaller county road angled off from the highway I was on. I turned. I followed this road another half mile until there was a break in the trees and I could get a clear view of the building. I didn't want a window. I wanted a wall. I was sweating like an amateur thief. The back of my shirt was stuck to the car seat, and the car was jerking because my foot was trembling with excited shock on the accelerator.

Through the thin trees, I saw the solid wall of the south building, whatever it held. There's a kind of architecture that makes you ashamed of human beings, and in my generic rage, my secret craziness that felt completely sensible, I took the gun and held my arm out of the window. It felt good to do that. I was John Wayne. I fired four times at that building, once for me, once for Ann, and once for each of my two boys. I don't know what I hit. I don't care. I probably hit that wall. It was the only kind of heroism I could imagine, the Don Quixote kind. But I hadn't fired the gun before and wasn't used to the recoil action, with the result that after the last shot, I lost control of the car, and it went off the road. In any other state my Chevy would have flipped, but this is southern Michigan, where the ditches are shallow, and I was bumped around—in my excitement I had forgotten to wear my seat belt—until the engine finally stalled in something that looked like a narrow offroad parking area.

I opened my door, but instead of standing up I fell out. With my head on the ground I opened my eyes, and there in the stones and pebbles in front of me was a shiny penny. I brought myself to a standing position, picked up the penny, a lucky penny, for my purposes, and surveyed the landscape where my car had stopped. I walked around to the other side of the car and saw a small pile of beer cans and a circle of ashes, where some revelers, sometime this summer, had enjoyed their little party of pleasure there in the darkness, close by the inaudible hum of the Holbein reactor. I dropped the penny in my trouser pocket, put the gun underneath the front seat again, and I started the car. After two tries I got it out, and before the constables came to check on the gunshots, I had made my escape.

I felt I had done something in the spirit of Westland. I sang, feeling very good and oddly patriotic. On the way back I found myself behind a car with a green bumpersticker.

CAUTION: THIS VEHICLE
EXPLODES UPON IMPACT!

That's me, I said to myself. I am that vehicle.

There was still the matter of the gun, and what to do with it. Fun is fun, but you have to know when the party's over. Halfway home, I pulled off the road into one of those rest stops, and I was going to discard the gun by leaving it on top of a picnic table or by dropping it into a trash can. What I actually did was to throw it into the high grass. Half an hour later, I walked into our suburban kitchen with a smile on my face. I explained the scratch on my cheek as the result of an accident while playing racquetball at the health club. Ann and the boys were delighted by my mood. That evening we went out to a park, and, sitting on a blanket, ate our picnic dinner until the darkness came on.

MANY of the American stories I was assigned to read in college were about anger, a fact that would not have surprised my mother, who was British, from Brighton. "Warren," she used to say to me, "watch your tongue in front of these people." "These people" always meant "these Americans." Among them was my father, who had been born in Omaha and who had married her after the war. "Your father," my mother said, "has the temper of a savage." Although it is true that my mind has retained memories of household shouting, what I now find queer is that my mother thought that anger was peculiar to this country.

Earl called me a few more times, in irate puzzlement over his life. The last time was at the end of the summer, on Labor Day. Usually Ann and I and the boys go out on Labor Day to a Metropark and take the last long swim of the summer, but this particular day was cloudy, with a forecast for rain. Ann and I had decided to pitch a tent on the back lawn for the boys, and to grill some hot dogs and hamburgers. We were hoping that the weather would hold until evening. What we got was drizzle, off and on, so that you couldn't determine what kind of day it was. I resolved to go out and cook in the rain anyway. I often took the weather personally. I was standing there, grim-faced and wet, firing up the coals, when Ann called me to the telephone.

It was Earl. He apologized for bringing me to the phone on Labor Day. I said it was okay, that I didn't mind, although I *did* mind, in fact. We waited. I thought he was going to tell me something new about his daughter, and I was straining for him not to say it.

"So," he said, "have you been watching?"

"Watching what? The weather? Yes, I've been watching that."

"No," he said, "not the sky. The Jerry Lewis telethon."

"Oh, the telethon," I said. "No, I don't watch it."

"It's important, Warren. We need all the money we can get. We're behind this year. You know how it's for Jerry's kids."

"I know it, Earl." Years ago, when I was a bachelor, once or twice I sat inside drinking all weekend and watching the telethon and making drunken pledges of money. I didn't want to remember such entertainment now.

"If we're going to find a cure for this thing, we need for everybody to contribute. It's for the kids."

"Earl," I said, "they won't find a cure. It's a genetic disorder, some scrambling in the genetic code. They might be able to prevent it, but they won't *cure* it."

There was a long silence. "You weren't born in this country, were you?"

"No," I said.

"I didn't think so. You don't sound like it. I can tell you weren't born here. At heart you're still a foreigner. You have a no–can–do attitude. No offense. I'm not criticizing you for it. It's not your fault. You can't help it. I see that now."

"Okay, Earl."

Then his voice brightened up. "What the hell," he said. "Come out anyway. You know where Westland is? Oh, right, you've been here. You know where the shopping center's located?"

"Yes," I said.

"It's the clown races. We're raising money. Even if you don't believe in the cure, you can still come to the clown races. We're giving away balloons, too. Your kids will enjoy it. Bring 'em along. *They'll* love it. It's quite a show. It's all on TV."

"Earl," I said, "this isn't my idea of what a person should be doing on a holiday. I'd rather—"

"I don't want to hear what you'd rather do. Just come out here and bring your money. All right?" He raised his voice after a quick pause. "Are you listening?"

"Yes, Earl," I said. "I'm listening."

SOMEHOW I put out the charcoal fire and managed to convince my two boys and my wife that they should take a quick jaunt to Westland. I told them about Earl, the clown races, but what finally persuaded the boys was that I claimed there'd be a remote TV unit out there, and they might turn up with their faces on Channel 2. Besides, the rain was coming down a little harder, a cool rain, one of those end-of-summer drizzles that make your skin feel the onset of autumn. When you feel like that, it helps to be in a crowd.

They had set up a series of highway detours around the shopping center, but we finally discovered how to get into the north parking lot. They'd produced the balloons, tents, and lights, but they hadn't produced much of a crowd. They had a local TV personality dressed in a LOVE NETWORK raincoat trying to get people to cheer. The idea was, you made a bet for your favorite clown and put your money in his fishbowl. If your clown won, you'd get a certificate for a free cola at a local restaurant. It wasn't much of a prize, I thought; maybe it *was* charity, but I felt that they could do better than that.

Earl was clown number three. We'd brought three umbrellas and were standing off to the side when he came up to us and introduced himself to my wife and the boys. He was wearing an orange wig and a clown nose, and he had painted his face white, the way clowns do, and he was wearing Bozo shoes, the size eighteens, but one of his sleeves was rolled up, and you could see the tattoo of that impaled rose. The white paint was running off his face a bit in the rain, streaking, but he didn't seem to mind. He shook hands with my children and Ann and me very formally. He had less natural ability as a clown than anyone else I've ever met. It would never occur to you to laugh at Earl dressed up in that suit. What you felt would be much more complicated. It was like watching a family member descend into a weakness like alcoholism. Earl caught the look on my face.

"What's the matter, Warren?" he asked. "You okay?"

I shrugged. He had his hand in a big clown glove and was shaking my hand.

"It's all for a good cause," he said, waving his other hand at the four lanes they had painted on the parking lot for the races. "We've made a lot of money already. It's all for the kids, kids who aren't as lucky as ours." He looked down at my boys. "You have to believe," he said.

"You sound like Jaynee," I told him. My wife was looking at Earl. I had tried to explain him to her, but I wasn't sure I had succeeded.

"Believe what?" she asked.

"You've been married to this guy for too long," he said, laughing his big clown laugh. "Maybe your kids can explain it to you, about what the world needs now." There was a whistle. Earl turned around. "Gotta go," he said. He flopped off in those big shoes.

"What's he talking about?" my wife asked.

They lined up the four clowns, including Earl, at the chalk, and those of us who were spectators stood under the tent and registered our bets while the LOVE NETWORK announcer from Channel 2 stood in front of the cameras and held up his starter's gun. I stared for a long time at that gun. Then I placed my bet on Earl.

The other three clowns were all fat, middle-aged guys, Shriners or Rotarians, and I thought Earl had a good chance. My gaze went from the gun down to the parking lot, where I saw Jaynee. She was standing in the rain and watching her old man. I heard the gun go off, but instead of watching Earl, I watched her.

Her hair was stuck to the sides of her head in that rain, and her cotton jacket was soaked through. She had her eyes fixed on her father. By God, she looked affectionate. If he wanted his daughter's love, he had it. I watched her clench her fists and start to jump up and down, cheering him on. After twenty seconds I could tell by the way she raised her fist in the air that Earl had clumped his way to victory. Then I saw the new woman, Jody, standing behind Jaynee, her big glasses smeared with rain, grinning.

I looked around the parking lot and thought: everyone here understands what's going on better than I do. But then I remembered that I had fired shots at a nuclear reactor. All the desperate remedies. And I remembered my mother's first sentence to me when we arrived in New York harbor when I was ten years old.

She pointed down from the ship at the pier, at the crowds, and she said, "Warren, look at all those Americans." I felt then that if I looked at that crowd for too long, something inside my body would explode, not metaphorically but literally: it would blow a hole through my skin, through my chest cavity. And it came back to me in that shopping center parking lot, full of those LOVE NETWORK people, that feeling of pressure of American crowds and exuberance.

We collected our free cola certificates, and then I hustled my wife and kids back into the car. I'd had enough. We drove out of the Westland parking lot, then were directed by a detour sign into a service drive that circled the entire shopping center and reentered the lot on the north side, back at the clown races. I saw Jaynee again, still in the rain, hugging her American dad, and Jody holding on to his elbow, looking up at him, pressing her thigh against him. I took another exit out of the lot but somehow made the same mistake I had made before, and, once again, found myself back in Westland. Every service drive seemed designed to bring us back to this same scene of father, daughter, and second wife. I gave them credit for who they were and what they were doing—I give them credit now—but I had to get out of there immediately. I don't know how I managed to get out of that place, but on the fourth try, I succeeded.

Prowlers

⟋⟋⟋

"FEAR NOT. This phrase, from the tenth chapter of Matthew, is the cornerstone of . . ." He touches a button. The cursor runs through the words and erases them.

"Fear not. These words are . . ."

Robinson stares at the amber screen of his word processor. The first two words of his sermon for the following Sunday—"Fear not"—are fixed in white block letters on the display's upper left margin. Downstairs his wife and Benjamin, once his best friend, have fallen silent. It is the third day of Benjamin's visit. Robinson strains to hear their voices. He can't think, and if he can't think, he can't write his sermon. He hates to catch himself eavesdropping. After all, he trusts them, and they trust him. They've all said so to one another, many times.

He stands up and walks to the window. A blizzard has been predicted for this evening: six or more inches of snow, winds up to forty miles an hour. So far, no sign of it. The sky is so clear that Robinson can see stars, the constellation of Orion. And down below, on the sidewalk, Mr. Hammerstein, a retired patent lawyer, is walking Sasha, his terrier.

He turns away from the window and tries not to listen, but, yes, they *are* whispering downstairs. He catches the hushed sibilance. This whispering seems uncalled-for: his wife and his friend love each other and have never kept their feelings a secret from anyone. Love falls, someone said—he can't remember who it was—like rain. And, after all, night after night, Angie sleeps next to her husband, not Benjamin. That's what counts, he thinks; that's what counts, that's what counts, that's what . . .

To drown out their conversation, Robinson turns on his radio: first Beethoven, then something more raucous, Jimi Hendrix's "Are You Experienced?" Da dum, da dum dum dum, ahheeeeeeeee . . .

"Daddy?" He feels his elbow being picked at. "Daddy!" His daughter is holding her clarinet as if she is about to hit him with it. Behind her brown-rimmed glasses her eyes are fierce. She looks like a twelve-year-old district attorney with a good case and witnesses. "I was going to practice," she says.

"It is not that loud," he tells her.

She taps her foot on the floor. He doesn't know where she picked up this gesture. "Well, it bothers me," Beth tells him. "Can you stop, please?"

"Yes, I can. You say 'please,' and I can do almost anything." He reaches over and switches off the radio.

"Whew." Beth sighs in mock relief. She wipes imaginary sweat off her brow. She is full of symbolic gestures tonight. "You writing your sermon?"

"Yup. That's it. That's what I'm doing."

"What's it about?"

"Faith," he says. "Faith, and not being fearful." He smiles at her. When he says such things, he sometimes feels the awesome banality of his efforts to be a good man.

She glances at the video display. "There's nothing there."

"I've just started. Now go back to your room and do some practicing. What're you working on this week?"

"Trills," she says. She walks toward the window. Watching

her, Robinson wonders how and why she has become overweight in the last year. What does she want from food that she can't get elsewhere? "I can see Mr. Hammerstein," she says. "Daddy, how long is Benjamin staying?"

Robinson shrugs. "He's leaving tonight. He has business. He has to be in Milwaukee tomorrow."

His daughter crosses the room and leans against the doorframe, tapping her left leg with her clarinet. "He and Mommy are sitting in the living room doing that yoga stuff. He tried to get me to do it, but I wouldn't. He called me a grouch. I wish he weren't leaving."

"Me too," Robinson says. "He's our friend and your godfather and all that, but when he says he has to go, he has to go."

"In the blizzard?" She doesn't wait for him to answer. "Daddy, how come they're whispering?"

"They have secrets," Robinson says. "Everyone has secrets." He gets up and walks toward his daughter. "Benjamin has known Mommy all her life. He knew her before I did. They were kids together."

"Do they love each other?"

Robinson scans his daughter's face. "Yes."

"Well, I love him too," she says. "I wish he wouldn't leave in a blizzard. Maybe if I tied him up he couldn't go anywhere."

"No," Robinson says, in his pastor's voice. "That wouldn't be right. We have to let him go when he wants to."

She walks backward down the dark hallway toward her room. "What if I let the air out of his tires?" she asks. "Do you think he'd mind?"

WHEN he has given them a few more minutes to say whatever they need to say to each other, Robinson comes downstairs. He sees his wife and his friend sitting in the middle of the living-room floor, leaning back. They have looks on their faces that are private and guilty and intimate. Someone has started a fire in the fireplace. Robinson sits down in the sofa and gazes at them, deciding on a tone. He settles for affectionate irony. "I'm out of the room for an hour, and this is what happens. Yoga. The postures of the East."

From the floor, Benjamin scowls. "Michael, don't be so earnest. You don't like yoga? Fine. It's *not* yoga. It's just relaxation."

Both Benjamin and Angie are wearing jeans, flannel shirts, and white socks. Probably they don't plan to dress alike, but when they're together, it often happens.

Angie glances quickly at her husband. "Benjamin was advising me about tension. He said that if I did this for ten minutes a day, I'd be more relaxed. No more antacids. *You* should try it, Mickey."

"You look like a couple of Buddhas," Robinson says. He leans back and covers his eyes with his hand, feeling the lump of his wedding ring on his forehead. "So relaxed. So happy. Just like old times."

"Don't be snooty," Benjamin says. "I know you. You don't trust happiness. You think it's shallow. You think I'm shallow. And you're absolutely right." He stands up and makes a motion of brushing invisible cracker crumbs off his lap, a salesman's gesture. Angie remains seated on the floor in a contorted position. "All right, everybody," Benjamin says. "I'm leaving in a little while, but first, I'm going outside to check the sky for snow. Michael, you're coming with me. You're good at forecasts and prophecy. It's your vocation."

"It's winter. It's *nighttime,* Benjamin. I don't want to go out."

"All the more reason." He pulls his parka out of the front-hall closet and then hands Robinson his blue ski jacket. "Come on, padre. We have to check the sky for impending blizzards." The two men stand in the hallway looking over at Angie, who is now gazing at Benjamin. The expression on her face is naked and fixed.

"Hurry on back," she says.

"Five minutes," Benjamin tells her, holding out his hand with his fingers spread. When he does this, she smiles quickly and directly at him, but he turns and reaches the front door before he appears to notice.

NOW THEY are on the sidewalk in front of the house, looking at the sky. Robinson watches his breath rise straight up. "I don't see any clouds," he says. When he turns to look at Benjamin, he sees him staring in the direction of Robinson's front window, through which Angie is still visible.

"I love that woman so much," Benjamin says, oddly rapt and expressionless at the same time. He stomps one foot on the sidewalk. "What an amazing joke on me. The one woman I could love in the world is married to you. I can't get over how I can't get over it. Happens every time I see her."

"It's only because she's married to me. That's why you feel that way."

"Don't psychoanalyze me, Michael. I can't stand it when straight people do that. It's very time-consuming and very very passé."

"All right. Sorry." Robinson feels his fingers getting cold. "You did know her first, Benjamin. You two were pals before I even met either of you. And we've had this conversation before. You dated her; you just didn't marry her. I did that. You did something else. You became . . . you. So don't let"—he notices his breath's vapor in the cold air—"your pain get so theatrical."

"Yes." Benjamin sounds exasperated. "Yes yes yes yes yes yes." He grabs Robinson by the shoulders and stares into his face. This intimate gesture makes Robinson nervous. "Michael," Benjamin says, "come back and talk to me when you've lain down with demons. I'll introduce you. I know a few by their first names. Clog onto a few obsessions. Then you can tell me it was a mistake for me not to marry your wife before you did, all right?"

He begins to walk toward the street corner. A dog two doors down growls and then barks at him. Robinson glances at the source of the noise. "Celestine," he says, "it's just us." The dog, a sheltie, sitting on the front snowy stoop, immediately stops barking and wags its tail. "I know the names of all the dogs in my neighborhood," Robinson says proudly, as he catches up to his friend. "Pepper, Brock, Maggie, Dazzle, Sasha, Bingo, Nero, Florida, Mr. Chips, Geronimo—"

"All right, all right," Benjamin says, looking down at his shoes. "We know you're very good at names. You're very good with dogs. You can identify trees, too. I've seen you do it. You're a child of God, Michael, admit it."

"I'm a child of God," Robinson says.

"That's nice for you," Benjamin says, "but it kind of leaves the rest of us in the lurch."

"Everyone is a child of God," Robinson says. "Everyone—"

"Save it. Save it for Sunday. Everyone is not a child of God. I'm not. And I won't go into it any further."

At the corner Benjamin stops and scratches his head. "I shouldn't come here, Michael. I shouldn't even come to visit." Under the streetlight, Benjamin's thinning hair looks stained, almost yellowish. "I'm too confusing for you. But I didn't come out here into the cold to tell you that. I came out to tell you something else."

He bends down to pick up some snow; then he begins to pat it into a snowball.

"What?"

Now that the snowball is formed, Benjamin packs it down. "Angie's been talking."

"Has she? I heard you whispering. Are you two finally going to make a break for it?"

"No." Behind his glasses Benjamin actually smiles. Then his smile vanishes completely. "She says she's frightened."

"She said that to you?"

"Yes. I asked her what she was frightened of."

"I know what she told you."

"Well. She said she was scared of prowlers. That was the word she used."

Benjamin lifts his snowball, and with a quick sidearm movement throws it toward the telephone pole, missing it by a foot. "Bad eyesight," he says. He takes off his glasses and rubs the lenses on the sleeve of his parka. "Look at these houses you and your neighbors live in. Little rectangular temples of light. Nothing here but families and fireplaces and Duraflame logs and children of God. Not the sort of place where a married woman ought to be worried about prowlers."

"I suppose not."

"Well?"

"Well what?"

"Well, are you going to tell me why your wife is suddenly afraid of prowlers?"

"No, I'm not."

"How come?"

"Because I don't know. Because even if I knew, I might not tell you."

Before he realizes it, Robinson is pushed from behind into a snowbank. He falls into the loose snow with a sensation, completely pleasurable, of sinking into darkness and ice. Snow is the only earthly substance that makes him feel like a child. When he rolls over, Benjamin bends down and helps him up.

"Sorry," he says. "I couldn't help myself."

They walk back until they are standing on the sidewalk in front of Robinson's house. All the lights in the living room are burning. "She never turns them off now," Robinson says. "When she gets home from work, she turns them on and keeps them on. She tries to leave them on all night. When I talk to her about the electric bill, I sound like my own father."

Benjamin links his hands together and puts them over a bald spot. Frustration radiates out of him heavily. It is as if the earth's gravity is pulling at his knees. "Michael," Benjamin says, "you're too innocent to be a minister. You recognize suffering but you don't understand it. *She* understands it. *She* understands about prowlers. Look at how beautiful she is." Robinson glances at Benjamin and sees his front window reflected on Benjamin's glasses, and, infinitely reduced in scale, his wife's image in the center of that reflection. "She's so beautiful," Benjamin says, as if his friend were not there, "it's enough to make a man lie down and sleep in the snow. She's the only woman I've ever lost sleep over. Michael," he says, grabbing Robinson by the shoulder, "don't ever let me come here again. You married people are the death of me. Do you promise?"

"Sure, Benjamin." He smiles. "I know you're leaving now because you always say that before you go. Benjamin, you're as predictable as a clock."

"Don't sermonize," Benjamin says, holding up his hand. "That's one of your weak points."

ONE HOUR later, Benjamin stands in the front hallway, having showered and put on his traveling clothes. His plaid suitcase, bulging with mysterious lumps, is at his right foot. Angie comes out of the kitchen, holding a cup of coffee. He takes it from her, sips, and hands the cup back. He smiles quickly; then he leans forward and gives her a plain, neutralized kiss. Robinson is off to the side of the window, watching them.

At this moment the thought occurs to him that God is no better and no worse than the sum of everything that happens and has happened on earth. As soon as he has thought of this idea, he tries to shove it out of his mind.

"Where's that goddaughter of mine?" Benjamin shouts. "Beth! Come down here and give me a smack right on my face!"

They hear her as she runs out of her room. She jumps down four stairs from the landing and then leaps into Benjamin's arms. His knees buckle but do not give way. He holds on to her, turns his cheek, and she kisses him.

"'Bye, Benjamin," she says. "Thanks for all the stuff."

"Trash and trinkets," he says. "Will you practice that clarinet while I'm gone?" She nods. "Good," he says, letting her down. "Okay," he announces, "I'm going now." He leans forward and gives Angie a hug and a kiss; then—this is new for him—he embraces Robinson and kisses him on the cheek. Robinson tries not to flinch. And then he thinks: from him, I accept it.

Without saying anything else, he is gone. The three of them go to the window, pull the curtains away, and watch him unlock his car, and they continue to watch until the car's taillights have disappeared down the street.

His sermon on fear is now waiting for him upstairs. He visualizes the video display covered with white words. "At least he's got front-wheel drive." No one is moving away from the window. "For the blizzard, I mean." He hears Beth clumping despondently up to her room. Robinson turns away from the window, sees Angie's face, and takes her hands in his.

"I won't ask," he says. "This time I won't ask."

"I might not tell you if you did. So don't." The overhead light makes quick lines under her eyes. Robinson waits for the tears to scald out of them and to be absorbed in his shirt. It is part of his job to watch people cry. But of course she does not do what he expects. She turns away, walks into the kitchen.

FOUR HOURS LATER, he wakes. He can feel Angie trembling silently next to him in the bed. He wonders how long he can wait until he has to say something. He stares at the ceiling, at the dull purposeless shadows thrown across it. There is almost no light coming through the curtains from the street. It must be snowing. His wife's spasms come in irregularly spaced waves, like shivering. He can hear the wind against the frames of the storm windows. He says, "It's here," and then realizes his mistake.

"What? What's here?"

"I only meant the blizzard. The one they predicted."

"Oh." She moves closer to him and he feels the taut motions of her breasts on his back. "I was worried about him."

"He'll be all right. He'll make it."

"There's this other thing."

"Downstairs?" he asks.

He can feel her nodding. He twists around in the bed so that he is facing her in the dark. "There's nothing downstairs. You know it and I know it." His voice is just above the level of a whisper, in the register where the vocal tones crack. "You've been dreaming. You know there's no one down there." He puts a hand on the side of her face.

"Mickey," she says, "I know what you're trying to tell me, but I dreamed about it, those terrible people, and they all had green caps with visors, but crooked, put on wrong. They were going through the rooms with crowbars. They were smashing everything. I know how bizarre this is, but they said they wanted to make the rooms hurt, and they did."

"All right," he says. "I know what to do. Come on."

He throws the covers of the bed back and switches on the bedside light. Angie blinks at him and at the lamp, irritably dazed. "Put your bathrobe on, honey, and we'll do a tour of the house, room by room. We'll see what we see." He helps her up. She passes her hand through her hair, makes a guttural noise, walks to the closet, and begins to knock the hangers against each other. At the window, Robinson is watching the snow, thrown from the sky and then lifted in sealike crests by the winds.

"Here," she says, standing behind him. She has her own bathrobe on and is holding his out for him. He puts it on, takes her hand, and walks to the top of the stairs. He flicks on the switch for the downstairs front hallway.

"Lights, Angie. The lights are on. The lights are taking care of everything." Still holding her hand, he tugs at her. As they walk, the stairs creak in all the familiar places. When they reach the last step, where a reed from Beth's clarinet has been mislaid, they look into the living room: the ashy orange light from the

fireplace glows dimly along the south wall. Robinson takes his
hand away from hers and walks over to a gooseneck lamp they
bought four years ago at a midnight madness sale. He switches
it on. "Now you can see," he says, holding out his arm, "all our
things. Our own living room. And there's nobody here but us.
Just you and me. We're the only prowlers here. Of course, there
are all these *things.*" He points to the clutter of a table, magazines,
and books. Then he touches her on the back, as gently as he can.
"There's nothing here," he says. "Nothing here but us."

They step past Angie's table of plants. He notices that the
geranium is about to bud. "Now," he says, "are you scared?
There's nothing unusual here." She replies with silence. All at
once Robinson feels the entire weight of his life pulling him
down into anger and hopelessness. He shakes his head, waiting for
the feeling to lift, and it does, as he knows it will. He points to
an abstractionist print on the wall, then asks Angie to turn on the
lamp at the other side of the sofa. "Now," he says, "put your
fingers on the lampshade." It's such an odd request that she doesn't
quarrel with it. "You see? Nothing special. Nothing here except
all these things we know." Together they glance down at three
shelves he has made as storage for Beth's lost or homeless items,
and the whole family's collection of adhesive-tape rolls, scissors,
pens, memo pads, and coffee cups. Angie heads toward the piano,
where a Bach partita is propped up on the music stand, and she
leans against the piano's side, with her arms crossed and her eyes
closed.

"It's not the *things,*" she says.

"I know." He takes her elbow and pilots her into a small
addition built by the house's last owner. "Here we are in the sun
room. No sun tonight, of course. There's the mess we've made
and all the bric-a-brac."

"We really ought to get Beth to take her Monopoly game
upstairs," Angie says. The game board has been left open on the
floor, and just as she finishes her sentence, Robinson feels under
his right foot the sharp edge of a Monopoly hotel. He shifts his

weight quickly, just as Angie is saying, "That's her science work-book." She points to a blue plastic milk crate on which Beth's workbook, called *Our Natural World,* lies open, a piece of teeth-indented bubble gum stuck inside the page close to the binding. Angie bends over her sewing table to stare out toward the yard. "My gosh," she says, "look at the wind."

"In grade school they always used to say that you can't see wind."

"Oh," she says, "of course, but you can see everything it does."

He takes her hand and guides her into the dining room. "We need new wallpaper in here," he says. "But there's nothing else. The prowlers are all home, asleep, snoring outlaw snores. It's just us, here." He makes a fist and knocks three times on the table. As soon as he's done it, he realizes it's a mistake: it sounds like someone knocking on the door. He and Angie exchange glances. "Now," he says quickly, "we can go into the kitchen and examine the blender for fingerprints."

"No," Angie says, "wait."

She approaches him and puts her right arm around his waist. She leans against him with great tenderness. "Now listen to me." At last she looks directly at him. "You've done the right thing: it's in your nature. You let your friend Benjamin into this house for three days, and then you let him go, and then you try to give me a tour to wash away the demons." She waits, shaking her head as if to negate something she has said. "Prowlers. You really don't get it, do you?"

Robinson looks down at his wife. "If I did, would I say?"

"No," she says, "you wouldn't."

They gaze at each other for a moment.

"Let me tell you a story," she says. "In high school Benjamin dressed as if he didn't notice his clothes: terrible yellow shirts and smudgy pants. But he had that sweet face that would melt stone. Then, the first time he took me to his house, there were his birds, his parakeets and his finches, all over his room. I loved hearing the sound of wings in that room. I'd doze off in that room and wake up to the sound of his birds." She crosses her arms and leans against the wall. "The boys you love in high school are the ones you don't quite get over."

"Yes."

She touches the light switch so that the chandelier is off and the room in semidarkness. He cannot quite see her face.

"He wasn't a very good lover," she says, her voice coming out of the darkness. "Of course he was young, but I don't think that was it. He . . . well, he tried hard. And sometimes it was okay. But he was upset with himself. I'd tell him he was trying to prove something, and he'd say, yes, that was it. We would lie there, and he'd say things that didn't make any sense to me then."

He takes her hand. "They do now?"

She leans her head back so that her hair falls loosely. "Why do men think that if they don't become men, they become nothing?"

"He said that?"

"Why do they, Mickey?" She clutches his hand tightly. "Girls grow up to be women, and boys grow up to be men, right? They *all* do, if they live."

"Come over here." He leads his wife into the center of the living room; a bit of light from the street flows over them, and they hear the furnace go on.

"And then you came along," she says. "The Reverend Prince Charming."

"Yes."

"You know how we broke up?"

"You and Benjamin?"

"Who else are we talking about?"

He says nothing. He waits for her to say whatever she intends to say, although he thinks he knows, almost word for word, what it will be.

"It was a long night. He and I went to a restaurant on campus, and I told him I was falling in love with you. Then we sat in a car. Then we went somewhere else. A room. A bare white room

with a water glass and a window on an alley. It was the strangest
night of my life. We . . . no, I think he thought it would work,
if we hurt each other, hour after hour."

"Why did you do it?"

"I asked him to."

"You said he thought it would work."

"After I . . . don't you get it? Don't you ever understand?"

"No," he says, "I don't."

"Well, you can give me all the tours you want through the
house, but you'll never get it. That's because all you want to do
is turn on the lights. Benjamin wanted them off. There wasn't a
secret of his I didn't know, and he knew every secret of mine."

"You know my secrets," Robinson says helplessly.

"Sweetheart, you don't have any secrets. You've never wanted
a single bad thing in your life. So here you are, and here I am,
the minister's wife. How about that?"

Robinson separates himself from her and walks into the
kitchen, where he pours himself a glass of milk. It has a disturbed,
sour taste. As he puts the glass on the dishwasher rack, he hears
Angie say from the direction of the living room, "Mickey, come
here."

"What is it?"

"Come here, to the window."

He turns off the kitchen light, then goes to where she is
standing in front of the west window that faces the street. The
snow is like a bedsheet: solid but two-dimensional, a blinder.

"Really coming down," he says, heartsick.

"That's not it. Look."

"Look where? There's nothing to see."

"Across the street. There's someone there."

He squints and follows the line of her pointing finger. He
begins at the snowy halation around the street light and then
glances down to where the sidewalk probably is. Then he sees the
bleared outline of a man. Next to this outline is the outline of
a dog.

"My God," Robinson says. "It's Mr. Hammerstein."

"Mr. Hammerstein?" Angie stares. "Mickey," she says, "it *is* him. You've got to go get him."

Robinson is already heading up the stairs. "I saw him hours ago. He must be half frozen." He hears Beth muttering in her sleep as he passes by her door.

In three minutes he has rushed downstairs, wearing jeans, a heavy flannel shirt, and a worn pair of shoes. He rummages in the closet and pulls out an old overcoat; goosefeather points are sticking out of pinholes in the lining. He opens the front door, feels the wind strike him, and heads down the front steps.

He is conscious of snow pelting his face and making its way into his ears. It blows into his shoes and attaches itself to his socks. He tilts his head, curious about the sky. Instantly snow falls into his eyes, and he has to wipe his face on his coat sleeve. The wind in the trees behind his house moans; the dense snowy air has, to Robinson, the smell of aluminum. Four steps down the driveway he realizes that he has no boots, no gloves. He turns his head and in the white blur, seeing the lights of his house, he shrugs it off.

In the street he slips on a patch of ice, and falls. He lands on his right side with his right hand raised near his face. He picks himself up and feels a match-burst of pain in his ankle. He makes his way slowly across the street toward Mr. Hammerstein, who is covered, on his hat and shoulders, with a half inch of snow. The dog is yipping quietly.

"Mr. Hammerstein," he says.

The old man looks at him. "Evening, Reverend."

"I . . . I came down to the kitchen for a drink of milk and I saw you out here. I thought maybe you'd been here since eight o'clock."

"Eight?" The old man laughs. "I'd be frozen stiff. No, what it was, my dog here woke me up a little while ago, wanted to go out and see the snowstorm. So I took him. I have insomnia, you know." He examines Robinson. "You're not dressed for this."

"No." Robinson at once notices that the old man's glasses are covered with snow; he isn't sure how he can see.

"I brought my hat and gloves and boots, which is more than I can say for you, Reverend. What in the world is a family man like yourself doing out here without gloves?"

Robinson holds his hands out and looks at them as if they belong to someone else. "I don't know," he says.

"Well, get back into your house before you catch your death. It's late." A wind swirling up from the ground blows into their faces and clears the snow scattered on Mr. Hammerstein's spectacles, moving from the left side of the lenses to the right. Behind the glasses Mr. Hammerstein's blue eyes gaze at Robinson's with amused wonderment. "Imagine," he says, "anyone but a silly old man and his dog being out here at two-thirty."

Robinson bends down to pat Sasha. "Your dog is shivering."

"Yes, he told me he wanted to come out here and now he wants to go back, the little cur." A gust of wind clears Mr. Hammerstein's eyebrows of snow. The dog barks twice. Robinson feels the hair on his own head being lifted by the wind, and the horizontally blowing snow clumping inside his collar.

"HE WAS all right." Robinson drops his overcoat in the front hallway. "He just came out to walk his dog. He told me to go home." He pulls at his shoes and socks, before running his hand through his hair. Snow drops out in flakes and pellets.

"Well, that's good. Did he tell you that you were dutiful? Did he say any of the other obvious things?" She watches him trying to shed his wet clothes. "The faithful shepherd. You've always had a calling for duty." She smiles, and he catches instantly the calm sadness behind the smile.

"Yeah, well," he says, trying to grin, and failing. It is too much effort. "Duty calls me into the shower." Limping up the stairs, he feels her gaze on him. Ever since his childhood, he has had a sixth sense for the gaze of others; when people looked at him, even if his back was turned, he had known. As soon as he reaches the top of the stairs—fifteen steps, counted—he feels the weight of her gaze lifting from his body. It is always this way; it has always been. His deepest experience from childhood onward has been that of being watched. He believes that it is what sent him into the ministry.

His shower finished, he puts on his pajamas, hanging on a knob of the bathroom cupboard where Angie has moved them from the bedroom floor. Outside the bathroom, he sees the light on in his study. He walks down the hall to turn it off.

Angie is sitting at his desk, wearing only her nightgown, a red plastic mechanical pencil in her hand. She is writing on a white sheet of paper, line after line. Her left hand, in the light, is bare: she has taken off her wedding ring. In thirteen years she has not taken it off, but Robinson knows better than to make an issue of it and ask where it is.

"What are you doing?"

"I'm writing your sermon," she says. She doesn't look up from the paper. Her hand moves as she speaks. He can see her body through the thin gown.

He says nothing.

"I know how you started it," she says. "You told me. Well, now I'm finishing it."

"I just had two words."

"I know that," she says. Robinson sees indistinctly the words the pencil is leaving on the paper, but he cannot read them. " 'Fear not.' That's how you started. Well, I'm giving you the rest." The Book of Common Prayer, with its red cover, is the only object on the desk, except for the keyboard, display, and the white sheet of paper on which Angie is writing. "I'm giving you something you can use."

Robinson begins to walk toward her. "May I see it?"

"No," she says, glancing toward him. "Not now."

"When?"

"On Sunday, of course."

"Sunday morning?"

"Yes."

"I don't read sermons," he says. "I speak to the congregation. You know that."

"Start with this. Then speak."

"How will I know what it says until then?"

"You won't. It's going to be my secret. You'll just have to wait before you discover it."

"I don't know if I can do that," Robinson says.

Angie turns in the chair to face him. "Oh Mickey," she says, looking at him, her bare right arm making a diagonal across the light as she props her head with her fist. She does love him; he sees how clear it is, how she will not, in her sleeplessness, let him go for now. "Oh Mickey," she repeats, "won't you read what I've written, and then believe me?"

A Relative Stranger

I WAS SEPARATED from my biological mother when I was four months old. Everything from that period goes through the wash of my memory and comes out clean, blank. The existing snapshots of my mother show this very young woman holding me, a baby, at arm's length, like a caught fish, outside in the blaring midday summer sunlight. She's got clothes up on the clothesline in the background, little cotton infant things. In one picture a spotted dog, a mongrel combination of Labrador and Dalmation, is asleep beside the bassinet. I'd like to know what the dog's name was, but time has swallowed that information. In another picture, a half-empty bottle of Grain Belt beer stands on the lawn near a wading pool. My mother must have figured that if she could have me, at the age of seventeen, she could also have the beer.

My mother's face in these pictures is having a tough time with daylight. It's a struggle for her to bask in so much glare. She squints and smiles, but the smile is all on one side, the right. The left side stays level, except at the edge, where it slips down. Because of the sunlight and the black-and-white film, my mother's face in other respects is bleached, without details, like a sketch for a face. She's a kid in these pictures and she has a kid's face, with hair pulled back with bobby pins and a slight puffiness in the cheeks, which I think must be bubble gum.

She doesn't look like she's ever been used to the outdoors, the poor kid. Sunlight doesn't become her. It's true she smiled, but then she did give me up. I was too much serious work, too much of a squalling load. Her girlish smile was unsteady and finally didn't include me. She gave me away—this is historical record— to my adoptive parents, Harold and Ethel Harris, who were older and more capable of parental love. She also gave them these photographs, the old kind, with soft sawtooth borders, so I'd be sure to know how she had looked when the unfamiliar sunlight hit her in a certain way. I think her teenaged boyfriend, my father, took these pictures. Harold and Ethel Harris were my parents in every respect, in love and in their care for me, except for the fact of these pictures. The other children in the family, also adopted, looked at the snapshots of this backyard lady with curiosity but not much else.

My biological father was never a particle of interest to me compared to my adoptive father, Harold Harris, a man who lived a life of miraculous calm. A piano tuner and occasional jazz saxophonist, Harold liked to sit at home, humming and tapping his fingers in the midst of uproar and riot, kids shouting and plaster falling. He could not be riled; he never made a fist. He was the parental hit of any childhood group, and could drive a car competently with children sitting on his shoulders and banging their hands on the side of his head. Genetic inheritance or not, he gave us all a feeling for pitch. Ask me for an F-sharp, I'll give you one. I get the talent from Harold.

I WENT to high school, messed around here and there, did some time in the Navy, and when I was discharged I married my sweetheart of three years, the object of my shipboard love letters, Lynda Claire Norton. We had an apartment. I was clerking at Meijer's Thrifty Acres. I thought we were doing okay. Each night I was sleeping naked next to a sexual angel. At sunrise she would wake me with tender physical comfort, with hair and fingertips. I was working to get a degree from night school. Fourteen months after we were married, right on the day it was due, the baby came. A boy, this was. Jonathan Harold Harris. Then everything went to hell.

I was crazy. Don't ask me to account for it. I have no background or inclination to explain the human mind. Besides, I'm not proud of the way I acted. Lynda moved right out, baby and all, the way any sensible woman would have, and she left me two empty rooms in the apartment in which I could puzzle myself out.

I had turned into the damnedest thing. I was a human monster movie. I'd never seen my daddy shouting the way I had; he had never carried on or made a spectacle of himself. Where had I picked up this terrible craziness that made me yell at a woman who had taken me again and again into her arms? I wrote long letters to the world while I worked at home on my model ships, a dull expression on my face. You will say that liquor was the troublemaker here and you would be correct, but only so far. I had another bad ingredient I was trying to track down. I broke dishes. My mind, day and night, was muzzy with bad intentions. I threw a light bulb against a wall and did not sweep up the glass for days. Food burned on the stove and then I ate it. I was committing outrageous offenses against the spirit. Never, though, did I smash one of the model ships. Give me credit for that.

I love oceans and the ships that move across them. I believe in man-made objects that take their chances on the earth's expanses of water. And so it happened that one weekday afternoon I was watching a rerun of *The Caine Mutiny,* with my workboard set up in front of me with the tiny pieces of my model *Cutty Sark* in separated piles, when the phone rang. For a moment I believed that my wife had had second thoughts about my behavior and was going to give me another chance. To tell the truth, whenever the phone rang, I thought it would be Lynda, announcing her terms for my parole.

"Hello? Is this Oliver Harris?" a man's voice asked.

"This is him," I said. "Who's this?"

"This is your brother." Just like that. Very matter-of-fact. This is your brother. Harold and Ethel Harris had had two other adopted sons, in addition to me, but I knew them. This voice was not them. I gripped the telephone.

Now—and I'm convinced of this—every adopted child fears and fantasizes getting a call like this announcing from out of the blue that someone in the world is a relative and has tracked you down. I know I am not alone in thinking that anyone in the world might be related to me. My biological mother and father were very busy, urgent lovers. Who knows how much procreation they were capable of, together and separately? And maybe they had brothers and sisters, too, as urgent in their own way as my mother and father had been in theirs, filling up the adoption agencies with their offspring. I could never go into a strange city without feeling that I had cousins in it.

Therefore I gripped the telephone, hoping for reason, for the everyday. "This is not my brother," I said.

"Oh yes, it is. Your mother was Alice Barton, right?"

"My mother was Ethel Harris," I said.

"Before that," the voice said, "your mother was Alice Barton. She was my mother, too. This is your brother, Kurt. I'm a couple of years younger than you." He waited. "I know this is a shock," he said.

"You can't find out about me," I said. The room wasn't spinning, but I had an idea that it might. My mouth was open halfway and I was taking short sweaty breaths through it. One shiver took its snaky way down and settled in the lumbar region. "The records are sealed. It's all private, completely secret."

"Not anymore, it isn't," he said. "Haven't you been keeping

up? In this country you can find out anything. There are no secrets worth keeping anymore; nobody *wants* privacy, so there isn't any."

He was shoving this pile of ideas at me. *My* thoughts had left me in great flight, the whole sad flock of them. "Who are you?" I asked.

"Your brother Kurt," he said, repeating himself. "Listen, I won't bore you to explain what I had to do to find you. The fact is that it's possible. Easy, if you have money. You pay someone and someone pays someone and eventually you find out what you want to know. Big surprise, right?" He waited, and when I didn't agree with him, he started up again, this time with small talk. "So I hear that you're married and you have a kid yourself." He laughed. "And I'm an uncle."

"What? No. Now you're only partly right," I said, wanting very hard to correct this man who said he was my brother. "My wife left me. I'm living here alone now."

"Oh. I'm sorry about that." He offered his sympathies in a shallow, masculine way: the compassion offered by princes and salesmen. "But listen," he said, "you're not alone. It's happened before. Couples separate all the time. You'll get back. It's not the end of the world. Oliver?"

"What?"

"Would you be willing to get together and talk?"

"Talk? Talk about what?"

"Well, about being brothers. Or something else. You can talk about anything you please." He waited for me to respond, and I didn't. This was my only weapon—the terrible static of telephone silence. "Look," he said, "this is tough for me. *I'm not a bad person.* I've been sitting by this phone for an hour. I don't know if I'm doing the right thing. My wife . . . you'll meet her . . . she hasn't been exactly supportive. She thinks this is a mistake. She says I've gone too far this time. I dialed your number four times before I dialed it to the end. I make hundreds of business calls but this one I could not do. It may be hard for you, also:

I mean, I take a little getting used to. I can get obsessive about little things. That's how I found you."

"By being obsessive."

"Yeah. Lucille . . . that's my wife . . . she says it's one of my faults. Well, I always wanted a brother, you know, blood-related and everything, but I couldn't have one until I found you. But then I thought you might not like me. It's possible. Are you following me?"

"Yes, I am." I was thinking: here I am in my apartment, recently vacated by my wife, talking to a man who says he's my brother. Isn't there a law against this? Someone help me.

"You don't have to like me," he said, his brusque voice starting to stumble over the consonants. That made me feel better. "But that isn't the point, is it?" Another question I didn't have to answer, so I made him wait. "I can imagine what's in your head. But let's meet. Just once. Let's try it. Not at a house. I only live about twenty miles away. I can meet you in Ann Arbor. We can meet in a bar. I *know* where you live. I drove by your building. I believe I've even seen your car."

"Have you seen me?" This brother had been cruising past my house, taking an interest. Do brothers do that? What *do* they do?

"Well, no, but who cares about looks where brothers are concerned? We'll see each other. Listen, there's this place a couple of miles from you, the Wooden Keg. Could we meet there? Tomorrow at three? Are you off tomorrow?"

"That's a real problem for me," I said. "Booze is my special poison."

"Hell, that's all right," he said. "I'll watch out for you. I'm your brother. Oh. There's one other thing. I lied. I look like you. That's how you'll recognize me. I have seen you."

I held on to the telephone a long time after I hung up. I turned my eyes to the television set. José Ferrer was getting drunk and belligerent at a cocktail party. I switched off the set.

I WAS IN that bar one hour before I said I would be, and my feelings were very grim. I wasn't humming. I didn't want him to be stationed there when I came in. I didn't want to be the one who sauntered in through the door and walked the long distance to the bar stool. I didn't want some strange sibling checking out the way I close the distance or blink behind my glasses while my eyes adjust to the light. I don't like people watching me when they think they're going to get a skeleton key to my character. I'm not a door and I won't be opened that easily.

Going into a bar in the midsummer afternoon takes you out of the steel heat and air-hammer sun; it softens you up until you're all smoothed out. This was one of those wood-sidewall bars with air that hasn't recirculated for fifty years, with framed pictures of thoroughbreds and cars on the walls next to the chrome decorator hubcaps. A man's bar, smelling of cigarettes and hamburger grease and beer. The brown padded light comes down on you from some recessed source, and the leather cushions on those bar stools are as soft as a woman's hand, and before long the bar is one big bed, a bed on a barge eddying down a sluggish river where you've got nothing but good friends lined up on the banks. This is why I am an alcoholic. It wasn't easy drinking Coca-Cola in that place, that dim halfway house between the job and home, and I was about to slide off my wagon and order my first stiff one when the door cracked open behind me, letting in a trumpet blast of light, and I saw, in the doorframe outline, my brother coming toward me. He was taking his own time. He had on a hat. When the door closed and my eyes adjusted, I got a better look at him, and I saw what he said I would see: I saw instantly that this was my brother. The elves had stolen my shadow and given it to him. A version of my face was fixed on a stranger. From the outdoors came this example of me, wearing a coat and tie.

He took a bar stool next to mine and held out his hand. I held out mine and we shook like old friends, which we were a long way from becoming. "Hey," we both said. He had the eyes, the cheek, and the jaw in a combination I had seen only in the mirror. "Oliver," he said, refusing to let my hand go. "Good to meet you."

"Kurt," I said. "Likewise." Brother or no brother, I wasn't giving away anything too fast. This is America, after all.

"What're you drinking?" he asked.

"Coke."

"Oh. Right." He nodded. When he nodded, the hat nodded. After he saw me looking at it, he said, "Keeps the sun out of my eyes." He took it off and tried to put it on the bar, but there wasn't enough room for it next to the uncleared beer glasses and the ashtrays, so he stood up and dropped it on a hook over by the popcorn machine. There it was, the only hat. He said, "My eyes are sensitive to light. What about yours?" I nodded. Then he laughed, hit the bar with the broad flat of his hand, and said, "Isn't this great?" I wanted to say, yes, it's great, but the true heart of the secret was that no, it was not. It was horrifyingly strange without being eventful. You can't just get a brother off the street. But before I could stop him from doing it, he leaned over and put his right arm, not a large arm but an arm all the same, over my shoulders, and he dropped his head so that it came sliding in toward my chest just under the chin. Here was a man dead set on intimacy. When he straightened up, he said, "We're going to have ourselves a day today, that's for sure." His stutter took some of the certainty out of the words. "You don't have to work this afternoon, right?"

"No," I said, "I'm not scheduled."

"Great," he said. "Let me fill you in on myself."

INSTEAD of giving me his past, he gave me a résumé. He tried to explain his origins. My biological mother, for all the vagueness in her face, had been a demon for good times. She had been passionate and prophylactically carefree. Maybe she had had twenty kids, like old Mother Hubbard. She gave us away like presents to a world that wanted us. This one, this Kurt, she had kept for ten months before he was adopted by some people called Sykes. My brother said that he understood that we—he and I—had two other siblings in Laramie, Wyoming. There might be more he didn't know about. I had a sudden image of Alice Barton as a human stork, flying at tree level and dropping babies into the arms of waiting parents.

Did I relax as my brother's voice took me through his life? Were we related under the skin, and all the way around the block? He talked; I talked. The Sykes family had been bookish types, lawyers, both of them, and Kurt had gone to Michigan State University in East Lansing. He had had certain advantages. No falling plaster or piano tuning. By learning the mysterious dynamics of an orderly life, he had been turned out as a salesman, and now he ran a plastics factory in Southfield, north of Detroit. "A small business," he said in a friendly, smug way. "Just fifteen employees." I heard about his comfortably huge home. I heard about his children, my nephews. From the wallet thick with money and credit cards came the lineup of photos of these beautiful children.

So what was he doing, this successful man, sitting on a bar stool out here, next to his brother, me, the lowly checkout clerk?

"Does anybody have enough friends?" he asked me. "Does anyone have enough *brothers?*" He asked this calmly, but the questions, as questions, were desperate. "Here's what it was," he said. "Two or three times a week I felt like checking in with someone who wasn't a wife and wasn't just a friend. Brothers are a different category, right there in the middle. It's all about *relatedness,* you know what I mean?" I must have scowled. "We can't rush this," he said. "Let's go have dinner somewhere. My treat. And then let's do something."

"Do what?" I asked.

"I've given that a lot of thought," he said. "What do you do the first time out with your brother? You can't just eat and drink. You can't shop; women do that." Then he looked me square in the eye, smiled, and said, "It's summer. Maybe we could go bowling or play some baseball." There was a wild look in his eye. He let out a quick laugh.

WE WENT in his Pontiac Firebird to a German restaurant and loaded up on sauerbraten. I had a vague sense he was lowering himself to my level but did not say so. He ordered a chest-sized decorated stein of beer but I stayed on the cola wagon. I tried to talk about my wife, but it wouldn't come out: all I could say was that I had a problem with myself as a family man. That wasn't me. The crying of babies tore me up. Feeding time gave me inexplicable jitters. I had acted like Godzilla. When I told him this, he nodded hard, like a yes man. It was all reasonable to him.

"Of course," he said. "Of course you were upset and confused." He was understanding me the way I wanted to be understood. I talked some more. Blah blah blah. Outside, it was getting dark. The bill came, and he paid it: out came the thick wallet again, and from a major-league collection of credit cards came the white bank plastic he wanted. I talked more. He agreed with everything I said. He said, "You're exactly right." Then I said something else, and he responded, "Yes, you're exactly right."

That was when I knew I was being conned. In real life people don't say that to you unless they're trying to earn your love in a hurry. But here he was, Kurt Sykes, visibly my brother, telling me I was exactly right. It was hard to resist, but I was holding on, and trying.

"Here's how," he said. He lifted his big stein of beer into the air, and I lifted my glass of Coke. Click. A big blond waitress watched us, her face disciplined into a steel-helmet smile.

AFTER THAT, it was his idea to go outside and play catch. This activity had all sorts of symbolic meanings for him, but what was

I going to do? Go home and watch television? I myself have participated in a few softball leagues and the jock way of life is not alien to me, but I think he believed he could open up if we stayed at my level, throwing something back and forth, grunting and sweating. We drove across town to Buhr Park, where he unloaded his newly purchased baseball, his two brand-new gloves, and a shiny new bat. Baseball was on the agenda. We were going to play ball or die. "We don't have to do any hitting," he said. While I fitted the glove to my left hand—a perfect fit, as if he had measured me—he locked the car. I have never had a car worth locking; it was not a goal.

The sun having set, I jogged out across a field of darkening grass. The sky had that blue tablecloth color it gets at dusk just before the stars come out. I had my jeans, sweatshirt, and sneakers on, my usual day-off drag. I had not dressed up for this event. In fact, I was almost feeling comfortable, except for some growing emotional hot spot I couldn't locate that was making me feel like pushing the baseball into my brother's face. Kurt started to toss the ball toward me and then either noticed his inappropriate dress-for-success formality or felt uncomfortable. He went back to the car and changed into his sweat clothes in the half-dark. He could have been seen, but wasn't, except by me. (My brother could change his clothes out in the open, not even bothering to look around to see who would see. What did this mean?)

Now, dressed down, we started to hustle, keeping the rhythms up. He threw grounders, ineptly, his arm stiff and curious. I bent down, made the imaginary play, and pivoted. He picked up the bat and hit a few high flies toward me. Playing baseball with me was his way of claiming friendship. Fine. Stars came out. We moved across the field, closer to a floodlit tennis court, so we had a bit of light. I could see fireflies at the edge of where we were playing. On the court to my right, a high school couple was working their way through their second set. The girl let out little cries of frustration now and then. They were pleasurable to hear.

Meanwhile, Kurt and I played catch in the near-dark, following the script that, I could see, he had written through one long sleepless night after another.

As we threw the ball back and forth, he talked. He continued on in his résumé. He was married but had two girlfriends. His wife knew about them both. She did not panic because she expected imperfection in men. Also, he said, he usually voted Republican. He went to parent-teacher-organization meetings.

"I suppose you weren't expecting this," he said.

No, I thought, I was *not* expecting you. I glanced at the tennis court. Clouds of moths and bright bugs swarmed in insect parabolas around the high-voltage lights. The boy had a white Huron high school T-shirt on, and white shorts and tennis shoes, and a blue sweatband around his thick damp hair. The girl was dressed in an odd assortment of pink and pastel blue clothes. She was flying the colors and was the better player. He had the force, but she had the accuracy. Between his heat and her coolness, she piled up the points. I let myself watch her; I allowed myself that. I was having a harder and harder time keeping my eyes on my brother.

"You gonna play or look at them?" Kurt asked.

I glanced at him. I thought I'd ignore his question. "You got any hobbies?" I asked.

He seemed surprised. "Hobbies? No. Unless you count women and making money."

"How's your pitch?"

"You mean baseball?"

"No. Music. How's your sense of pitch?"

"Don't have one."

"I do," I said. "F-sharp." And I blew it at him.

He leaned back and grimaced. "How do you know that's F-sharp?"

"My daddy taught me," I said. "He taught me all the notes on the scale. You can live with them. You can become familiar with a note."

"I don't care for music," he said, ending that conversation. We were still both panting a bit from our exertions. The baseball idea was not quite working in the way he had planned. He seemed to be considering the possibility that he might not like me. "What the hell," he said. "Let's go back to that bar."

WHY DID I hit my brother in that bar? Gentlemen of the bottle, it is you I address now. You will understand when I tell you that when my brother and I entered the bar, cool and smoky and filled with midsummer ballplayers, uniformed men and women, and he thoughtlessly ordered me a Scotch, you will understand that I drank it. Drank it after I saw his wad of money, his credit cards, his wallet-rubbed pictures of the children, my little nephews. He said he would save me from my alcoholism but he did not. Gentlemen, in a state of raw blank irritation I drank down what God and nature have labeled "poison" and fixed with a secret skull and crossbones. He bought me this drink, knowing it was bad for me. My mind withdrew in a snap from my brain. The universe is vast, you cannot predict it. From the great resources of anger I pulled my fund, my honest share. But I do not remember exactly why I said something terrible, and hit my brother in the jaw with my fist. And then again, higher, a punch I had learned in the Navy.

HE STAGGERED back, and he looked at me.

HIS NOSE was bleeding and my knuckles hurt. I was sitting in the passenger side of his car. My soul ached. My soul was lying facedown. He was taking me back to my apartment, and I knew that my brother would not care to see me from now on. He would reassert his right to be a stranger. I had lost my wife, and now I had lost him, too.

WE STUMBLED into my living room. I wobbled out to the kitchen and, booze-sick, filled a dish towel with ice cubes and brought it to him. My right hand felt swollen. We were going to have ugly bruises, but his were facial and would be worse. Holding the ice to his damaged face, he looked around. Above the ice his eyes flickered on with curiosity. "Ships," he said. Then he pointed at the work table against the wall. "What's all that?"

"It's my hobby," I said. The words came slow and wormlike out of my puzzled mouth.

He squinted above the ice. "Bottles? And glue?"

"I build ships in bottles." I sounded like a balloon emptying itself of air. I pointed at the decorator shelf on the west wall, where my three-masted clipper ship, the *Thermopylae,* was on display.

"How long have you done this?" he asked.

"So long I can't remember."

"How do you do it?"

He gave me a chance. Even a bad drunk is sometimes forced to seize his life and to speak. So I went over to the worktable. "You need these." I held up the surgical forceps. I could hardly move my fingers for the pain. Alcoholic darkness sat in a corner with its black bag waiting to cover me entirely. I went on talking. "And these. Surgical scissors." Dried specks of glue were stuck to the tips. "Some people cheat and saw off the bottom of the bottle, then glue it back on once the ship is inside. I don't do it that way. It has to grow inside the bottle. You need a challenge. I build the hull inside. I have used prefab hulls. Then you've got to lay the deck down. I like to do it with deck furnishings already in place: you know, the cabin doors and hatch covers and cleats and riding bits already in place on the deck. You put the glue on and then you put the deck in, all in one piece, folded up, through the neck; then you fold it out. With all that glue on, you only have one shot. Then you do the rigging inside the bottle. See these masts? The masts are laid down inside the bottle with the bottom of the mast in a hole."

I pointed to the *Cutty Sark,* which I was working on. I did not care if my hands were broken; I would continue this, the only lecture in my head, even if I sounded like a chattering magpie.

"You see, you pull the mast up inside the bottle with a string attached to the mast, and there's a stop in the hole that'll keep the mast from going too far forward. Then you tie the lines that are already on the mast off on the belaying pins and the bits and the cleats." I stopped. "These are the best things I do. I make ships in bottles better than anything else I do in my life."

"Yes." He had been standing over my worktable, but now he was lying on the sofa again.

"I like ships," I said. "When I was growing up, I had pictures on the wall of yachts. I was the only person in the Harris family who was interested in ships."

"Hmm."

"I like sailboats the most." I was talking to myself. "They're in their own class."

"That's interesting," he said. "That's all very interesting, but I wonder if I could lie down here for a while."

"I think you're already doing it."

"I don't need a pillow or a blanket," Kurt said, covered with sweat. "I can lie here just as is."

"I was going to turn on the air conditioner."

"Good. Put it on low."

I went over to the rattletrap machine and turned it on. The compressor started with a mechanical complaint, a sound like *orrr orrr orrr,* and then faster, *orrorrorr.* By the time I got back into the living room, my brother's eyes were closed.

"You're asleep," I said.

"No," he said, "no, I'm not. My eyes are just closed. I'm bruised and taking a rest here. That's all. Why don't you talk to me for a minute while I lie here with this ice. Say anything."

SO I talked against the demons chittering in the corners of the room. I told my brother about being on a carrier in the Navy. I talked about how I watched the blue lifting swells of the Pacific even when I wasn't supposed to and would get my ass kicked for it. I was hypnotized by seawater, the crazy majesty of horizontal lines. I sleepwalked on that ship, I was so happy. I told him about the rolling progress of oceanic storms, and how the cumulonimbus clouds rose up for what looked like three or four miles into the atmosphere. Straight-edged curtains of rain followed us; near the Straits of Gibraltar it once rained for thirty minutes on the forward part of the ship, while the sun burned down on the aft.

I talked about the ship's work, the painting and repairing I did, and I told him about the constant metallic rumble vibrating below decks. I told him about the smell, which was thick with sterile grease stink that stayed in your nostrils, and the smell of working men. Men away from women, men who aren't getting any, go bad, and they start to smell like metal and fur and meat.

Then I told him about the ships I built, the models, and the originals for them, about the masts and sails, and how, in the water, they had been beautiful things.

"What if they fell?" my brother said.

I didn't understand the question, but thought I would try to answer it anyway. It was vague, but it showed he was still awake, still listening. I wanted to ask, fell from where? But I didn't. I said if a man stood on the mainmast lookout, on a whaler, for example, he could lose his balance. If he tumbled from that height, he might slap the water like he was hitting cement. He might be internally damaged, but if he did come up, they'd throw him a lifebuoy, the white ones made out of cork and braided with a square of rope.

I brought one of the ships toward him. "I've got one here," I said, "tiny, the size of your fingernail."

He looked at it, cleated to the ship above the deck. He studied it and then he gazed at me. "Yes," he said. It was the most painful smile I'd ever seen in an adult human being, and it reminded me of me. I thought of the ocean, which I hadn't viewed for years and might not, ever again. "Yes," my brother said from under the icepack. "Now I get it."

LIKE strangers sitting randomly together in a midnight peeling-gray downtown bus depot smelling of old leather shoes, we talked until four in the morning, and he left, his face bruised dark, carrying one of my ships, the *Lightning,* under his arm. He came back a week later. We sat in the park this time, not saying much. Then I went to see him, and I met his wife. She's a pleasant woman, a tall blonde who comes fully outfitted with jewels I usually see under glass in display cases. My brother and I know each other better now; we've discovered that we have, in fact, no subjects in common. But it's love, so we have to go on talking, throwing this nonsense into the air, using up the clock. He has apologized for trying to play baseball with me; he admits now that it was a mistake.

When I was small, living with Harold and Ethel Harris and the other Harris children, I knew about my other parents, the aching lovers who had brought me into my life, but I did not miss them. They'd done me my favor and gone on to the rest of their lives. No, the only thing I missed was the world: the oceans, their huge distances, their creatures, the tides, the burning water-light I heard you could see at the equator. I kept a globe nearby my boy's bed. Even though I live here, now, no matter where I ever was, I was always homesick for the rest of the world. My brother does not understand that. He thinks home is where he is now. I show him maps; I tell him about Turkey and the Azores; I have told him about the great variety and beauty of human pigmentation. He listens but won't take me seriously.

When my brother talks now, he fingers his nose, probably to remind me where I hit him. It's a delicate gesture, with a touch of self-pity. With this gesture he establishes a bit of history between us. He wants to look up to me. He's twenty-eight years old, hasn't ever seen Asia, and he says this to me seriously. Have you ever heard the sound of a man's voice from a minaret? I ask him, but he just smiles. He's already called my wife; he has a whole series of happy endings planned, scene by scene. He wants to sit in a chair and see me come into the room, perfected, thanking the past for all it has done for me.

Shelter

COOPER had stopped at a red light on his way to work and was adjusting the dial on his radio when he looked up and saw a man in a filthy brown corduroy suit and a three-day growth of beard staring in through the front windshield and picking with his fingernails at Cooper's windshield wiper. Whenever Cooper had seen this man before, on various Ann Arbor street corners, he had felt a wave of uneasiness and unpleasant compassion. Rolling down the window and leaning out, Cooper said, "Wait a minute there. Just wait a minute. If you get out of this intersection and over to that sidewalk, I'll be with you in a minute"—the man stared at him—*"I'll have something for you."*

Cooper parked his car at a meter two blocks up, and when he returned, the man in the corduroy suit was standing under a silver maple tree, rubbing his back against the bark.

"Didn't think you'd come back," the man said, glancing at Cooper. His hair fell over the top of his head in every direction.

"How do you do?" Cooper held his hand out, but the man—who seemed rather old, close up—

didn't take it. "I'm Cooper." The man smelled of everything, a bit like a municipal dump. Cooper tried not to notice it.

"It doesn't matter who I am," the man said, standing unsteadily. "I don't care who I am. It's not worth anybody thinking about it." He looked up at the sky and began to pick at his coat sleeve.

"What's your name?" Cooper asked softly. "Tell me your name, please."

The old man's expression changed. He stared at the blue sky, perfectly empty of clouds, and after a moment said, "My mother used to call me James."

"Good. Well, then, how do you do, James?" The man looked dubiously at his own hand, then reached over and shook. "Would you like something to eat?"

"I like sandwiches," the man said.

"Well, then," Cooper said, "that's what we'll get you."

As they went down the sidewalk, the man stumbled into the side of a bench at a bus stop and almost tripped over a fire hydrant. He had a splay-footed walk, as if one of his legs had once been broken. Cooper began to pilot him by touching him on his back.

"Would you like to hear a bit of the Gospels?" the man asked.

"All right. Sure."

He stopped and held on to a light pole. "This is the fourth book of the Gospels. Jesus is speaking. He says, 'I will not leave you desolate; I will come to you. Yet a little while, and the world will see me no more, but you will see me; because I live, you will live also.' That's from John," the man said. They were outside the Ann Arbor Diner, a neon-and-chrome Art Deco hamburger joint three blocks down from the university campus. "There's more," the old man said, "but I don't remember it."

"Wait here," Cooper said. "I'm going to get you a sandwich."

The man was looking uncertainly at his lapel, fingering a funguslike spot.

"James!" Cooper said loudly. "Promise me you won't go away!"

The man nodded.

When Cooper came out again with a bag of french fries, a carton of milk, and a hamburger, the man had moved down the street and was leaning against the plate-glass window of a seafood restaurant with his hands covering his face. "James!" Cooper said. "Here's your meal." He held out the bag.

"Thank you." When the man removed his hands from his face, Cooper saw in his eyes a moment of complete lucidity and sanity, a glance that took in the street and himself, made a judgment about them all, and quickly withdrew from any engagement with them. He took the hamburger out of its wrapping, studied it for a moment, and then bit into it. As he ate, he gazed toward the horizon.

"I have to go to work now," Cooper said.

The man glanced at him, nodded again, and turned his face away.

"WHAT are we going to do?" Cooper said to his wife. They were lying in bed at sunrise, when they liked to talk. His hand was on her thigh and was caressing it absently and familiarly. "What are we going to do about these characters? They're on the street corners. Every month there are more of them. Kids, men, women, everybody. It's a horde. They're sleeping in the arcade, and they're pushing those terrible grocery carts around with all their worldly belongings, and it makes me nuts to watch them. I don't know what I'm going to do, Christine, but whatever it is, I have to do it." With his other hand, he rubbed his eyes. "I dream about them."

"You're such a good person," she said sleepily. Her hand brushed over him. "I've noticed that about you."

"No, that's wrong," Cooper said. "This has nothing to do with good. Virtue doesn't interest me. What this is about is not feeling crazy when I see those people."

"So what's your plan?"

He rose halfway out of bed and looked out the back window at the treehouse he had started for Alexander, their seven-year-old. Dawn was breaking, and the light came in through the slats of the blinds and fell in strips over him.

When he didn't say anything, she said, "I was just thinking. When I first met you, before you dropped out of law school, you always used to have your shirts laundered, with starch, and I remember the neat creases in your trouser legs, from somebody ironing them. You smelled of after-shave in those days. Sexually, you were ambitious. You took notes slowly. Fastidious penmanship. I like you better now."

"I remember," he said. "It was a lecture on proximate cause."

"No," she said. "It was contribution and indemnification."

"Whatever."

He took her hand and led her to the bathroom. Every morning Cooper and his wife showered together. He called it soul-showering. He had picked up the phrase from a previous girlfriend, though he had never told Christine that. Cooper had told his wife that by the time they were thirty they would probably not want to do this anymore, but they were both now twenty-eight, and she still seemed to like it.

Under the sputter of the water, Christine brushed some soap out of her eyes and said, "Cooper, were you ever a street person?"

"No."

"Smoke a lot of dope in high school?"

"No."

"I bet you drank a lot once." She was an assistant prosecutor in the district attorney's office and sometimes brought her professional habits home. "You tapped kegs and lay out on the lawns and howled at the sorority girls."

"Sometimes I did that," he said. He was soaping her back. She had wide flaring shoulders from all the swimming she had done, and the soap and water flowed down toward her waist in a pattern of V's. "I did all those things," he said, "but I never became that kind of person. What's your point?"

She turned around and faced him, the full display of her smile. "I think you're a latent vagrant," she said.

"But I'm not," he said. "I'm here. I have a job. *This* is where I am. I'm a father. How can you say that?"

"Do I love you?" she asked, water pouring over her face. "Stay with me."

"Well, sure," he said. "That's my plan."

THE SECOND one he decided to do something about was standing out of the hot summer sun in the shade of a large catalpa tree near a corner newsstand. This one was holding what seemed to be a laundry sack with the words AMERICAN LINEN SUPPLY stenciled on it. She was wearing light summer clothes—a Hawaiian shirt showing a palm tree against a bloody splash of sunset, and a pair of light cotton trousers, and red Converse tennis shoes—and she stood reading a paperback, beads of sweat falling off her face onto the pages.

This time Cooper went first to a fast-food restaurant, bought the hamburger, french fries, and milk, and then came back.

"I brought something for you," Cooper said, walking to the reading woman. "I brought you some lunch." He held out a bag. "I've seen you out here on the streets many times."

"Thank you," the woman said, taking the bag. She opened it, looked inside, and sniffed appreciatively.

"Are you homeless?" Cooper asked.

"They have a place where you can go," the woman said. She put down the bag and looked at Cooper. "My name's Estelle," she said. "But we don't have to talk."

"Oh, that's all right. If you want. Where's this shelter?"

"Over there." The woman gestured with a french fry she had picked out. She lifted the bag and began to eat. Cooper looked down at the book and saw that it was in a foreign language. The cover had fallen off. He asked her about it.

"Oh, that?" she said. She spoke with her mouth full of food, and Cooper felt a moment of superiority about her bad manners. "It's about women—what happens to women in this world. It's in French. I used to be Canadian. My mother taught me French."

Cooper stood uncomfortably. He took a key ring out of his pocket and twirled it around his index finger. "So what happens to women in this world?"

"What *doesn't?*" the woman said. "Everything happens. It's terrible but sometimes it's all right, and, besides, you get used to it."

"You seem so normal," Cooper said. "How come you're out here?"

The woman straightened up and looked at him. "My mind's not quite right," she said, scratching an eyelid. "Mostly it is but sometimes it isn't. They messed up my medication and one thing led to another and here I am. I'm not complaining. I don't have a bad life."

Cooper wanted to say that she *did* have a bad life, but stopped himself.

"If you want to help people," the woman said, "you should go to the shelter. They need volunteers. People to clean up. You could get rid of your guilt over there, mopping the floors."

"What guilt?" he asked.

"All men are guilty," she said. She was chewing but had put her bag of food on the ground and was staring hard and directly into Cooper's face. He turned toward the street. When he looked at the cars, everyone heading somewhere with a kind of fierce intentionality, braking hard at red lights and peeling rubber at the green, he felt as though he had been pushed out of his own life.

"You're still here," the woman said. "What do you want?"

"I was about to leave." He was surprised by how rude she was.

"I don't think you've ever seen the Rocky Mountains or even

the Swiss Alps, for that matter," the woman said, bending down to inspect something close to the sidewalk.

"No, you're right. I haven't traveled much."

"We're not going to kiss, if that's what you think," the woman said, still bent over. Now she straightened up again, glanced at him, and looked away.

"No," Cooper said. "I just wanted to give you a meal."

"Yes, thank you," the woman said. "And now you have to go."

"I was . . . I *was* going to go."

"I don't want to talk to you anymore," the woman said. "It's nothing against you personally, but talking to men just tires me out terribly and drains me of all my strength. Thank you very much, and goodbye." She sat down again and opened up her paperback. She took some more french fries out of the sack and began to eat as she read.

"THEY'RE polite," Cooper said, lying next to his wife. "They're polite, but they aren't nice."

"Nice? Nice? Jesus, Cooper, I prosecute rapists! Why should they be nice? They'd be crazy to be nice. Who cares about nice except you? This is the 1980s, Cooper. Get real."

He rolled over in bed and put his hand on her hip. "All right," he said.

They lay together for a while, listening to Alexander snoring in his bedroom across the hall.

"I can't sleep, Cooper," she said. "Tell me a story."

"Which one tonight?" Cooper was a good improviser of stories to help his wife relax and doze off. "Hannah, the snoopy cleaning woman?"

"No," Christine said. "I'm tired of Hannah."

"The adventures of Roderick, insurance adjuster?"

"I'm sick of him, too."

"How about another boring day in Paradise?"

"Yeah. Do that."

For the next twenty minutes, Cooper described the beauty and tedium of Paradise—the perfect rainfalls, the parks with roped-off grassy areas, the sideshows and hot-air balloon rides, the soufflés that never fell—and in twenty minutes, Christine was asleep, her fingers touching him. He was aroused. "Christine?" he whispered. But she was sleeping.

THE NEXT MORNING, as Cooper worked at his baker's bench, rolling chocolate-almond croissants, he decided that he would check out the shelter in the afternoon to see if they needed any help. He looked up from his hands, with a trace of dough and sugar under the fingernails, over toward his boss, Gilbert, who was brewing coffee and humming along to some Coltrane coming out of his old radio perched on top of the mixer. Cooper loved the bakery where he worked. He loved the smell and everything they made there. He had noticed that bread made people unusually happy. Customers closed their eyes when they ate Cooper's doughnuts and croissants and danishes. He looked up toward the skylight and saw that the sky had turned from pale blue to dark blue, what the 64 Crayola box called blue-indigo. He could tell from the tint of the sky that it was seven o'clock, time to unlock the front doors to let in the first of the customers. After Gilbert turned the key and the Firestone mechanics from down the street shuffled in to get their morning doughnuts and coffee in Styrofoam cups, Cooper stood behind the counter in his whites and watched their faces, the slow private smiles that always registered when they first caught the scent of the baked dough and the sugared fruit.

THE SHELTER was in a downtown furniture store that had gone out of business during the recession of '79. To provide some privacy, the first volunteers had covered over the front plate-glass window with long strips of paper from giant rolls, with the result that during the daytime the light inside was colored an unusual tint, somewhere between orange and off-white. As soon as he volunteered, he was asked to do odd jobs. He first went to work in the evening ladling out food—stew, usually, with ice-cream-scoop mounds of mashed potatoes.

The director of the shelter was a brisk and slightly overweight woman named Marilyn Adams, who, though tough and efficient, seemed vaguely annoyed about everything. Cooper liked her officious irritability. He didn't want any baths of feeling in this place.

Around five o'clock on a Thursday afternoon—the bakery closed at four—Cooper was making beds near the front window when he heard a voice from behind him. "Hey," the voice said. "I want to get in here."

Cooper turned around. He saw the reddest person he had ever laid eyes on: the young man's hair was red, his face flamed with sunburn and freckles, and, as if to accentuate his skin and hair tone, he was wearing a bright pink Roxy Music T-shirt. He was standing near the window, with the light behind him, and all Cooper could see of him was a still, flat expression and deeply watchful eyes. When he turned, he had the concentrated other-worldliness of figures in religious paintings.

Cooper told the young man about the shelter's regulations and told him which bed he could have. The young man—he seemed almost a boy—stood listening, his right foot thumping against the floor and his right hand shaking in the air as if he were trying to get water off it. When the young man nodded, his head went up and down too fast, and Cooper thought he was being ironic. "Who are you?" he finally asked. "My name's Cooper."

"Billy Bell," the young man said. "That's a real weird name, isn't it?" He shook his head but didn't look at Cooper or wait for him to agree or disagree. "My mother threw me out last week. Why shouldn't she? I'm twenty-three. She thought I was doing drugs. I wasn't doing drugs. Drugs are so boring. Look at those awful capitalist lizards using them and you'll know what I mean. But I *was* a problem. She was right. She had to get on my case. She decided to throw me away for a while. Trash trash. So I've been sleeping in alleys and benches and I slept for a couple of nights in the Arboretum, but there are too many mosquitoes this time of year for that and I've got bites. I was living with a girl but all my desires left me. You live here, Cooper? You homeless yourself, or what?"

"I'm a volunteer," he said. "I just work here. I've got a home."

"I don't," Billy Bell said. "People should have homes. I don't work now. I lost my job. I'm full of energy but I'm apathetic. Very little appeals to me. I guess I'm going to start some of those greasy minimum-wage things if I can stand them. I'm smart. I'm not a loser. I'm definitely not one of these messed-up ghouls who call this place home."

Cooper stood up and walked toward the kitchen, knowing that the young man would follow him. "They aren't ghouls," he said. "Look around. They're more normal than you are, probably. They're down on their luck."

"Of course they are, of course they are," Billy said, his voice floating a few inches behind Cooper's head. Cooper began to wipe off the kitchen counter, as the young man watched him. Then Billy began waving his right hand again. "My problem, Cooper, my problem is the problem of the month, which is pointlessness and the point of doing anything, which I can't see most of the time. I want to heal people but I can't do that. I'm stalled. What happened was, about a year ago, there was this day. I remember it was sunny, I mean the sun was out, and I heard these wings flapping over my head because I was out in the park with my girlfriend feeding Cheerios to the pigeons. Then this noise: *flap flap flap*. Wings, Cooper, *big* wings, taking my soul away. I didn't want to look behind me because I was afraid they'd taken my shadow, too. It could happen, Cooper, it could happen to anybody. Anyhow, after that, what I knew was, I didn't want what everybody else did, I mean I don't have any desires for anything, and at some times of day I *don't* cast a shadow. My desires just went away like that—poof, poor desires. I'm a saint now but I'm not enjoying it one bit. I can bless people but not heal them. Anybody could lose his soul the way I did. Now all I got is that sad robot feeling. You know, that five-o'clock feeling? But all day, with me."

"You mentioned your mother," Cooper said. He dropped some cleanser into the sink and began to scour. "What about your father?"

"Let me do that." Billy nudged Cooper aside and started to clean the sink with agitated, almost frantic hand motions. "I've done a *lot* of this. My father died last year. I did a lot of housecleaning. I'm a man-maid. My father was in the hospital, but we took him out, and I was trying to be, I don't know, a sophomore in college, which is a pretty dumb thing to aspire to, if you think about it. But I was also sitting by my father's bed and taking care of him—he had pancreatic cancer—and I was reading *Popular Mechanics* to him, the home-improvement section, and feeding him when he could eat, and then when he died, the wings flew over me, though that was later, and there wasn't much I wanted to do. What a sink."

As he talked, Billy's hand accelerated in its motions around the drain.

"Come on," Cooper said. "I'm going to take you somewhere."

HIS IDEA was to lift the young man's spirits, but he didn't know quite how to proceed. He took him to his car and drove him down the river road to a park, where Billy got out of the car, took his shoes off, and waded into the water. He bent down, and, as Cooper watched, cupped his hands in the river before splashing it over his face. Cooper thought his face had a strange expression, something between ecstasy and despair. He couldn't think of a word in English for this expression but thought there might be a word in another language for it. German, for example. When Billy was finished washing his face, he looked up into the sky. Pigeons and killdeer were flying overhead. After he had settled back into the front seat of Cooper's car, drops of water from his face dripping onto the seat, Billy said, "That's a good feeling, Cooper. You should try it. You wash your face in the flowing water and then you hear the cries of the birds. I'd like to think it makes me a new man but I know it doesn't. How old are you, Cooper?"

"I'm twenty-eight."

"Five years older than me. And what did you say you did?"

"I'll show you."

He drove Billy to the bakery and parked in the back alley. It was getting close to twilight. After Cooper had unlocked the back door, Billy walked into the dark bakery kitchen and began to sniff. "I like this place," he said. "I like it very much." He shook some invisible water off his hand, then ran his finger along the bench. "What's this made of?"

"Hardrock maple. It's like the wood they use in bowling alleys. Hardest wood there is. You can't dent it or break it. Look up."

Billy twisted backwards. "A skylight," he said. "Cooper, your life is on the very top of the eggshell. You have grain from the earth and you have the sky overhead. Ever been broken into?"

"No."

Cooper looked at Billy and saw, returning to him, a steady gaze made out of the watchful and flat expression he had first seen on the young man's face when he had met him a few hours before. "No," he repeated, "never have." He felt, suddenly, that he had embarked all at once on a series of misjudgments. "What did your father do, Billy?"

"He was a surgeon," Billy said. "He did surgery on people."

They stood and studied each other in the dark bakery for a moment.

Sunday magazine section with a spatula in his hand, and, like, I'll be flipping hamburgers and telling my kids to keep their hands out of the chive dip and go run in the sprinkler or do some shit like that. I'll belong to do-good groups like Save the Rainforests, and I'll ask my wife how she likes her meat, rare or well-done, and she'll say well-done with that pretty smile she has, and that's how I'll do it. A wonderful fucking barbecue, this is, with folding aluminum chairs and paper plates and ketchup all over the goddamn place. Oceans of vodka and floods of beer. Oh, and we've sprayed the yard with that big spray that kills anything that moves, and all the flies and mosquitoes and bunnies are dead at our feet. Talk about the good life. That has got to be it."

Alexander had turned around and was staring at Billy, and Christine's face had become masklike and rigid. "Finish your beer, Mr. Bell," she said. "I think you absolutely have to go now. Don't let's waste another minute. Finish the beer and back you go."

"Yes," he said, nodding and grinning.

"I suppose you think what you just said was funny," Cooper said, from where he was standing in the back of the kitchen.

"No," Billy said. "I can't be funny. I've tried often. It doesn't work. No gift for that."

"Have you been in prison, Mr. Bell?" Christine asked, looking down at her legal pad and writing something there.

"No," Billy said. "I have not."

"Oh good," Christine said. "I was afraid maybe you had been."

"Do you think that's what will become of me?" Billy asked. His voice had lowered from its previous manic delivery and become soft.

"Oh, who knows?" Christine said, running her hand through her hair. "It could happen, or maybe not."

"Because I think my life is out of my hands," Billy said. "I just don't think I have control over it any longer."

"Back you go," Christine said. "Goodbye. Fare thee well."

"Thank you," Billy said. "That was a nice blessing. And thank you for the beer. Goodbye, Alexander. It was nice meeting you."

"Nice to meet you," the boy said from the floor.

"Let's go," Cooper said, picking at Billy's elbow.

"Back I go," Billy said. "Fare thee well, Billy, goodbye and Godspeed. So long, Mr. Human Garbage. Okay, all right, yes, now I'm gone." He did a quick walk through the kitchen and let the screen door slam behind him. Christine gave Cooper a look, which he knew meant that she was preparing a speech for him, and then he followed Billy out to the car.

ON THE WAY to the shelter, Billy slouched down on the passenger side. He said nothing for five minutes. Then he said, "I noticed something about your house, Cooper. I noticed that in the kitchen there were all these glasses and cups and jars out on the counter, and the jars weren't labeled, not the way they usually label them, and so I looked inside one of them, one of those jars, and you know what I saw? I suppose you must know, because it's your kitchen."

"What?" Cooper asked.

"Pain," Billy said, looking straight ahead and nodding. "That jar was full of pain. I had to close the lid over it immediately. Now tell me something, because I don't have the answer to it. Why does a man like you, a baker, have a jar full of pain in his kitchen? Can you explain that?"

Out through the front windows, Cooper saw the reassuring lights of the city, the lamplights shining out through the front windows, and the streetlights beginning to go on. A few children were playing on the sidewalks, hopscotch and tag, and in the sky a vapor trail from a jet was beginning to dissolve into orange wisps. What was the price one paid for loving one's own life? He felt a tenderness toward existence and toward his own life, and felt guilty for that.

At the shelter, he let Billy out without saying good night. He watched the young man do his hop-and-skip walk toward the front door; then he put the car into gear and drove home. As he expected, Christine was waiting up for him and gave him a lecture, in bed, about guilty liberalism and bringing the slime element into your own home.

"That's an exaggeration," Cooper said. He was lying on his side of the bed, his hip touching hers. "That's not what he was. I'm not wrong. I'm not." He felt her lips descending over him and remembered how she always thought that his failures in judgment made him sensual.

TWO DAYS later he arrived at work before dawn and found Gilbert standing motionless in front of Cooper's own baker's bench. Cooper closed the door behind him and said, "Hey, Gilbert."

"It's all right," Gilbert said. "I already called the cops."

"What?"

Gilbert pointed. On the wood table were hundreds of pieces of broken glass from the scattered skylight in a slice-of-pie pattern, and, over the glass, a circle of dried blood the width of a teacup. Smaller dots of blood, like afterthoughts, were scattered around the bench and led across the floor to the cash register, which had been jimmied open. Cooper felt himself looking up. A bird of a type he couldn't identify was perched on the broken skylight.

"Two hundred dollars," Gilbert said, overpronouncing the words. "Somewhere somebody's all cut up for a lousy two hundred dollars. I'd give the son of a bitch a hundred not to break in, if he'd asked. But you know what I really mind?"

"The blood," Cooper said.

"Bingo." Gilbert nodded, as he coughed. "I hate the idea of this guy's blood in my kitchen, on the floor, on the table and over there in the mixing pans. I really hate it. A bakery. What a fucking stupid place to break into."

"I TOLD you so," Christine said, washing Cooper's face. Then she turned him around and ran the soapy washcloth down his back and over his buttocks.

AUGUST. Three days before Christine's birthday. Cooper and his son were walking down Main Street toward a store called the Peaceable Kingdom to get Christine a present, a small stuffed pheasant that Alexander had had his eye on for many months. Alexander's hand was in Cooper's as they crossed at the corner, after waiting for the WALK sign to go on. Alexander had been asking Cooper for an exact definition of trolls, and how they differ from ghouls. And what, he wanted to know, *what exactly* is a goblin, and how are they born? In forests? Can they be born anywhere, like trolls?

Up ahead, squatting against the window of a sporting-goods store, was the man perpetually dressed in the filthy brown corduroy suit: James. His hands were woven together at his forehead, thumbs at temples, to shade his eyes against the sun. As Cooper and his son passed by, James spoke up. He did not ask for money. He said, "Hello Cooper."

"Hello, James," Cooper said.

"Is this your boy?" He pulled his hands apart and pointed at Alexander.

"Yes."

"Daddy," Alexander said, tugging at his father's hand.

"A fine boy," James said, squinting. "Looks a bit like you." The old man smelled as he had before: like a city dump, like everything.

"Thank you," Cooper said, beaming. "He's a handsome boy, isn't he?"

"Indeed," James said. "Would you like to hear a bit of the Gospels?"

"No, thank you, James," Cooper said. "We're on our way to get this young man's mother a birthday present."

"Well, I won't keep you," the old man said.

As Cooper reached for his wallet, Alexander suddenly spoke: "Daddy, don't."

"What?"

"Don't give him any money," the boy said.

"Why not?"

Alexander couldn't say. He began to shake his head, looking at James, then at his father. He backed away, down the sidewalk, his lower lip beginning to stick out and his eyes starting to grow wet.

"Here, James," Cooper said, watching his son, who had retreated down the block and was hiding in the doorway of a hardware store. He handed the old man five dollars.

"Bless you," James said. "And bless Jesus." He put the money in his pocket, then placed his hands together in front of his chest, lowered himself to his knees, and began to pray.

"Goodbye, James," Cooper said. With his eyes closed, James nodded. Cooper ran down the block to catch up with his son.

After Alexander had finished crying, he told his father that he was afraid—afraid that he was going to bring that dirty man home, the way he did with the red-haired guy, and let him stay, maybe in the basement, in the extra room.

"I wouldn't do that," Cooper said. "Really. I wouldn't do that."

"WOULDN'T you?" his wife asked, that night, in bed. "Wouldn't you? I think you might."

"No. Not home. Not again."

But he had been accused, and he rose up and walked down the hall to his son's room. The house was theirs, no one else's; his footsteps were the only audible ones. In Alexander's room, in the dim illumination spread by the Swiss-chalet nightlight, Cooper saw his son's model airplanes and the posters of his baseball heroes, but in looking around the room, he felt that something was missing. He glanced again at his son's dresser. The piggy bank, stuffed with pennies, was gone.

He's frightened of my charity, Cooper thought, looking under the bed and seeing the piggy bank there, next to Alexander's favorite softball.

Cooper returned to bed. "He's hidden his money from me," he said.

"They do that, you know," Christine said. "And they go on doing that."

"You can't sleep," Cooper said, touching his wife.

"No," she said. "But it's all right."

"I can't tell you about Paradise," Cooper told her. "I gave you all the stories I knew."

"Well, what *do* you want?" she asked.

He put his hands over hers. "Shelter me," he said.

"Oh, Cooper," she said. "Which way this time? Which way?"

To answer her, he rolled over, and, as quietly as he could, so as not to wake their son in the next room, he took her into his arms and held her there.

Snow

TWELVE years old, and I was so bored I was
combing my hair just for the hell of it. This
particular Saturday afternoon, time was stretch-
ing out unpleasantly in front of me. I held the
comb under the tap and then stared into the
bathroom mirror as I raked the wave at the front
of my scalp upward so that it would look casual
and sharp and perfect. For inspiration I had my
transistor radio, balanced on the doorknob, tuned
to an AM Top Forty station. But the music was
making me jumpy, and instead of looking casual
my hair, soaking wet, had the metallic curve of
the rear fins of a De Soto. I looked aerodynamic
but not handsome. I dropped the comb into the
sink and went down the hallway to my brother's
room.

Ben was sitting at his desk, crumpling up papers and tossing them into a wastebasket near the
window. He was a great shot, particularly when
he was throwing away his homework. His stainless-steel sword, a souvenir of military school,
was leaning against the bookcase, and I could see
my pencil-thin reflection in it as I stood in his
doorway. "Did you hear about the car?" Ben

asked, not bothering to look at me. He was gazing through his window at Five Oaks Lake.

"What car?"

"The car that went through the ice two nights ago. Thursday. Look. You can see the pressure ridge near Eagle Island."

I couldn't see any pressure ridge; it was too far away. Cars belonging to ice fishermen were always breaking through the ice, but swallowing up a car was a slow process in January, though not in March or April, and the drivers usually got out safely. The clear lake ice reflected perfectly the flat gray sky this drought winter, and we could still see the spiky brown grass on our back lawn. It crackled and crunched whenever I walked on it.

"I don't see it," I said. "I can't see the hole. Where did you hear about this car? Did Pop tell you?"

"No," Ben said. "Other sources." Ben's sources, his network of friends and enemies, were always calling him on the telephone to tell him things. He basked in information. Now he gave me a quick glance. "Holy smoke," he said. "What did you do to your hair?"

"Nothing," I said. "I was just combing it."

"You look like that guy," he said. "The one in the movies."

"Which guy?"

"That Harvey guy."

"Jimmy Stewart?"

"Of course not," he said. "You know the one I mean. Everybody knows that guy. The Harvey guy." When I looked blank, he said, "Never mind. Let's go down to the lake and look at that car. You'd better tell them we're going." He gestured toward the other end of the house.

In the kitchen I informed my parents that I was headed somewhere with my brother, and my mother, chopping carrots for one of her stews, looked up at me and my hair. "Be back by five," she said. "Where did you say you were off to?"

"We're driving to Navarre," I said. "Ben has to get his skates sharpened."

My stepfather's eyebrows started to go up; he exchanged a glance with my mother—the usual pantomime of skepticism. I turned around and ran out of the kitchen before they could stop me. I put on my boots, overcoat, and gloves, and hurried outside to my brother's car, a 1952 Rocket 88. He was already inside. The motor roared.

The interior of the car smelled of gum, cigarettes, wet wool, analgesic balm, and after-shave. "What'd you tell them?" my brother asked.

"I said you were going to Navarre to get your skates sharpened."

He put the car into first gear, then sighed. "Why'd you do that? I have to explain everything to you. Number one: my skates aren't in the car. What if they ask to see them when we get home? I won't have them. That's a problem, isn't it? Number two: when you lie about being somewhere, you make sure you have a friend who's there who can say you *were* there, even if you weren't. Unfortunately, we don't have any friends in Navarre."

"Then we're safe," I said. "No one will say we *weren't* there."

He shook his head. Then he took off his glasses and examined them as if my odd ideas were visible right there on the frames. I was just doing my job, being his private fool, but I knew he liked me and liked to have me around. My unworldliness amused him; it gave him a chance to lecture me. But now, tired of wasting words on me, he turned on the radio. Pulling out onto the highway, he steered the car in his customary way. He had explained to me that only very old or very sick people actually grip steering wheels. You didn't have to hold the wheel to drive a car. Resting your arm over the top of the wheel gave a better appearance. You dangled your hand down, preferably with a cigarette in it, so that the car, the entire car, responded to the mere pressure of your wrist.

"Hey," I said. "Where are we going? This isn't the way to the lake."

"We're not going there first. We're going there second."

"Where are we going first?"

"We're going to Five Oaks. We're going to get Stephanie. Then we'll see the car."

"How come we're getting her?"

"Because she wants to see it. She's never seen a car underneath the ice before. She'll be impressed."

"Does she know we're coming?"

He gave me that look again. "What do they teach you at that school you go to? Of course she knows. We have a date."

"A date? It's three o'clock in the afternoon," I said. "You can't have a date at three in the afternoon. Besides, I'm along."

"Don't argue," Ben said. "Pay attention."

By the time we reached Five Oaks, the heater in my brother's car was blowing out warm air in tentative gusts. If we were going to get Stephanie, his current girlfriend, it was fine with me. I liked her smile—she had an overbite, the same as I did, but she didn't seem self-conscious about it—and I liked the way she shut her eyes when she laughed. She had listened to my crystal radio set and admired my collection of igneous rocks on one of her two visits to our house. My brother liked to bring his girlfriends over to our house because the house was old and large and, my brother said, they would be impressed by the empty rooms and the long hallways and the laundry chutes that dropped down into nowhere. They'd be snowed. Snowing girls was something I knew better than to ask my brother about. You had to learn about it by watching and listening. That's why he had brought me along.

BEN parked outside Stephanie's house and told me to wait in the car. I had nothing to do but look at houses and telephone poles. Stephanie's front-porch swing had rusted chains, and the paint around her house seemed to have blistered in cobweb patterns. One drab lamp with a low-wattage bulb was on near an upstairs window. I could see the lampshade: birds—I couldn't tell what kind—had been painted on it. I adjusted the dashboard clock. It didn't run, but I liked to have it seem accurate. My brother had said that anyone who invented a clock that would really work in a car would become a multimillionaire. Clocks in cars never work, he said, because the mainsprings can't stand the shock of potholes. I checked my wristwatch and yawned. The inside of the front window began to frost over with my breath. I decided that when I grew up I would invent a new kind of timepiece for cars, without springs or gears. At three-twenty I adjusted the clock again. One minute later, my brother came out of the house with Stephanie. She saw me in the car, and she smiled.

I opened the door and got out. "Hi, Steph," I said. "I'll get in the backseat."

"That's okay, Russell," she said, smiling, showing her overbite. "Sit up in front with us."

"Really?"

She nodded. "Yeah. Keep us warm."

She scuttled in next to my brother, and I squeezed in on her right side, with my shoulder against the door. As soon as the car started, she and my brother began to hold hands: he steered with his left wrist over the steering wheel, and she held his right hand. I watched all this, and Stephanie noticed me watching. "Do you want one?" she asked me.

"What?"

"A hand." She gazed at me, perfectly serious. "My other hand."

"Sure," I said.

"Well, take my glove off," she said. "I can't do it by myself." My brother started chuckling, but she stopped him with a look. I took Stephanie's wrist in my left hand and removed her glove, finger by finger. I hadn't held hands with anyone since second grade. Her hand was not much larger than mine, but holding it gave me an odd sensation, because it was a woman's hand, and where my fingers were bony, hers were soft. She was wearing a bright-green cap, and when I glanced up at it she said, "I like your

hair, Russell. It's kind of slummy. You're getting to look dangerous. Is there any gum?"

I figured she meant in the car. "There's some up there on the
dashboard," Ben said. His car always had gum in it. It was a
museum of gum. The ashtrays were full of cigarette butts and
gum, mixed together, and the floor was flecked silver from the
foil wrappers.

"I can't reach it," Stephanie said. "You two have both my
hands tied down."

"Okay," I said. I reached up with my free hand and took a
piece of gum and unwrapped it. The gum was light pink, a
sunburn color.

"Now what?" I asked.

"What do you think?" She looked down at me, smiled again,
then opened her mouth. I suddenly felt shy. "Come on, Russell,"
she said. "Haven't you ever given gum to a girl before?" I raised
my hand with the gum in it. She kept her eyes open and on me.
I reached forward, and just as I got the gum close to her mouth
she opened wider, and I slid the gum in over her tongue without
even brushing it against her lipstick. She closed and began chewing.

"Thank you," she said. Stephanie and my brother nudged each
other. Then they broke out in short quick laughs—vacation
laughter. I knew that what had happened hinged on my igno-
rance, but that I wasn't exactly the butt of the joke and could
laugh, too, if I wanted. My palm was sweaty, and she could
probably feel it. The sky had turned darker, and I wondered
whether, if I was still alive fifty years from now, I would
remember any of this. I saw an old house on the side of the
highway with a cracked upstairs window, and I thought, that's
what I'll remember from this whole day when I'm old—that one
cracked window.

Stephanie was looking out at the dry winter fields and suddenly said, "The state of Michigan. You know who this state is
for? You know who's really happy in this state?"

"No," I said. "Who?"

"Chickens and squirrels," she said. "They love it here."

MY BROTHER parked the car on the driveway down by our dock, and we walked out onto the ice on the bay. Stephanie was stepping awkwardly, a high-center-of-gravity shuffle. "Is it safe?" she asked.

"Sure, it's safe," my brother said. "Look." He began to jump up and down. Ben was heavy enough to be a tackle on his high-school football team, and sounds of ice cracking reverberated all through the bay and beyond into the center of the lake, a deep echo. Already, four ice fishermen's houses had been set up on the ice two hundred feet out—four brightly painted shacks, male hideaways—and I could see tire tracks over the thin layer of sprinkled snow. "Clear the snow and look down into it," he said.

After lowering herself to her knees, Stephanie dusted the snow away. She held her hands to the side of her head and looked. "It's real thick," she said. "Looks a foot thick. How come a car went through?"

"It went down in a channel," Ben said, walking ahead of us and calling backward so that his voice seemed to drift in and out of the wind. "It went over a pressure ridge, and that's all she wrote."

"Did anyone drown?"

He didn't answer. She ran ahead to catch up to him, slipping, losing her balance, then recovering it. In fact I knew that no one had drowned. My stepfather had told me that the man driving the car had somehow—I wasn't sure how a person did this—pulled himself out through the window. Apparently the front end dropped through the ice first, but the car had stayed up for a few minutes before it gradually eased itself into the lake. The last two nights had been very cold, with lows around fifteen below zero, and by now the hole the car had gone through had iced over.

Both my brother and Stephanie were quite far ahead of me, and I could see them clutching at each other, Stephanie leaning against him, and my brother trying out his military-school peacock walk. I attempted this walk for a moment, then thought better of it. The late-afternoon January light was getting very raw: the sun came out for a few seconds, lighting and coloring what there was, then disappeared again, closing up and leaving us in a kind of sour grayness. I wondered if my brother and Stephanie actually liked each other or whether they were friends because they had to be.

I ran to catch up to them. "We should have brought our skates," I said, but they weren't listening to me. Ben was pointing at some clear ice, and Stephanie was nodding.

"Quiet down," my brother said. "Quiet down and listen."

All three of us stood still. Some cloud or other was beginning to drop snow on us, and from the ice underneath our feet we heard a continual chinging and barking as the ice slowly shifted.

"This is exciting," Stephanie said.

My brother nodded, but instead of looking at her he turned slightly to glance at me. Our eyes met, and he smiled.

"It's over there," he said, after a moment. The index finger of his black leather glove pointed toward a spot in the channel between Eagle Island and Crane Island where the ice was ridged and unnaturally clear. "Come on," he said.

We walked. I was ready at any moment to throw myself flat if the ice broke beneath me. I was a good swimmer—Ben had taught me—but I wasn't sure how well I would swim wearing all my clothes. I was absorbent and would probably sink headfirst, like that car.

"Get down," my brother said.

We watched him lowering himself to his hands and knees, and we followed. This was probably something he had learned in military school, this crawling. "We're ambushing this car," Stephanie said, creeping in front of me.

"There it is," he said. He pointed down.

This new ice was so smooth that it reminded me of the thick glass in the Shedd Aquarium, in Chicago. But instead of seeing a loggerhead turtle or a barracuda I looked through the ice and saw this abandoned car, this two-door Impala. It was wonderful to see—white-painted steel filtered by ice and lake water—and I wanted to laugh out of sheer happiness at the craziness of it. Dimly lit but still visible through the murk, it sat down there, its huge trunk and the sloping fins just a bit green in the algae-colored light. This is a joke, I thought, a practical joke meant to confuse the fish. I could see the car well enough to notice its radio-antenna, and the windshield wipers halfway up the front window, and I could see the chrome of the front grille reflecting the dull light that ebbed down to it from where we were lying on our stomachs, ten feet above it.

"That is one unhappy automobile," Stephanie said. "Did anyone get caught inside?"

"No," I said, because no one had, and then my brother said, "Maybe."

I looked at him quickly. As usual, he wasn't looking back at me. "They aren't sure yet," he said. "They won't be able to tell until they bring the tow truck out here and pull it up."

Stephanie said, "Well, either they know or they don't. Someone's down there or not, right?"

Ben shook his head. "Maybe they don't know. Maybe there's a dead body in the backseat of that car. Or in the trunk."

"Oh, no," she said. She began to edge backward.

"I was just fooling you," my brother said. "There's nobody down there."

"What?" She was behind the area where the ice was smooth, and she stood up.

"I was just teasing you," Ben said. "The guy that was in the car got out. He got out through the window."

"Why did you lie to me?" Stephanie asked. Her arms were crossed in front of her chest.

"I just wanted to give you a thrill," he said. He stood up and walked over to where she was standing. He put his arm around her.

"I don't mind normal," she said. "Something could be normal and I'd like that, too." She glanced at me. Then she whispered into my brother's ear for about fifteen seconds, which is a long time if you're watching. Ben nodded and bent forward and whispered something in return, but I swiveled and looked around the bay at all the houses on the shore, and the old amusement park in the distance. Lights were beginning to go on, and, as if that weren't enough, it was snowing. As far as I was concerned, all those houses were guilty, both the houses and the people in them. The whole state of Michigan was guilty—all the adults, anyway—and I wanted to see them locked up.

"Wait here," my brother said. He turned and went quickly off toward the shore of the bay.

"Where's he going?" I asked.

"He's going to get his car," she said.

"What for?"

"He's going to bring it out on the ice. Then he's going to drive me home across the lake."

"That's really stupid!" I said. "That's really one of the dumbest things I ever heard! You'll go through the ice, just like that car down there did."

"No, we won't," she said. "I know we won't."

"How do you know?"

"Your brother understands this lake," she said. "He knows where the pressure ridges are and everything. He just *knows*, Russell. You have to trust him. And he can always get off the ice if he thinks it's not safe. He can always find a road."

"Well, I'm not going with you," I said. She nodded. I looked at her, and I wondered if she might be crazed with the bad judgment my parents had told me all teenagers had. Bad judgment of this kind was starting to interest me; it was a powerful antidote for boredom, which seemed worse.

"You don't want to come?"

"No," I said. "I'll walk home." I gazed up the hill, and in the distance I could see the lights of our house, a twenty-minute walk across the bay.

"Okay," Stephanie said. "I didn't think you'd want to come along." We waited. "Russell, do you think your brother is interested in me?"

"I guess so," I said. I wasn't sure what she meant by "interested." Anybody interested him, up to a point. "He says he likes you."

"That's funny, because I feel like something in the Lost and Found," she said, scratching her boot into the ice. "You know, one of those gloves that don't match anything." She put her hand on my shoulder. "One glove. One left-hand glove, with the thumb missing."

I could hear Ben's car starting, and then I saw it heading down Gallagher's boat landing. I was glad he was driving out toward us, because I didn't want to talk to her this way anymore.

Stephanie was now watching my brother's car. His headlights were on. It was odd to see a car with headlights on out on the ice, where there was no road. I saw my brother accelerate and fishtail the car, then slam on the brakes and do a 360-degree spin. He floored it, revving the back wheels, which made a high, whining sound on the ice, like a buzz saw working through wood. He was having a thrill and soon would give Stephanie another thrill by driving her home across ice that might break at any time. Thrills did it, whatever it was. Thrills led to other thrills.

"Would you look at that," I said.

She turned. After a moment she made a little sound in her throat. I remember that sound. When I see her now, she still makes it—a sign of impatience or worry. After all, she didn't go through the ice in my brother's car on the way home. She and my brother didn't drown, together or separately. Stephanie had two marriages and several children. Recently, she and her second husband adopted a Korean baby. She has the complex dignity of many small-town people who do not resort to alcohol until well after night has fallen. She continues to live in Five Oaks, Michigan, and she works behind the counter at the post office, where I buy stamps from her and gossip, holding up the line, trying to make her smile. She still has an overbite and she still laughs easily, despite the moody expression that comes over her when she relaxes. She has moved back to the same house she grew up in. Even now the exterior paint on that house blisters in cobweb patterns. I keep track of her. She and my brother certainly didn't get married; in fact, they broke up a few weeks after seeing the Chevrolet under ice.

"What are we doing out here?" Stephanie asked. I shook my head. "In the middle of winter, out here on this stupid lake? I'll tell you, Russell, I sure don't know. But I do know that your brother doesn't notice me enough, and I can't love him unless he notices me. You know your brother. You know what he pays attention to. What do I have to do to get him to notice me?"

I was twelve years old. I said, "Take off your shoes."

She stood there, thinking about what I had said, and then, quietly, she bent down and took off her boots, and, putting her hand on my shoulder to balance herself, she took off her brown loafers and her white socks. She stood there in front of me with her bare feet on the ice. I saw in the grayish January light that her toenails were painted. Bare feet with painted toenails on the ice—this was a desperate and beautiful sight, and I shivered and felt my fingers curling inside my gloves.

"How does it feel?" I asked.

"You'll know," she said. "You'll know in a few years."

My brother drove up close to us. He rolled down his window and opened the passenger-side door. He didn't say anything. I watched Stephanie get into the car, carrying her shoes and socks and boots, and then I waved goodbye to them before turning to walk back to our house. I heard the car heading north across the ice. My brother would be looking at Stephanie's bare feet on the floor of his car. He would probably not be saying anything just now.

When I reached our front lawn, I stood out in the dark and looked in through the kitchen window. My mother and stepfather were sitting at the kitchen counter; I couldn't be sure if they were speaking to each other, but then I saw my mother raise her arm in one of her can-you-believe-this gestures. I didn't want to go inside. I wanted to feel cold, so cold that the cold itself became permanently interesting. I took off my overcoat and my gloves. Tilting my head back, I felt some snow fall onto my face. I thought of the word "exposure" and of how once or twice a year deer hunters in the Upper Peninsula died of it, and I bent down and stuck my hand into the snow and frozen grass and held it there. The cold rose from my hand to my elbow, and when I had counted to forty and couldn't stand another second of it, I picked up my coat and gloves and walked into the bright heat of the front hallway.

Silent Movie

SHE WAS tired of men's voices, of their volume
and implacability. She had the idea that she
would spend the day not listening to any of
them. She would just shut them off. She would
try to spend the day inside images, instead. She
wasn't sure it was possible.

She was in the bathroom when he started talking to her. While she stood in front of the mirror, he soaped himself off in the shower, and his
words came out of the stall toward her, like
clouds of steam: Maureen this, Maureen that.
They were like clouds in their humidity, in the
way they blocked her view of her own face.

She concentrated on the swirling of the water
in the sink, the clear musky brown of the oval
soap in the dish, the articulated joints of her own
hands and feet.

At the breakfast table his words came at her
again: he was like a television set, except that
there was no way you could unplug him. And
he looked almost always like someone trying to
be serious, as if his face were being stretched or
pulled to the sides for emphasis, and some iron
weight were resting on top of his head. He

talked. The talk was supposed to be about the problem, but the talk *was* the problem. For him, the solution would follow from her listening, and then her agreement.

She gazed at the sun coming in through the window. Its rays fell on the rusty checkerboard-pattern floor tile and passed through the blue glass vase she had set on the windowsill. She sliced some strawberries into a bowl with cereal and was studying the way the white of the milk surrounding them intensified their redness. The cereal glowed gold with its beautiful assortment of random shapes.

He talked on and on. He talked while eating. He never looked at his food; it was there on his plate—toast, whatever—and then it disappeared inside him. She saw his mouth opening and closing.

When she had had more than enough, she put on her boots, overcoat, and gloves. She took the path out to the woods behind the house. The snowfall during the night had left a layering of soft powder on the surface, on which she could see the tracks of rabbits or squirrels, like little arrows. The early-morning sun, as she walked, pecked at her with light through the variously moving branches. The sun is a woman, she thought; the sun has always been a woman, and I don't care if that sounds crazy or not. Ahead of her on the path was a dead bird, a bluejay. Against the snow its feathers looked faded and muddy. In her gloves she picked up the stiffened bird. After gazing for a moment at its iridescent blue feathers, she flung it with both hands into the woods where it would decompose.

She kept the radio off in the car, on the way to work, studying instead the flag hanging limply in front of the post office, the exhaust from the other cars rising in disappearing puffs into the ice blue morning air.

If he had been in the car, he would have said: This is about the doctor, isn't it? This is about your appointment this afternoon. That's why you're not listening to me, that's why you're tuning me out, that's why that's why that's why . . .

She silenced the memory of his voice by studying the patterns

of white road salt, arranged almost like a painting, a Jackson
Pollock, on the trunk of the green Chevy waiting at the light
in front of her. She had never appreciated the hot glassy red of
brake lights before, placed this way next to spatterings of road
salt.

HER APPOINTMENT with the doctor was at two o'clock.

In the meantime she sat or stood in the back room of the florist,
cutting roses and chrysanthemums and arranging them for display
in the refrigerated cases. When an order came in, she would also
wrap potted flowers, paper-white narcissus and gloxinia, in green
tissue paper, for shipment to hospitals and residences. The room
smelled of water and roses and cigarette smoke. She worked with
a fierce old woman, Loretta, who smoked Viceroys and dressed
in black day after day. The purple gloxinias looked beautiful
against her black dress. She would talk to the flowers, giving
them pet names. "Oh, Donald," she'd say, arranging some daisy
pomps for a hospital room, "don't be like that, get *with* it."

She was happy to look at the old woman's face: it had the
resignation of accepted age: bright wide eyes behind the glasses,
hair going every which way, not giving a damn, and a wide smile
showing yellow teeth. She had a little mole almost hidden behind
her left cheek. And she was mostly deaf, so she pretended to hear
what Maureen said to her by nodding and shouting replies. "It's
all profit, darling, every sunrise," she'd say, her voice rising from
a mumble and ending in something close to a shout.

The old woman and Maureen would share their lunches: Maureen would hand Loretta a ripe purple plum and get an odd
yellow-orange miniature brick of cheese in return. Just before
lunch Maureen ran in place, did jumping jacks and push-ups
while the old woman watched and counted, nodding her head.
"You young women are so tough," she'd say. "Like farm
women."

IN THE doctor's waiting room she gazed at the painting opposite her: something in green and flesh tones that looked like a
broken fender. The room smelled of rubbing alcohol. Opposite
her a woman in a red plaid flannel shirt and jeans was reading
a copy of *Life* and looking vaguely apprehensive. The room's
wallpaper had a burlap texture; the carpeting was light gray. We
have to get used to these textures, Maureen thought; they're
everywhere. A tropical fish aquarium gurgled on a table by the
entrance. Inside the aquarium were tiny fish with neon colors,
brilliant blues and reds, radiating along them lengthwise.

The doctor stood her in front of a white wall panel lit from
inside. With careful measured violence he shoved her X-rays up
so that they were clamped at the top of the panel.

She noticed a pot of paper-white narcissus on the side table.
Possibly it had come from her nursery. In front of her was the
examining table.

He was saying that she was in good health, after all.

She stared at the X-rays of her upper torso. She saw her own
bone structure, the rib cage, the collarbone, the bones of the upper
arm. On the X-ray her body looked like the fields of snow in
which she had walked this morning and discovered the dead
bluejay. There were indications in outlined snowy light of where
her breasts were, and her heart, and her lungs.

Only a man, she thought, would invent an X-ray. It would
take a man's mind to unite technology with the desire to see not
only in but through the body, past the flesh.

His fingers were pointing at images on the X-ray. His hand
swept back and forth across the negative image of her breasts. He
wore a small diamond ring on the little finger of his right hand.
She considered this an affectation, a failure of taste, déclassé, a
vanity. She would get another doctor.

SMALL BIRDS fluttered for warmth at the tops of chimneys.
She noticed that some people in the residential areas hadn't

taken down their Christmas lights. One month after Christmas and still the lights stayed up, colored electric bulbs fighting the despair brought on by snow and ice and daylight that concluded at five-thirty P.M.

She noticed a plastic Santa on somebody's roof. His right arm was lifted, as if waving at her.

What would she do about him, his endless talk, his relentless seriousness, his face that seemed stretched out to the sides out of pure rage and earnestness, his bag of presents, his reindeer, his hands, his trips down the chimney, all his invasions.

"Loretta," she asked, back at the florist's, "how do I get rid of this guy?"

"Darling," Loretta shouted, "first ignore him and then just move out."

WHAT she wanted was a vacation from words spoken by voices below middle C. After work, she was running in her sweatsuit and shoes on the dark sidewalks. She ran for the silence and the sweat; she ran for the priceless hard breathing.

She ran so effortlessly that streetlights, trees, and stationary dogs seemed to move past her on a moving treadmill. She felt so strong that she had the sensation that she wasn't moving; they were.

Back in the house, he was there, sitting on the sofa, talking; then he was in the kitchen, under the electric light, talking; then he was sitting or standing outside the bathroom, talking; and she pretended to be Russian, not understanding a word, because she didn't understand what he was getting at anyway.

Now, at nighttime, the blue vase in the kitchen was a darker blue color, and the soap in the shower was a darker white.

LEAVING a man, calmly and peacefully, looks like this.

It looks like soap and fingernail clippers and emery boards and tampons and one bottle of perfume placed inside a yellow plastic kit.

It is a brown suitcase. It is the clothes for the week, the underwear and blouses and skirts and shirts and jeans and the sweatsuit, folded nicely so that they fit snugly inside the brown— that color again!—corduroy bag.

Meanwhile, of course, he is talking, talking and eating. Food disappears inside him and then reappears, this time as words. Now he is waving his arms at her. He is saying the usual things.

She is giving him a few days to collect his possessions, his prized objects, and leave, because the house, after all, is hers.

A mahogany table, with a flow-blue plate in the center. A brindle cat, named Jesse, sleeping on a wool blanket near the doorway. Her fingers, their articulated joints, articulating themselves away from the house, where the hallway light flickers as she walks past it. There is no shouting. There are no words. It is peaceful here. Inside, where it matters, the quietness is like snow falling in a forest, where Santa has never visited with his terrible sack of presents.

She didn't want any flowers; she only wanted to lie with her hands turned up and be utterly empty. The silence there is large; it dazes her.

And a happy ending: the cat beside her, the lights of the house growing smaller in the rearview mirror as she drives away, the happy ending of a silent movie as the headlights of the little car guide her toward her friend's house, where she will stay tonight. And the images of snow falling and resting quietly on the school playground, falling on the swings, the jungle gym, the teeter-totter, the merry-go-round, the slide, all of them seen quickly, by moonlight.

Her heart beats in the car, beats out of sheer love of her, and it is that love, and not any sorrow over the separation, that makes her cry now out of happiness, but only one tear, which is enough.

That is how it looks.

The Old Fascist
in Retirement

"DO YOU know that story about Nietzsche?"

The voice rose to the old poet out of the darkness.

"You know that story about Nietzsche, don't you, what he was doing just before his mind gave way?"

The old man nodded. Yes, everybody knows that story.

The voice continued as if it had not paid any attention to his response. Below the balcony where the old man was sitting, a vaporetto steamed southward on the far side of the canal, its engine making a two-note slur as it rocked on the waves. "You know that on the day Nietzsche lost his mind, he saw on the streets of Turin a cart horse being whipped. We can imagine, if we choose to, small droplets of blood clinging to the horse's flanks, to the smooth hairs. What we imagine is always our choice. Nietzsche rushed toward the horse and threw his arms around the beast's neck. Something broke in the philosopher's mind at that moment, some small crucial relay of synapses. Nietzsche collapsed to the ground. From that moment on he never uttered a completely lucid sentence."

Yes, the old man said. I know that story.

"I thought so," the voice said. "And what else do you remember?"

The voice faded back into the water: a clawed winged voice. He didn't know to whom it belonged. He could not see anyone sitting with him on the balcony overlooking the canal and the stone jetty. And yet the voice came and departed regularly as if he had given it a special status. The voice would have to be dealt with. He would have to speak to it. Sharp flagellant light whirled above the horizon. Specks of blood on a flogged horse. False dawn? If so, according to what authority?

IN HIS TIME, the old man had often seen paradise: jagged panes, lightning angles, the unformulated glory of smashed leaded glass. In Paris in 1924 he had watched a workman accidentally drop from a second-story scaffolding a windowpane, which had broken on the boulevard of the Quai Voltaire. The shattered glass on the sidewalk contained the geometrical shapes of paradise: transparent isosceles edges, razors: glass made beautiful by fracture and the accidents of force.

He had wanted his poems to be as beautiful as that broken glass. He wanted them to cut into the skin and evoke the blood-flow. That day, he had planted his cane in the gutter of the Quai Voltaire and studied those glass shards while the oblivious pedestrians made their dulled ways around him.

He knew his poetry had no pity and that all tenderness had been expunged from its light. There, in poetry, the light was as hard and as brutal as purity required. He had told everyone this and explained it patiently. He wanted to wean the world. He wanted humankind to grow up, to see the beauty of pitilessness and broken glass. The point was to damn fear and softness forever, not to give in to the temporary comforts.

He suspected that he had grown stupid trying to tell them.

IN THE ROOMS behind him his caretakers came and went, the women and the visitors, his society. He closed his eyes, and his mind, which had once been his ally and confederate, flashed up Chinese ideograms which, when he tried to read them, denounced him. In Chinese, the lettering of heaven, he read that he had been a fool. He had left the spectrum of intelligence at one end, the genius end, and reentered it again at the other end, the fool end. There he was now, a fool, and he was damned if he would open up his mouth in public one more time.

Somehow he rose, put on his cape and scarf, and found himself out on the sidewalk, heading who-knows-where. By accident he had sneaked past the women and the visitors to his decrepit salon, and now here he was outside, the night air smelling of history, a damp and fishy smell. As he walked, his mossy gray hair rising like aging fire from his head, the citizens of Venice saluted him. They bowed. "Maestro," they said.

He walked long enough through the alleyways and past the shuttered vegetable markets to lose himself. He had stepped into a cobbled street he didn't recognize, with closed grocers' shops and a bleak café with a crackling blue neon sign. The usual cats prowled near the gutters, and the old man reached into his pockets for pieces of cheese and bread. The cats mewled and slithered around his ankles. At the end of the street was a fountain with a broken stone dish through whose cracks water dribbled; above it was a statue of a lion, one of its legs broken off.

None of this was familiar to him. He stopped for a breath and wrapped his burgundy wool scarf closer around his neck. Darkness here. He felt something on the back of his neck and looked up. Snow was falling in the dark, a rarity. Pennsylvania: those afternoon cloud snowstorms with sun burning in another part of the sky: light ridging the snow. Bright air descending.

> *white dust the prismatic light seeks*
> *while Pomona rests under amethyst branches*

He waited on the sidewalk for his eyesight to clear, to clarify. Seeing a single lamp, fire butter yellow, he walked toward it. It receded ahead of him. Laughter, which he took at once to be American tourist laughter, echoed on stone and green canal water. He kept his eyes on the pavement, but from the sound of it two Americans, a boy and a girl, passed him. Still laughing. Pain, which he had spent a lifetime studiously ignoring, rose from his ankle, inhabited his kneecap for a moment, then actually lifted his right leg at the hip. A pain step.

He stopped to breathe. His old hatreds returned to him, the old friends. Coming to the end of the street, he turned left into a dank blank alleyway where the four-story houses seemed to tilt toward him, and he heard the sound of a radio playing Mascagni accompanied by two women bickering about opera. A dog came up to the old man, barked, wagged its tail; the poet rolled the bread in his pocket into a ball and dropped it straight down into the dog's dark mouth.

As he patted the dog, he felt the anger against the young Americans achieving a level. Against such people, the bourgeoisie, he had thrown his poems like bricks. Obstreperous box dwellers, the bourgeoisie devoured and consumed, leaving behind their filth. The dog, sensing rage rising in the old man, turned its head away from his hand and trotted down the alley.

He watched the dog go

> *that after borrowing, after the eating and tearing*
> *hoc caverat mens provida Reguli*
> *dissentientis condicionibus*

For a moment his mind caught fire and burned, like an old warehouse. It was an animal pleasure to feel it burning.

He found himself walking into a peculiarly lit square where late-night strangers could be seen inside a café drinking apéritifs. Despite the snow of a few moments before, the old man felt revived by the small fire of his hatred. Seeing the long receding plane of the sidewalk, the unsettled lamps electrically sputtering, he let the wings of his mind extend; he unsheathed the claws; and as he crossed diagonally another futile-looking square, he saw two Jews pass by him without seeing him. They were speaking heavily accented Italian.

He had once had thoughts about Jews, lengthy serpentine thoughts, but there were no thoughts there anymore.

He leaned against a wall between two drainpipes, which in the darkness had a brittle and crustacean sheen. He had once tried to set everybody straight about the Jews. On the radio. Elsewhere. The trouble was, since the time when silence had swallowed him up—it now seemed to have been all his life but maybe it was only last year or even yesterday—a small suspicion had fallen. The canal water lapped ahead of him; he thought he saw a rat scuttling in front of him, smooth glossy creature, crawling headfirst cheerfully ratlike down toward the water. The old man smiled, observing the rat. Yes, a suspicion had fallen. The suspicion was that he himself was a Jew. Had always been a Jew. Had not been informed about it. Had been kept in the dark. *Nunc retrosum vela dare atque iterare cursus cogor relictos.* In the dark about being a Jew, and, a prank, had been brought around to give speeches against them. Now that he was living in the trash can, an old piece of human rubbish, it had come to him, and it had a woman's face. Not smooth: angles and jags. She came to him in the street here in this city on a crepuscular Sunday and she had said, Henceforth you are a Jew. And she had left him, all but the memory of her face. Five efficient lines, but he recognized her. She had touched him and he knew. Canst thou see?

"Do you know that story about Nietzsche?"

The voice rose out of the paving stones, without footsteps. Like a thief, he would have yellowish eyes. The old man could see the eyes without looking.

"Do you know what he was doing before his mind gave way?"

THE OLD MAN accelerated. Against the paving stones his cane tapped a Provençal poetry rhythm, a beat of three against two. He was entering a mostly darkened street with one tavern. Beyond it, out of season, was an ice cream pushcart, with tin sides—aluminum? chrome? he couldn't remember materials— reflecting the sidewalk lights, a white dress, and, distorted, the legs of a woman standing close by. But after all it was not deep winter. Approaching, he stood head down near the woman, hoping to breathe in that rare green scent of oak leaves that American women sometimes carried with them: the odor of innocence, the odor of what-if-everybody.

He inhaled the woman's presence and thought of American trees, oaks and elms. Like those trees, the woman stood like something antecedent to the human reign. With her was a young man, so American that he wore a cap with a visor in the streets of Venice.

"Yes?" The ice cream vendor looked down into his cart, wanting the old man's order. Simple: he wanted vanilla. But he could not say it, not in any of the several languages that he knew, not a single syllable. Each one of the syllables had left him, taken its leave. He looked at the ice cream vendor.

"Ah, Maestro!" The Italian smile of recognition. The vendor spread his hand over his cart: anything here is yours, Maestro. Any flavor for the great man, the illustrious poet.

Sound—crickets, locusts crawling from their discarded shells—broke and shattered and echoed in his throat. It was the trench warfare of sound and silence: and words filling him with nausea. The words were eyes, gazing at him, floating halfway between the street and the windows. The words were the splinters around which this infection had grown. They were beetles; they were eyeless statues. Under his tongue the words had at last fallen to pieces like dried mushrooms. So that now—and this was hell, the inability to perform the smallest acts—he was unable to say what flavor ice cream he preferred.

The woman with the aroma of the oak tree grasped his arm. "Hey," she said, "are you all right? What's the matter? Jerry, come here."

The old man shook his head and freed his arm. He would not let himself be pitied by a couple of normal Americans wandering around the streets of Venice after dark. He would rather be pitied by a walled garden of eyeless statues. These Americans spoke English with such flat vowels that the sounds seemed to have come out of a plow cutting through topsoil. The normal Americans were consulting. Drawn together, they whispered, glancing at the old man with expressions of predatory helpfulness.

He bent his head. It occurred to him that he had not known many normal Americans. Perhaps none.

"Il poeta," the ice cream vendor explained, obviously pleased to be in the old man's company. "The famous and renowned poet. Of your country." He raised his palm toward the old man as if he were blessing him. "Of your country, America."

"Why doesn't he say anything?" the American woman asked.

Struggling with his English, the vendor said, "He says nothing, signora. For many years now nothing." He handed the old man an ice cream cone. Vanilla: what he wanted: he took it and reached with his other hand into his pocket for coins. Nothing there, all money removed by the women for the protection of himself. The vendor held up his hand again, this time like a traffic cop: no money, Maestro. Not from you.

"Why doesn't he say anything?" the visored American asked, taking off his cap and scratching his hair.

"Not for years," the vendor said. Then, in a scandalized whisper, he said, "Arrested!"

"Arrested?" the woman repeated. "A poet under arrest? I never heard of a poet being arrested. They don't arrest poets in America. Besides, I never heard of him. He couldn't have been *that* bad!" She said this as if the old man were not only mute, but also deaf. Giving him a last smile, she took her husband's crooked arm and led him off into foreign dark.

The old man bowed to the vendor. "Grazie," he said.

Sometimes he could say it.

"You spoke," the vendor said.

The old man nodded. Then, holding what was left of his ice cream, he took himself into the shadows, where he was comfortable.

SOMETHING about the night in Venice: one never saw stars here: a relief. He hated the stars. Overhead only the universe of the earthly atmosphere—smoke, haze, and breath. Though he had struggled only for light

> *the hawk form wing gathering*
> *and the integers poured from gold cups*
> *Ratio: ash, elm, and the thick sap drying*

the light had abandoned him. He had been a terrorist for light. He had taken up with The Boss in the cause of light: of order and economic hierarchy and the shapely organization of the affairs of state. And the light had flayed them both. They had lifted The Boss up on the hook, in the light, stripping him down to the bloody cartilage in the public square.

As for the old man, after caging him, they had left him with his life, so that he could cultivate a proper respect for hell. In the Victorian melodramas of his youth, the ones he had seen in Chicago and Philadelphia, they had lit the villain with a green light, the light of vanity and envy. They had been quite intelligent in those days.

He had learned a mild respect for the green precincts of hell. He was now so old that he knew the gods had decided to let him live so that he could suffer properly, in a timely manner. He was now four hundred years old and would live at least for another two hundred years.

UNDER a streetlight he felt himself shriveling. He took two steps to the right and leaned against a wall, damp like all the other stonework and now snowy, and he bowed his head as one of his hands picked at the skin of the other hand. Was this the place? He had an idea that he was out here on this cold evening for a rendezvous with a woman who was almost as old as he was but who had not somehow aged, who was unaging and therefore beautiful. Above all she was deeply and terrifyingly symmetrical. Out of another window came another swell of music, this time Wagner, the dripping poison of *Parsifal.*

He had a headache. He could not remember when he had not had one. And—this was the strange quality to his headaches— they were in both his head and his hands. He plucked at his hands in order to get the headache out of them. His ideas were stuffed down inside his hands. It came from too much writing.

He waited for her, watching the occasional snow; he tried to clear the phlegm out of his throat but failed. In this side street only a few couples passed, smoking cigarettes, but not speaking. He thought of language with nostalgia, a country house, all its doors locked.

Possibility for a long poem: a poet—an American!—takes over the country of language and becomes its ruler but then is violently deposed and cannot return, even to speak. The dictator robbed of words who cannot dictate. *Dicto, dictare.* To take dictation. The old man felt a sweet nostalgia for terror. And a warmer nostalgia for cleanliness, the purifying light.

"Do you know that story about Nietzsche? in the streets of Turin . . ."

"Leave me alone," the old man muttered.

"No: listen. Listen to me. He raised his arms around the horse's neck. He embraced the horse. He hugged it."

The old man swayed from side to side.

"The bright specks of blood . . . Nietzsche Caesar . . . the flogged horse . . . and the last act, *the one you of all people should be aware of,* Nietzsche's last act, of purest tenderness . . ."

The old man raised his hands to his face. But did not weep.

IN THE darkness of his hands he saw the lost American order. He had thought of his native country as a semicomical circus, a joke-society where men and women ran around in public in their underwear. America was a place of tunnels, and, more recently, of mental hospitals where he had been, for rather too many years, detained. He had wanted to put his hands to America and shape it as a child shapes putty. For a time he thought he would succeed to the place of John Adams and Thomas Jefferson as a theorist of societal arrangements.

But something had gone wrong. He was still trying to understand where: in some location there had been fissures.

America had put its hands on *him* and shaped *him* like putty. The fissures were in his own head. It occurred to him that he was Roderick Usher, an expatriate American like himself, and that the rotting palace consisted of his ideas: all the ideas, the ideas that had gone into the letters and speeches and reviews and essays and poems. False friends, they had moved away, one and all. Economics, history, poetics, politics, they had sprouted wings and flown. Now—and he saw this, too—in his old age he was mixing metaphors: the ideas could not be birds and houses at the same time.

He could remember his ideas but they felt meaningless to him.

It was an odd sensation to remember meaningless ideas. It was a bit like trying to eat wax fruit.

HE TOOK his hands away from his face and proceeded to march down the sidewalk, his cape swirling behind him and his cane once again tapping out one beat to the dactyl of his steps. Wherever one was in Venice (and he could not be sure, ever since he had eaten the ice cream cone, where he was), one could smell the decadence of history, the bloodletting of the Council of Ten and its secret police, the movement of prisoners across the bridges, the eastward flow of the filthy Adriatic. Commerce and trade and usury, Marco Polo and Shylock.

He came to a place where he already was. He leaned back against another wall. Not wanting to, he nevertheless breathed out, a small breath. He remembered lakes and trees of the American Midwest, perhaps the only blues and greens he had ever owned outright. He had traded them in for some European statues with which he cluttered up his mind, and a few Chinese characters that no longer expressed what he meant to say. He was the victim of a wonderful joke perpetuated by the gods, in which the natural tendency of intelligence toward mania was perfectly expressed. He was known worldwide not as a poet but as a maniac.

Here, standing inside this labyrinth of cities, old and raging, both the Minotaur and Theseus, he saw his old beard and old hair and old eyes reflected in the glass of a shop window. He looked like an elderly human goat. He had looked like a goat for several years now. He had once looked like an intellectual hero and his friends the sculptors had done his head in bronze and stone and marble. Now he looked like a goat and young people he didn't know came to take his photograph. Once as a joke they asked to see his hooves.

He accepted himself as a barbarian. If one was an American, one remained a barbarian, no matter how many books one read.

Because finally they would not be American books and slowly and certainly one turned oneself into a museum of foreign acquisitions.

Finally this world was too corrupt for him to fix. He remembered the urge to save and purify as a deep and satisfying source of energy. The Industrial Revolution had been a mistake; profits won on a massive scale were a mistake; banking in its modern form was a mistake. They must see that. But he himself was the greatest mistake; and there was now no fixing him apart from the silence that he himself had entered as a retreat from the mafiosi of meaning.

He had seen the world despoiled. He had eyes. Had seen the masses falling ever further into rootlessness. Deprived of dignity, they had been sent off to war to fight for the bankers and brought back to be injured in industrial servitude. Everything clean in nature had been pulled down out of the light and besmirched, fouled. There had once been a realm of light. But the light and its masters were being extinguished. What had surprised him was that everyone knew it. Everyone welcomed this sputtering of the light. The arrival of the uncreating word, the shit of chaos, was an occasion for joy! He saw that first in the prison and then in the hospital.

The puzzle: all his life he had campaigned for light and purity. But somehow he had found himself on the wrong side. He had never mastered the techniques of intellectual terror. So that when they came, in their uniforms, to arrest him, they had used terror effectively against him.

HE FOUND himself walking again. He had managed to move away from the glass and was approaching one of the larger canals. For ten seconds snow fell, then stopped. It was an abstract snow, an idea of snow. In the canal, ahead of him, a gondolier was watching him with a sleepy but still attentive look.

The old man gazed at him. The gondolier had the face of Titian's Pietro Aretino, though without the beard. Often in

Venice he saw these time-spiral tricks. One walked out of a museum or gallery and saw a face from a painting by Tintoretto transferred to a waiter serving tea in the public square.

The gondolier, Pietro Aretino, helped the old man into the boat. The old man felt the gondolier's hands and realized with pleasure that the gondolier had no ideas in his hands; if he had any ideas, they would be in his head.

He asked the old man where he wanted to go. The old man pointed forward.

From the pier behind him he heard the yellow voice calling out about Nietzsche and the horse. Then the voice began to recite Nietzsche's poem about the pigeons in St. Mark's Square.

> *Die Tauben von San Marco seh ich wieder:*
> *Still ist der Platz, Vormittag ruht darauf.*

Again I see the pigeons of St. Mark: the square lies still, in— what?—slumbering morning mood . . .? He felt a wave of nausea and forced the words down into his hands.

The waves lapped patiently against the boat in a patter of Vivaldian sixteenth notes. In the dark, heading nowhere through this tiny crooked canal that smelled of cheese and laundry, the old man closed his eyes and let darkness drop on darkness. He thought, for the barest moment, of paradise. This time it was pleasingly empty. Uninhabited by humankind and the messier forms of the vegetable realm, it manifested itself inside his eyelids as a single horizon line making a division of brilliant unclouded sky above and warmed earth below, green but not with grass, the green of a primordial element. A horizon line, blue sky, a sun. And no people at all.

He held his eyes closed for another moment while he wished in the innermost core cell of his heart for the obliteration of all human life.

When he opened his eyes again, he saw that the gondola was heading into some sort of fog, a halation effect surrounding the

few lights from windows that he was still able to see. Reaching
down to scratch an itch that had manifested itself on his knee, his
hand dropped by accident into the water. The water felt green
and cold, topped by oily foam. The water had flowed toward him
all the way from Byzantium. But at this moment it felt alien.
None of the water was his.

He opened his eyes wider. The halation effect increased. The
gondolier was taking him down a patchwork of ever-narrowing
one-way canals. But then it brought him into the Grand Canal,
past a palace with Moorish windows, and the old man thought
he saw the Palazzo Barbaro where Milly Theale had died of that
odd and delicate disease Henry James had thoughtfully given her
in *The Wings of the Dove.* But no: they were not in that part of
the Grand Canal at all. They were not approaching, as he had
thought, the Accademia Bridge. As the halation increased around
all of the lights—an effect of his cataracts, he thought—he could
not be sure where they were, or even that they were making a
progress down the Grand Canal at all.

Geography, in this city, anywhere, had become too much for
him.

Location had given way to age. He was so old and so out-of-
date everywhere that it didn't matter where he was.

Out of the haze of the misted lights hung on the piers and
attached to the walls of the calles, he saw a woman standing in
the distance, waiting for him. Without asking himself who it
was, he knew. Dressed as she was always dressed, in darkness, her
face radiating out of the cobalt-blue Persian silk scarves with
which she surrounded her face, she saw him and stepped toward
him. Of course she would say nothing: had never said anything:
could not. It was for her he had grown silent. His muteness was
intended as a response to hers, the last courtship of old age. Her
gaze clear, she waited for him, as she waited every night, on this
darkened pier.

The old man turned around to examine the gondolier's face.
It was the same face every night. It knew everything.

She was old and yet beautiful: unaging and terrifyingly symmetrical.

As he did every evening at this time, he thought of himself passing over another day and becoming eternal. But if he ever died—and he was not sure, now, that he ever would—he would die as a good and a bad American.

Slowly, with patient infirmity, the old man grasped the fringed cushion underneath him and brought himself to his feet. Standing in the gondola, his eyes fixed on the woman, the old man held himself erect, unappeased, and waited to arrive before her.

1 ❧ Lake Stephen

THE SECOND WEEK of their vacation, the young man got up early to make pancakes. When his girlfriend smelled breakfast being made, she reached down to the floor and put on her nightgown. She went out to the living room in her bare feet.

"Good morning," she said. "I thought we were going to sleep late."

"Want some pancakes?" he asked, flipping them over in the skillet. "They're not great, but they do have a sort of lumberjack appeal. They taste like trees and brush."

"Doesn't this place have an exhaust fan?" she asked. "It's smoky in here."

The young man looked around. "I don't see one."

"Why did you get up? I thought we were going to laze around in bed together."

"I was restless."

"But it's vacation," she said. "It's our first vacation together. And here we are, surrounded by trees, in the Deer Park Resort. What is there to be restless about?"

"I'm not used to this," he said.

"Used to what?"

"This." He spread his hand to indicate the cabin's small living room, the door to the bedroom, the pine trees outside the picture window, and the lake, visible a few hundred feet away. "It's too much of something."

"It's too beautiful," she suggested.

"No." He walked over to the dining-room table and dropped three pancakes on a plate. "There aren't any distractions. I'm used to distractions. I'm used to . . . I don't know. Craziness."

"Well, *I'm* a distraction," she said. She leaned back to let him see her in her nightgown. "I can be crazy."

"Yes," he said. "You're wonderful. That's been proved."

She nodded.

"But it all feels cooped up somehow," he said. "Even when we go canoeing or go for hikes or go swimming, it feels cooped up."

"I don't understand," she said. "How can it be cooped up when you're outside doing things?"

He looked at her for a moment. He seemed to be searching her face for some element there that was bothering him.

"I don't know," he said finally. "I think we have to get out more. Do things."

"Do what things? We've *been* doing things."

"What day is it?" he asked.

"Sunday."

"Well, if it's Sunday, we could go to church." He sat down with her after dishing out two pancakes on his own plate. He reached over for the can of maple syrup.

She laughed nervously. "Go to church? We don't go to church. We've never gone to church. We aren't Christians or anything. I don't think there's even a church around here."

"*I* saw one," he said. "About ten miles down the road, in that little crossroads village, where the grocery is, and that gas station."

"You're serious," she said. "You're really serious about this."

"Well, why not?" He smiled in her direction and laughed. "I mean, they don't keep strangers out, do they? Of course not. They *want* strangers to come in. It's a kind of show. It might be interesting. You could pretend you were an anthropologist."

"I've never been to a church," she said. "Except for weddings and funerals. My parents weren't religious."

"Same here," he said.

"They'll look at us," she said. She began eating his pancakes.

"That's all right," he said. "We'll look back at them."

THE CHURCH was just inside the village of Wilford and stood next to a small shaded hill and a cemetery. It was a plain white wooden structure with a sign outside giving its name and its pastor, the Rev. Cedric Banks. Sunday worship service was scheduled to be at ten o'clock. The young man and woman drove on the dirt roads close to the church, wasting time, until five minutes before ten, when they parked their car behind a line of other cars and went inside. A few members of the small congregation, mostly middle-aged couples, turned and looked at them with what seemed to be friendly curiosity. The church smelled of white pine and cedar. Trying to stay inconspicuous, the two young people sat in the back pew.

"I think this is wrong," she said. "This is supposed to be serious. It's not supposed to be entertainment."

"Do they kneel in this church?" he asked. He was whispering.

"How should I know?" She was looking up at the vaulted ceiling, the support beams, and the one stained-glass window at the back of the altar.

At the start of the service, a woman in a purple robe sat down at an electric organ at the front of the church and began the opening chords for a hymn. The congregation stood and began singing. Their voices were weak, except for one woman with a high, shrill soprano, and although the young woman strained to hear, she couldn't make out the words clearly. Her boyfriend was looking for the hymn in the hymnal but had still not found it by the time the music ended. When she next looked up, she saw the pastor standing in front of the altar. He had a hard-country face, she thought, a wide head and a crew cut, but somewhat tired eyes, like a boxer between rounds.

"He looks like a logger or something," the young man whispered. "Or maybe a plumber. He doesn't look very spiritual."

"How does spiritual look?" she asked, whispering back.

"Different," he said. "Like someone on television."

"Shh," she said. "Pay attention."

The minister began a series of prayers. Because of the reverberation in the church and his tendency to mumble, many of his prayers were incomprehensible to the two young people sitting in the back row. But when the young woman looked over at her boyfriend, she saw an oddly intense expression on his face.

"Do you *like* this?" she asked.

"Shh," he said. "You're just supposed to take it all in."

After several more minutes the pastor walked slowly to the right-hand side of the church, mounted a few steps, and stood behind a lectern. After a brief invocation, he began by quoting from the book of Jonah. He continued to mumble, so that his sentences went in and out of focus, but the expression on his face was earnest and direct. The subject of his sermon seemed to be surprises. The minister said that Jonah was repeatedly surprised by the persistence of God. Nothing that happened on earth was a surprise to the Almighty, he said, but then he said something that the young woman simply couldn't hear. At times he held his finger up as if to make a point. Once or twice he pounded his fist lightly on the lectern. We should contribute to the surprise of creation, the pastor said, by exercising charity, which is always outside the chain of inevitability.

"This doesn't make any sense," the young woman said in a whisper to her boyfriend. "It's all mixed up."

"He knows everyone here," the young man whispered back. "He doesn't have to explain everything to them."

"Maybe he's been drinking."

"No," the young man said. "He just mumbles."

When the service was over, the pastor stepped down the aisle and stood at the doorway to shake hands with the members of the congregation as they left. When the two young people approached him, the minister raised his eyebrows at them and smiled. Close up, he looked bulky and slightly overweight, like a man who had once played football and now drank a few beers in the evening to relax.

"I don't know you two," he said, holding out his hand toward them. "Welcome. Are you passing through?" His breath smelled of cigarettes, and the young woman found herself both pleased and slightly shocked by this.

"I *think* we're just passing through," the young man said.

"You think so?" the minister asked. "You're not sure?"

"We like it here," the young man went on. "We'd like to settle down somewhere around here, raise a family. It's such beautiful country."

"Yes, it is," the minister said, glancing down at their ring fingers. The young woman knew that she would look guilty and silly if she tried to hide the fact that she wore no wedding ring, so she looked back at the minister with a blank smile, her hand resting easily on her hip. "Well," the minister said at last, "enjoy yourselves while you're here."

Back in the car, headed in no particular direction, the young man said, "Well, what did you think of that?"

"It was all right," she said. "But why did you say that we were going to settle down and raise a family here? That's a kind of weird fantasy. We don't live here. And we aren't married."

"Oh, I know," he said. "I just think about it. I play with it." He waited. She knew these pauses were awkward for him and she didn't try to interrupt. "But he was saying that surprises were good things, so I decided to surprise him and to surprise you. It was stupid, I admit it. But I agreed with him. I like surprises. I love it when things are unexpected. I *love* it."

"I don't," she said. "I don't like it much."

"I know that," he said suddenly, and the way he said it, overenunciated so that the effort was like underlining the words, made her sit up straight. She waited inside the air pocket of silence for a moment, then put her hand on her boyfriend's thigh. She rested it there lightly. It wasn't for love or for sensuality's sake; it was to calm him.

"The trouble is," he began. Then he stopped. They both looked out through the front windshield at the pine trees on both sides of the road, and the occasional farm; the soil was mostly clay and rock up here, and the farming was poor. There were FOR SALE signs everywhere, on the front yards and nailed to the trees. "The trouble is," he started again, "that you anticipate every one of my moves. You anticipate everything I do. When we talk or make love or I cook or watch you or talk about the future or what I'm reading, you anticipate all of it. You nod and I can tell how predictable I'm already getting. That's why I feel cooped up. It gets to me. It's like I'm living out a script someone's written. Only, the thing is, you've already gotten the script and I haven't. You know everything I'm going to do. I look into the future and you still know everything I'm going to do, for years and years, and it doesn't matter if we're married or not. You know everything I'm going to do."

"I don't understand," she said. In fact, she did understand, but she thought the rest of their vacation would go better if she pretended that she didn't.

"It's like basketball," the young man said. He laughed, a quick intake of breath. But his face became serious again quickly. "You take Kareem Abdul-Jabbar. You watch him some night. The man is a genius. You know why?" The young woman shook her head. "The reason Jabbar is a genius is that you can't anticipate his moves. It's not speed. Speed's important in basketball but it's not the most important thing. The most important thing is to do the move, the logical move, so unexpectedly and gracefully that your opponent is faked out and can't guard against it."

"Basketball isn't the world," she said. "It's not about relationships."

"Oh yes it is," he said. "It's a relationship between individuals on two different teams. And the more you can't be anticipated, the more effective you are." He turned off the road onto a smaller dirt road that the young woman hadn't seen, and the car took some hard bounces as they proceeded through a cluster of thick trees.

"Where does this go?" she asked. "Where are we?"

The young man smiled. "I saw a sign for a lake back there," he said. "Faked you out, didn't I?"

"Yes," she said. "You certainly did."

"Never thought I'd take you to a lake, did you?" he asked.

"Nope," she said. "You got me this time."

The road came out in a clearing for public access. The young man stopped the car and got out, walking down to the shoreline to look into the water and then across the lake to the other side. In the distance they could see one broken-down cabin, its roof fallen in. The water was very clear; they could both see minnows swimming in schools in the shallow water.

"I wonder what the name of this lake is," he said.

"*We* can name it," she said. "Let's name it after you. Let's call it Lake Stephen."

"Okay," he said. "Now that it's mine, what do I do with it?"

"You don't do anything with it."

"Yes, you do," he said. "You have to do something with it, if it's named after you." All at once he straightened up. "I'll surprise you," he said.

"How?"

"If I told you," he said, "it wouldn't be a surprise."

At exactly that moment, she knew he was going to take all his clothes off and go swimming. She knew that he was going to take off his shirt first, button by button, and hang it on the end of a tree branch, and he did; that he was going to unbuckle his belt, then slip off his shoes and socks, put the socks inside the shoes and put the shoes together neatly at the base of the tree, and he did that, too; then he would lower his trousers and fold them at the knee and put the folded trousers over the shoes and socks; and then she knew, quite a bit in advance of his actually doing it, that he would grin at her, a happy smile breaking across his pleasant bearded face, and, with a yelp, lower his underwear and turn around and dash into the water, shouting as he went and making half-articulate exclamations like a man running into battle. He wanted to be dangerous and unpredictable, and so, watching him, she did her best to look amazed at what he was doing.

He swam back and forth in the water, splashing and barking like a happy seal. She watched the water passing over his pale skin. The rest of the year, he worked indoors at a desk, and he didn't believe in getting sun, so his body was visible underwater even when he dove down; it was that white. She watched him swimming parallel to the shoreline and was pleasantly lost in his physical form, which she liked. As bodies went, his was attractive; he swam regularly and worked out. But the final effect was of frailty. Men, when you got their clothes off, looked rather simple and frail, even the strong ones. The strength was all on the outside. This was no secret, and it became more apparent as they aged.

"Come on in," he shouted. "It's great."

"I don't know," she said, looking around. "Maybe there are people here."

"It's okay," he said. "It's my lake and my beach, and what I say goes. I'm the law here."

"Well, you sure have surprised me," she said. Then, once again, she knew that he would try to scare her, and pretend to drown. She knew, before he actually did it, that he would dive down and hold his breath; that he would stay underwater for as long as he could; and that he even might try to inhale some water so that he could choke a little, not much, but just enough to give her a scare. This was just like men, to try to scare you by being dangerous and vulnerable at the same time. She took off her shoes and socks and waded out into the water, soaking her dress as she went. She waited for Stephen to come up, out of the water. She waited for what she thought was a long time. She couldn't see any bubbles; she knew he was holding his breath down there, like a boy among the minnows. He would be curled up, his feet brushing against the sandy bottom. And now he would be feeling as if his lungs were about to explode, and she went farther out into the water, so that it came up to her knees.

Then he rose to the surface, coughing and choking. She waded out to where he was and took his hand. "Stephen," she cried, "are you all right?"

He smiled. "Did I frighten you?" he asked. "Good." He spat some water out of his mouth.

"Damn it," she said, pretending to be indignant, "don't do that again."

Another large grin broke across his face. "You should come in," he said. "Come on, Jan. Come in. Take your clothes off."

"I don't want to," she said.

And then, suddenly, both of them knee-deep in water, he put his bare arms around her, and she gasped. It wasn't his body. They were lovers, and she was used to that. It was that his skin was ice-cold; for a moment, it didn't feel like his, or like living flesh, but something else. It was puckered with goosebumps and felt clammy, as if it had come from some other world into this one, and when he put his lips to hers, she flinched.

"What's the matter?" he asked.

She could feel his wet hand soaking through the back of her blouse. He was soaking her down in small stages. Looking at him, at the water dripping off his beard and down his chest, she thought he looked a bit like a minor god or a monster, she couldn't decide which.

"Come in," he said, reaching for her.

She paused and looked at the future. She knew that he would not go on loving her if she didn't take her clothes off now; he would not, someday, propose to her; and they would not get married and have children. Unless she broke the rules now, he would not follow the rules later. He wanted her to be wild; all right: she would be wild. She grinned at him. She did a little shimmy, then unbuttoned her blouse and tossed it on the sand. She unhooked her bra, thinking: he'll still talk about this when we're old. He'll cherish this because it's our first secret. She threw her bra toward shore, then took off the rest of her clothes and dropped them on the sand. Then, knowing how beautiful she was, how physically breathtaking in sunlight, she walked toward him into the water, her back straight and her hips swaying, and, reaching him, pressed herself against him.

"You're something," he said. "I never thought you'd actually do that."

She was about to say, "I know," but stopped herself.

"I take it all back," he said, his fingers playing with her hair. "I take it all, all, all back. I never expected this. You're crazy. I love you. It's wonderful."

"Are you all talk?" she asked. "Or are we going to swim? Come on."

She took his hand and pulled at him. She dove in and felt him following her, as if he were one-tenth of a second off, behind her. Her hand was raised, holding his, until he was under the water next to her. Then she let him go.

2 ❧ Scissors

THE BARBER, whose name was Harold, had read the sports section, the business news, and was working his way down the front page when the boy and his mother came inside. The boy was wearing a spring coat too large for him, with mittens attached to the coat sleeves with alligator clips. The woman, upon entering, stood up straight as the barber looked at her and dropped his paper onto the floor. "Louise," he said, and the woman nodded. It was midday, and there were no other customers and no other barbers. Outside, the ice had melted into puddles, and the boy was stamping his feet. The woman and the barber stood looking at each other until finally he said, "Louise, it's been a coon's age."

"Has it been that long?" she asked. She dropped her coat on one of the chairs, helped her son out of his hat and coat, and led him toward the first barber chair. "Such a nice day," she said. "Like spring, even though it *isn't* spring yet. Time for Robbie's first professional haircut. And I thought, well, certainly, you should do it." She leaned forward and kissed the barber on the cheek.

"I've seen you around town," he said. "Sometimes I wave, but you never seem to see me."

She smiled. "Oh," she said, "I see you. And I always think, 'Well, there's Harold, and he's waving at me,' and what I do is, I sort of wave back, but, you know, mentally. Not so anyone would see."

They stood there for a moment, the barber looking at the woman's face, doing his best not to stare at it, and the woman turned in profile to him, gazing at the display of Pinaud Clubman after-shave and Lucky Tiger hair tonic on the windowsill. Her hands were on her son's shoulders.

"Did you know, Harold, that they're going to send a hot-air balloon down, well, I mean, just *over* the main street in a little while? I heard about it."

"It's a promotion," he said. "Tulip Days in Five Oaks. They're going to drop discount coupons from the balloon into the street. It's good for business." He was tugging nervously at his mustache. He stopped himself and went over to the counter near the mirror and came back with a board, which he put over the arms of the chair. He hoisted the boy up on the board and tucked the cloth in around his neck and spread it over his shirt and pants. The boy squirmed for a moment.

The barber bent down. "So, how old are you, young man?"

Three fingers poked up under the cloth.

"Can you say it?" the barber asked.

"He's very shy," the boy's mother said. "But he can say it. He knows. He's three, aren't you, Robbie?" The boy nodded.

The barber twirled the chair around twice. "Well, he certainly is handsome. Aren't you, Robbie? Aren't you the handsomest kid in all Five Oaks?"

The boy said, "No," and looked at the floor. He smiled for a split second, and, just as quickly as the smile had appeared, it vanished.

"Everyone's handsome at three," the barber said. "It's later that they aren't. Louise, how do you want his hair cut?"

"Sort of normal," she said. "Sort of like a normal boy."

Harold nodded and began clipping around the boy's ear. His knees were trembling slightly and he had to lean against the chair to steady himself. He noticed that his scissors weren't quite steady, either, so he stopped for a moment. His face, and Robbie's, and Louise's, were reflected, in the usual way of barber shops, forty or fifty times, accordionlike, back into darkness between the two wall mirrors.

"How's George?" the barber asked.

"George? George is fine. George is always fine. He's the definition of fine. Except he's losing his hair. You should know. You cut it. Don't you two talk?"

"Yes," Harold said. "About the weather. And sports."

"Sports? You always hated sports," she said. "You told me."

"I'm a barber, Louise. I have to talk to these men about something."

"Well," Louise said, standing by the window, "you could talk to George about me."

"What would I say? I don't see you anymore, except to wave. And I don't want to be curious, do I?" He stopped cutting the boy's hair to glance at her. She shrugged. "No, I do not talk to George about you. That's not even . . ." He thought of a word he never used. "Conceivable. That's not conceivable."

"Oh, you *could* say something about me. To him. But he wouldn't notice. He'd go right on sitting, having his hair cut, and not noticing."

Robbie squirmed, and Harold began to sing "Boris the Spider," walking his fingers across the top of the boy's head. Robbie laughed and said, "No Boris." When he had settled down again, Harold bent to clip the hair at the back of the boy's neck.

"Robbie's hair color is the same as yours," Louise said, "and his eyes, too, the exact same. You know, sometimes I have these thoughts, when I'm lying in bed, late at night, next to George, and he's snoring, you know, asleep and ignoring me, and anyway, I'm looking at the way my toes poke up under the blankets, so there are two little peaks down there at the end of the bed, and I'm having these thoughts, and the only trouble with them is, they're tricky. You can't say them around George, you know?"

"Sort of," Harold said. She was as beautiful and as crazy as ever. His craziness, his wildness, had once been able to match hers, and then it could not. "Have you ever tried to say them?"

"I'm trying to say them now," Louise said. "You remember in junior high, when we had that math teacher, Mr. Powers—"

"He taught shop class."

"He did that too. Anyway, once in science club, one of our meetings when you weren't there, he said that maybe the universe was imaginary. That maybe it was all made up. And that it could be a *thought* in someone's head. Or, maybe it was a *trick*, sort of like a practical joke."

"What are you saying, Louise?"

"You're so handsome, Harold, no wonder I fell in love with you. But you're so *mild*. You never took me anywhere. You never even drove me out of this town. You talked softly and you had nice hands but you didn't spirit me away. That was the one thing you had to do, and you never did it. You never even took me to a movie. Of course there was George by then, but you see what I'm getting at."

"Oh God, Louise," he said. "For God's sake."

"But that's it," she said, "that's what I'm *saying*. I'm not blaming you. You never took me away because I was married to George, that was the first thing, and the second thing was, you were yourself. Mild. A very very mild and pleasant-feeling man who never did anything except cut hair. Who couldn't take me away because he just couldn't, that's all. And that's what I mean about the universe. Those are my thoughts, when I'm lying awake at night."

"Your thoughts."

"Yes."

"I don't get the part about the universe." He was finishing up on Robbie's hair, trimming along the sides, going quickly so the boy wouldn't have to sit much longer. The fine, blondish curls fell over his fingers onto the floor.

"The universe, Harold, is a practical joke."

"On who?"

"Why, on us, of course. They put it together to be a joke on us."

"No, they didn't." He let himself take another glance at her. Her face had its customary intensity, which made her beautiful no matter what her thoughts were. Harold lightly brushed the hair away from the back of the boy's neck. "It's too complicated to be a joke. Let's get a look at you, young man." He swiveled the chair around so that he was face to face with Robbie. "He looks very good. Like a proud little boy." He touched the fingers of his right hand to his own lips, and then lightly placed the fingers on the side of the boy's cheek. A shiver ran down his back.

"I saw that," she said.

"What?"

"Don't think I didn't see it."

Harold lowered the chair, pulled the cloth away from around the boy, and flicked out the hairs onto the floor. The boy jumped down and went to the window.

"Up there," the boy said. At that moment one of Harold's regular customers, a teacher in the high school named Saul Bernstein, walked into the shop, ringing the bell over the door.

"Hey, Harold," he said. "See the balloon?" He pointed outside, toward the sky. Down at the other end of the main street a hot-air balloon with an enormous red tulip painted on its side was floating in a northerly direction just above treetop level toward Harold's barbershop. "Well, hello," he said to the boy.

The boy turned to look at Saul. "Hi," he said. Meanwhile, the boy's mother was reaching into her purse for money. From her pocketbook she drew out a ten-dollar bill and handed it to Harold.

"You can't give me money, Louise," he said quietly, handing it back to her. "You just can't." Saul watched the two of them for a moment, then walked to the back of the barbershop and began to search through the old copies of *Argosy* and *Sports Illustrated.*

By now, both the boy and his mother had their spring coats on. Louise touched Harold once on the arm, then turned toward the window. "It's dropping something," she said. "Little sheets of paper."

"Those are the coupons," Harold said, rubbing his hand across his eyes. "Like I told you. The whole thing's a promotion for Five Oaks businesses. We're trying—" He seemed to lose his thought for a moment. "We're trying to keep the businesses prosperous." He laughed, a faint and unhappy sound deep in his throat. "Two dollars off a haircut if you use the coupon before May first."

"Well," Louise said, "we'll just have to go out, Robbie and me, and search up and down the street till we find one of your coupons, Harold, and that way, the next time we come, we won't have to spend George's money at full price."

Harold didn't say anything.

"We'll come back," Louise said, "because I love the haircut you gave Robbie, it's just wonderful how he looks now, and I want you to be his barber. I don't mean just now; I mean from now on. Won't that be nice? Every month, you can cut Robbie's hair."

Harold seemed to nod at the floor.

"Mom?" the boy said. "Go out now?" His mother smiled, opened the door for him, and, as soon as he was out on the sidewalk, she walked over to Harold and kissed him on the cheek.

"Tulip Days," she said. "What a good way to welcome in the spring." She brushed a bit of her son's hair off Harold's shoulders and then turned to go. "See you," she said. "And God bless you, and I mean that."

When the bell rang again, announcing her exit, Saul put down the magazine he had been reading and walked over to the window, taking his time. Outside, white coupons were fluttering down out of the sky and landing on the sidewalk and in the street; some of the cars going by had their windshield wipers on. Louise's boy stood next to a parking meter in the snowstorm of paper, one coupon stuck to his forehead and another lodged in his shirt at the back of his neck. His mouth was open, as if he hoped a coupon would drop into it. His mother had turned to walk down the street; she was checking in the gutters and poking at the papers with the toe of her boot.

"You know," Saul said, standing beside Harold at the front of the window, "I love this town. They do this promotion, even remember to do it on Saturday, but then they forget about publicizing it, so no one's here, almost, except the usual layabouts like me, and a few others like that lady out there, grabbing up those coupons. What's the matter, Harold, you feeling a little faint?"

For a moment the barber had leaned forward, and he had had to reach out and touch the sill to straighten up. "I'm fine," he said. "I had a touch of the flu. But that was last month. I just feel a little bit of it now and then."

"Must be what screwed up your bowling last week," Saul said. "Another night like that, and we'll have to drum you out of the league. Ha." Saul had a laugh which was not a laugh, but a spoken word, which he sometimes put at the end of his sentences. "You guys running these businesses are going to have to think of something else next year instead of dumping all these trashy discount slips out of a hot-air balloon onto the street. It's not good for business. It's too weird. I don't care if it *is* Tulip Days."

"Saul, you want your hair cut, or what?"

"A trim. The usual trim so I don't look like a wildman and give all the other Jews in this town a bad name."

"Okay," Harold said. "I think I can do that. But you got to sit down in the chair."

"Torture by Mr. Harold of Paris," Saul said, settling himself in the chair. "And don't do any of that funny stuff with the hair dryer. That was a cute kid, that boy whose hair you just cut. You did a nice job. A real sweetie, that kid was. Harold? Hello? Hello?"

Harold was standing behind Saul, a pair of scissors in his right hand. He was staring at the floor and holding on to the chair with his other hand.

"Harold?"

"What?"

"Harold," Saul said. "Maybe you need a little air."

"Yes."

"Such as having the door open."

"Yes."

"Buck up, Harold. Life goes on. Listen, you want to close the shop for a minute and go out for a beer? Want to do a bit of basketball down at the high school? I've got keys, Harold, keys to the gym. You could practice that lousy lay-up of yours, and that jump shot. How about that?"

"That would . . . yes," Harold said. He was looking at himself in the mirrors, his reflections curving back into darkness.

"No more of this," Saul said, getting out of the chair and taking the cloth off from around his neck. "No more snipping hair this morning. Come on, Harold, we'll go have lunch." He stood at the door and turned the sign so that it read CLOSED. "Let's go."

"I should stay. It's supposed to be a big business day."

"Come on, Harold. A break. To relax."

"All right." He took off his smock and went over to the coatrack for his jacket. "You know," he said suddenly, "the coupons and the hot-air balloon were my idea. They were all my idea. The things I think of doing. Now it's all on the street, but we forgot about the wind. Imagine. It's spring, but we forgot about that."

"It was a good idea, Harold, a *good* idea, and very original." They went out to the sidewalk, and Harold closed the door behind him and locked it. Coupons were swirling in circle patterns and now stuck against his shoes. "It's a day of discounts,"

Saul said. "Everything's discounted today. The world is forty percent off. We should take advantage."

"Sun's out," Harold said.

"My point exactly." Saul bent down toward the gutter and gathered up two handfuls of coupons. "Bargains galore. What should we do with all these coupons, Harold?"

"Make them fly," Harold said.

"Anything you say." Saul threw a fistful of papers up into the air, and as they fell, Harold thought of the one time when he *had* taken Louise out for dinner, one weekend when George was gone. She must have forgotten. They had driven to a seafood restaurant thirty miles away, in Bay City, and Louise had ordered whitefish. All during the meal, she had held his hand. He hadn't noticed how awkward it had been, hadn't even thought about it until later, when he had patiently reimagined the dinner, minute by minute. The light from the candle had made her hair shine with a slightly reddish glow; the curls, and the way they fell over her shoulders, made him think that any kind of future might be possible. But they didn't talk about their future. Instead, they sat there describing each other, the small details each one liked. He had thought, in that moment, that he was perfectly happy, and, thinking of that moment now, Harold smiled and reached out to touch Saul's shoulder.

"Did you know that woman?" Harold asked.

"No, Harold, I never did."

"I knew her once."

"I know that." He reached for the barber's sleeve. "Hamburger time," he said, walking up the street toward the diner.

3 ✤ Scheherazade

SHE LEANED down to adjust his respirator tube and the elastic tie around his neck that kept it in place. "Don't," he said, an all-purpose warning referring to nothing in particular, and she heard Muzak from down the hall, a version of "Stardust" that made her think of cold soup. A puddle outside his window reflected blue sky and gave the ceiling of his room a faint blue tint.

He was looking sallow and breathing poorly; she would have to lie again to perk him up.

"Do you remember," she said, sitting in the chair next to his chair, "my goodness, this would have been fifty years ago, that trip we made to Hawaii?"

"Don't remember it," he said. "Don't think I've been there."

"Yes, you have," she said, patting his hand where the wedding ring was. "We took the train, it had 'Zephyr' in its name somewhere, one of those silver trains that served veal for dinner. We had a romantic night in the Pullman car; I expect you don't remember that."

"Not just now," he said.

"Well, we did. We took it to Oakland or San

Francisco, I forget which, and from there we took the boat to Honolulu."

"What boat? I don't remember a boat. Did it have a name?"

She leaned back and stared at the ceiling. Why did he always insist on the names? She couldn't invent names; that always caused her trouble. And her bifocals were hurting her. She would have to see that nice Dr. Hauser about them. "The name of the ship, dear, was *Halcyon Days*, not very original, I must say; we were on the C deck, second-class. The first night out you were seasick. Then you were all right. The ship had an orchestra and we danced the fox-trot. You flirted with that woman whose room was down the hall. You were quite awful about it."

The outline of a smile appeared on his face. "Who?"

She saw the smile and was pleased. "I don't remember," she said. "Why should I remember her name? She was just a silly woman with vulgar dark-red hair. She let it fly all over her shoulders."

"What was her name?"

"I told you I don't remember."

"Please," he said. His mouth was open. His filmy eyes looked in her direction.

"All right," she said. "Her name was Peggy."

"Peggy," he said, briefly sighing.

"Yes, Peggy," she said, "and you made yourself quite ridiculous around her, but I think she liked you, and I remember I once caught you two at the railing, looking at the waters of the Pacific go by as the ship churned westward."

"Was I bad?"

"You were all right, dear. You were just like any man. I didn't mind. Men are like that. You bought her drinks."

"What did she drink?"

"Old-fashioned," she said. "An odd drink for a single woman to order. I would have thought she might prefer martinis or Manhattans or gin and tonics. But no. She liked bourbon mixed with sugar water and bitters." She felt herself going too far in this improvisation and hauled herself back in. "What *I* minded was that she would not always close the door to her stateroom. You would look in, and there she was."

"Yes," he said. "There she was."

"There she was," she continued, "in her bathrobe, or worse, with that terrible red hair of hers billowing down to her shoulders. In her white bathrobe, and you, standing in the hallway like any man, staring at her."

"You caught me."

"Yes, I did, but I didn't blame you. You were attractive to women."

"I was?"

"Yes, you were. You were so handsome in those days, and so witty, and when you sat down at the piano and sang those Cole Porter tunes, it was hard for women to resist. Blandishments. That's what they call them. Your blandishments."

"Could I play the piano?" He was smiling, perhaps thinking of the Pacific, or Peggy.

"Very well, dear. You could play and sing. Though I've heard better, I have certainly heard worse. You sang to me. You'd sing to anybody."

"To Peggy?"

"To anyone," she said. When she saw his smile fade, she said, "And to her, too. In an effort to charm. You sang 'You're the Top.' I daresay she liked it. Who knows what trouble you two got into? I was not a spy. All I know now is, it's been over fifty years."

He closed his eyes and stretched his thin legs. She saw a smile cross his face again and was pleased with herself.

"In Hawaii," she said, "we stayed at the Royal Palm Hotel." Although she had once been on a ship, she had never been in Hawaii and was speaking more slowly now as she tried to see the scene. "It was on the beach, the famous one with the name, and the sands were white, as white as alabaster. We played shuffle-board."

"I remember that," he said.

"Good. We drove around the island and climbed the extinct volcano, Mount Johnson. There's a lake inside Mount Johnson, and you went swimming in it, and there were large birds, enormous blue birds, flying over our heads, and you called them the archangel birds and said that God had sent them to us as a sign."

"A sign of what?"

"A sign of our happiness."

"Were we happy?"

"Yes," she said. "We were."

"Always?"

"It seems so to me now. Anyway, Mount Johnson was one day, and on another day we went diving for pearls. You found an oyster with a pearl in it. I still wear it on a pin."

He looked over at her and searched her face and chest and arms.

"Just not today," she said. "I'm not wearing it today."

The sound of the oxygen hissing out of the respirator tube fatigued her. She would not be able to continue this much longer. It was like combat of a subtle kind. She hurried on. "On the island we picked enormous flowers, and every evening we sat down for dinner by the water, and you put a gardenia in my hair one night. We ate pineapples and broke open coconuts, and at moonrise the sea breezes came in through the window of our room where we were lying on the bed. We were so in love. We had room service bring us champagne and you read poetry to me."

"Yes," he said. "What did you look like?"

She clasped her hands in her lap. "I was beautiful." She paused. "You said so."

"The sound," he said.

"What sound?"

"There was a sound."

"I don't remember a sound," she said.

"There was one," he insisted.

"Where?"

"In the room."

"Yes?"

"It came in through the window," he whispered.

"From where?"

"From the sea."

"I don't remember it," she said. "What sort of sound was it?"

"A note."

"A musical note?"

"A note like this," he said. Then he made a terrible noise from his throat and his mouth.

"I don't remember it. Oh yes," she said suddenly, inspired. "There was an orchestra right outside our window, and one night it played all night long, violins, violins," she said, briefly swept away. "That's what you mean, dear, the medley of show tunes and a little piece, that piece by Mozart, 'A Little Night Music,' I think it's called."

"No," he said. "That wasn't it."

"It wasn't?"

"No," he said. "It came from the sea."

"The Pacific," she said.

"Yes. Far away. From over the horizon. From thousands of miles." He made the terrible noise again.

"That's a foghorn. That's the sound you're making."

"We were never in Hawaii."

"Yes, we were. You just don't remember. Oh yes. I remember that sound now. It was a siren, from downtown Honolulu."

"No," he said. "From the sea."

"How can you be sure?"

Suddenly he turned toward her and looked directly at her. "I hear it now," he said. "I hear it right this minute."

"You poor dear," she said, whispering. "Think of Hawaii."

"I will. Do you hear it?"

"What?"

"The sound."

"No."

"Listen."

She sat listening. The Muzak from the hallway had fallen silent. From outside there was a faint, low humming.

"Hear it?"

"Yes," she said faintly.

"I heard it first there."

"So did I."

"I feel a little better," he said. "I feel sleepy."

"Go to sleep, dear," she said. "Take a little nap."

"You'll be back?"

"Yes, tomorrow."

"Where else did we go?"

"We went," she said, "to Egypt, where we crawled through the pyramids. We went through the fjords in Norway. We saw wonders. We saw many wonders."

"Tell me tomorrow."

"I will." She kissed him on the forehead, stood up, and walked to the doorway. She looked back at him; he seemed to be about to fall asleep, but he also seemed to be listening to the sound. She gazed at him for a moment, and then went down the hallway, past the nurses, bowing her head for a moment before she went out the front door to the bus stop. She was thinking of tomorrow's story; she would say that they had traveled to Argentina—but what did people do there besides speak Spanish? Perhaps they had gardens. Why not the largest garden, the Garden of Branches and Twigs—it sounded better in Spanish—still, after all these years, and despite the vandals, geometrical and intact?

The Disappeared

WHAT he first noticed about Detroit and therefore America was the smell. Almost as soon as he walked off the plane, he caught it: an acrid odor of wood ash. The smell seemed to go through his nostrils and take up residence in his head. In Sweden, his own country, he associated this smell with autumn, and the first family fires of winter, the smoke chuffing out of chimneys and settling familiarly over the neighborhood. But here it was midsummer, and he couldn't see anything burning.

On the way in from the airport, with the windows of the cab open and hot stony summer air blowing over his face, he asked the driver about it.

"You're smelling Detroit," the driver said.

Anders, who spoke very precise school English, thought that perhaps he hadn't made himself understood. "No," he said. "I am sorry. I mean the burning smell. What is it?"

The cab driver glanced in the rearview mirror. He was wearing a knitted beret, and his deadlocks flapped in the breeze. "Where you from?"

"Sweden."

The driver nodded to himself. "Explains why," he said. The cab took a sharp right turn on the freeway and entered the Detroit city limits. The driver gestured with his left hand toward an electronic signboard, a small windowless factory at its base, and a clustered group of cramped clapboard houses nearby. When he gestured, the cab wobbled on the freeway. "Fires here most all the time," he said. "Day in and day out. You get so you don't notice. Or maybe you get so you do notice and you like it."

"I don't see any fires," Anders said.

"That's right."

Feeling that he was missing the point somehow, Anders decided to change the subject. "I see a saxophone and a baseball bat next to you," he said, in his best English. "Do you like to play baseball?"

"Not in this cab, I don't," the driver said quietly. "It's no game then, you understand?"

The young man sat back, feeling that he had been defeated by the American idiom in his first native encounter with it. An engineer, he was in Detroit to discuss his work in metal alloys that resist oxidation. The company that had invited him had suggested that he might agree to become a consultant on an exclusive contract, for what seemed to him an enormous, American-sized fee. But the money meant little to him. It was America he was curious about, attracted by, especially its colorful disorderliness.

Disorder, of which there was very little in Sweden, seemed sexy to him: the disorder of a disheveled woman who has rushed down two flights of stairs to offer a last long kiss. Anders was single, and before he left the country he hoped to sleep with an American woman in an American bed. It was his ambition. He wondered if the experience would have any distinction. He had an idea that he might be able to go home and tell one or two friends about it.

At the hotel, he was met by a representative of the automobile company, a gray-haired man with thick glasses who, to Anders's surprise, spoke rather good Swedish. Later that afternoon, and for the next two days, he was taken down silent carpeted hallways and shown into plush windowless rooms with recessed lighting. He showed them his slides and metal samples, cited chemical formulas, and made cost projections; he looked at the faces looking back at him. They were interested, friendly, but oddly blank, like faces he had seen in the military. He saw corridor after corridor. The building seemed more expressive than the people in it. The lighting was both bright and diffuse, and a low-frequency hum of power and secrecy seemed to flow out from the ventilators. Everyone complimented him on his English. A tall woman in a tailored suit, flashing him a secretive smile, asked him if he intended to stay in this country for long. Anders smiled, said that his plans on that particular point were open, and managed to work the name of his hotel into his conversation.

At the end of the third day, the division head once again shook Anders's hand in the foyer of the hotel lobby and said they'd be getting in touch with him very soon. Finally free, Anders stepped outside the hotel and sniffed the air. All the rooms he had been in since he had arrived had had no windows, or windows so blocked by drapes or blinds that he couldn't see out.

He felt restless and excited, with three days free for sightseeing in a wide-open American city, not quite in the wild West but close enough to it to suit him. He returned to his room and changed into a pair of jeans, a light cotton shirt, and a pair of running shoes. In the mirror, he thought he looked relaxed and handsome. His vanity amused him, but he felt lucky to look the way he did. Back out on the sidewalk, he asked the doorman which direction he would recommend for a walk.

The doorman, who had curly gray hair and sagging pouches under his eyes, removed his cap and rubbed his forehead. He did not look back at Anders. "You want my recommendation? Don't walk anywhere. I would not recommend a walk. Sit in the bar and watch the soaps." The doorman stared at a fire hydrant as he spoke.

"What about running?"

The doorman suddenly glanced at Anders, sizing him up. "It's a chance. You might be okay. But to be safe, stay inside. There's movies on the cable, you want them."

"Is there a park here?"

"Sure, there's parks. There's always parks. There's Belle Isle. You could go there. People do. I don't recommend it. Still and all you might enjoy it if you run fast enough. What're you planning to do?"

Anders shrugged. "Relax. See your city."

"You're seeing it," the doorman said. "Ain't nobody relaxed, seeing this place. Buy some postcards, you want sights. This place ain't built for tourists and amateurs."

Anders thought that perhaps he had misunderstood again and took a cab out to Belle Isle; as soon as he had entered the park, he saw a large municipal fountain and asked the cabbie to drop him off in front of it. On its rim, children were shouting and dangling their legs in the water. The ornamentation of the stone lions was both solemn and whimsical and reminded him of forced humor of Danish public sculpture. Behind the fountain he saw families grouped in evening picnics on the grass, and many citizens, of various apparent ethnic types, running, bicycling, and walking. Anders liked the way Americans walked, a sort of busyness in their step, as if, having no particular goal, they still had an unconscious urgency to get somewhere, to seem purposeful.

He began to jog, and found himself passing a yacht club of some sort, and then a small zoo, and more landscaped areas where solitaries and couples sat on the grass listening to the evening baseball game on their radios. Other couples were stretched out by themselves, self-absorbed. The light had a bluish-gold quality. It looked like almost any city park to him, placid and decorative, a bit hushed.

He found his way to an old building with a concession stand inside. After admiring the building's fake Corinthian architecture, he bought a hot dog and a cola. Thinking himself disguised as a native—America was full of foreigners anyway—he walked to the west windows of the dining area to check on the unattached women. He wanted to praise, to an American, this evening, and this park.

There were several couples on this side of the room, and what seemed to be several unattached men and women standing near the open window and listening to their various earphones. One of these women, with her hair partially pinned up, was sipping a lemonade. She had just the right faraway look. Anders thought he recognized this look. It meant that she was in a kind of suspension, between engagements.

He put himself in her line of sight and said, in his heaviest accent, "A nice evening!"

"What?" She removed the earphones and looked at him. "What did you say?"

"I said the evening was beautiful." He tried to sound as foreign as he could, the way Germans in Sweden did. "I am a visitor here," he added quickly, "and not familiar with any of this." He motioned his arm to indicate the park.

"Not familiar?" she asked. "Not familiar with what?"

"Well, with this park. With the sky here. The people."

"Parks are the same everywhere," the woman said, leaning her hip against the wall. She looked at him with a vague interest. "The sky is the same. Only the people are different."

"Yes? How?"

"Where are you from?"

He explained, and she looked out the window toward the Canadian side of the Detroit River, at the city of Windsor. "That's Canada, you know," she said, pointing a finger at the river. "They make Canadian whiskey right over there." She pointed at some high buildings and what seemed to be a grain elevator. "I've never drunk the whiskey. They say it tastes of acid rain. I've never been to Canada. I mean, I've seen it, but I've never been there. If I can see it from here, why should I go there?"

"To be in Canada," Anders suggested. "Another country."

"But I'm *here*," she said suddenly, turning to him and looking at him directly. Her eyes were so dark they were almost colorless. "Why should I be anywhere else? Why are *you* here?"

"I came to Detroit for business," he said. "Now I'm sightseeing."

"Sightseeing?" She laughed out loud, and Anders saw her arch her back. Her breasts seemed to flare in front of him. Her body had distinct athletic lines. "No one sightsees here. Didn't anyone tell you?"

"Yes. The doorman at the hotel. He told me not to come."

"But you did. How did you get here?"

"I came by taxi."

"You're joking," she said. Then she reached out and put her hand momentarily on his shoulder. "You took a taxi to this park? How do you expect to get back to your hotel?"

"I suppose," he shrugged, "I will get another taxi."

"Oh no you won't," she said, and Anders felt himself pleased that things were working out so well. He noticed again her pinned-up hair and its intense black. Her skin was deeply tanned or naturally dark, and he thought that she herself might be black or Hispanic, he didn't know which, being unpracticed in making such distinctions. Outside he saw fireflies. No one had ever mentioned fireflies in Detroit. Night was coming on. He gazed up at the sky. Same stars, same moon.

"You're here *alone?*" she asked. "In America? And in this city?"

"Yes," he said. "Why not?"

"People shouldn't be left alone in this country," she said, leaning toward him with a kind of vehemence. "They shouldn't have left you here. It can get kind of weird, what happens to people. Didn't they tell you?"

He smiled and said that they hadn't told him anything to that effect.

"Well, they should have." She dropped her cup into a trash

can, and he thought he saw the beginning of a scar, a white line, traveling up the underside of her arm toward her shoulder.

"Who do you mean?" he asked. "You said, 'they.' Who is 'they'?"

"Any they at all," she said. "Your guardians." She sighed. "All right. Come on. Follow me." She went outside and broke into a run. For a moment he thought that she was running away from him, then realized that he was expected to run *with* her; it was what people did now, instead of holding hands, to get acquainted. He sprinted up next to her, and as she ran, she asked him, "Who are you?"

Being careful not to tire—she wouldn't like it if his endurance was poor—he told her his name, his professional interests, and he patched together a narrative about his mother, father, two sisters, and his Aunt Ingrid. Running past a slower couple, he told her that his aunt was eccentric and broke china by throwing it on the floor on Fridays, which she called "the devil's day."

"Years ago, they would have branded her a witch," Anders said. "But she isn't a witch. She's just moody."

He watched her reactions and noticed that she didn't seem at all interested in his family, or any sort of background. "Do you run a lot?" she asked. "You look as if you're in pretty good shape."

He admitted that, yes, he ran, but that people in Sweden didn't do this as much as they did in America.

"You look a little like that tennis star, that Swede," she said. "By the way, I'm Lauren." Still running, she held out her hand, and, still running, he shook it. "Which god do you believe in?"

"Excuse me?"

"Which god?" she asked. "Which god do you think is in control?"

"I had not thought about it."

"You'd better," she said. "Because one of them is." She stopped suddenly and put her hands on her hips and walked in a small circle. She put her hand to her neck and took her pulse, timing it on her wristwatch. Then she placed her fingers on Ander's neck and took his pulse. "One hundred fourteen," she said. "Pretty good." Again she walked away from him and again he found himself following her. In the growing darkness he noticed other men, standing in the parking lot, watching her, this American with pinned-up hair, dressed in a running outfit. He thought she was pretty, but maybe Americans had other standards so that here, in fact, she wasn't pretty, and it was some kind of optical illusion.

When he caught up with her, she was unlocking the door of a blue Chevrolet rusting near the hubcaps. He gazed down at the rust with professional interest—it had the characteristic blister pattern of rust caused by salt. She slipped inside the car and reached across to unlock the passenger side, and when he got in—he hadn't been invited to get in, but he thought it was all right—he sat down on several small plastic tape cassette cases. He picked them out from underneath him and tried to read their labels. She was taking off her shoes. Debussy, Bach, 10,000 Maniacs, Screamin' Jay Hawkins.

"Where are we going?" he asked. He glanced down at her bare foot on the accelerator. She put the car into reverse. "Wait a minute," he said. "Stop this car." She put on the brake and turned off the ignition. "I just want to look at you," he said.

"Okay, look." She turned on the interior light and kept her face turned so that he was looking at her in profile. Something about her suggested a lovely disorder, a ragged brightness toward the back of her face.

"Are we going to do things?" he asked, touching her on the arm.

"Of course," she said. "Strangers should always do things."

SHE SAID that she would drop him off at his hotel, that he must change clothes. This was important. She would then pick him up. On the way over, he saw almost no one downtown. For some reason, it was quite empty of shoppers, strollers, or pedestrians of any kind. "I'm going to tell you some things you should know," she said. He settled back. He was used to this kind of talk on dates: everyone, everywhere, liked to reveal intimate details. It was an international convention.

They were slowing for a red light. "God is love," she said, downshifting, her bare left foot on the clutch. "At least I think so. It's my hope. In the world we have left, only love matters. Do you understand? I'm one of the Last Ones. Maybe you've heard of us."

"No, I have not. What do you do?"

"We do what everyone else does. We work and we go home and have dinner and go to bed. There is only one thing we do that is special."

"What is that?" he asked.

"We don't make plans," she said. "No big plans at all."

"That is not so unusual," he said, trying to normalize what she was saying. "Many people don't like to make—"

"It's not liking," she said. "It doesn't have anything to do with liking or not liking. It's a faith. Look at those buildings." She pointed toward several abandoned multistoried buildings with broken or vacant windows. "What face is moving behind all that? Something is. I live and work here. I'm not blind. *Anyone* can see what's taking place here. You're not blind either. Our church is over on the east side, off Van Dyke Avenue. It's not a good part of town but we want to be near where the face is doing its work."

"Your church?"

"The Church of the Millennium," she said. "Where they preach the Gospel of Last Things." They were now on the freeway, heading up toward the General Motors Building and his hotel. "Do you understand me?"

"Of course," he said. He had heard of American cult religions but thought they were all in California. He didn't mind her talk of religion. It was like talk of the sunset or childhood; it kept things going. "Of course I have been listening."

"Because I won't sleep with you unless you listen to me," she said. "It's the one thing I care about, that people listen. It's so damn rare, listening I mean, that you might as well care about it. I don't sleep with strangers too often. Almost never." She turned to look at him. "Anders," she said, "what do you pray to?"

He laughed. "I don't."

"Okay, then, what do you plan for?"

"A few things," he said.

"Like what?"

"My dinner every night. My job. My friends."

"You don't let accidents happen? You should. Things reveal themselves in accidents."

"Are there many people like you?" he asked.

"What do you think?" He looked again at her face, taken over by the darkness in the car but dimly lit by the dashboard lights and the oncoming flare of traffic. "Do you think there are many people like me?"

"Not very many," he said. "But maybe more than there used to be."

"Any of us in Sweden?"

"I don't think so. It's not a religion over there. People don't . . . They didn't tell us in Sweden about American girls who listen to Debussy and 10,000 Maniacs in their automobiles and who believe in gods and accidents."

"They don't say 'girls' here," she told him. "They say 'women.' "

SHE DROPPED him off at the hotel and said that she would pick him up in forty-five minutes. In his room, as he chose a clean shirt and a sport coat and a pair of trousers, he found himself laughing happily. He felt giddy. It was all happening so fast; he could hardly believe his luck. I am a very lucky man, he thought.

He looked out his hotel window at the streetlights. They had an amber glow, the color of gemstones. This city, this American

city, was unlike any he had ever seen. A downtown area emptied
of people; a river with huge ships going by silently; a park with
girls who believe in the millennium. No, not girls: women. He
had learned his lesson.

He wanted to open the hotel window to smell the air, but the
casement frames were welded shut.

After walking down the stairs to the lobby, he stood out in
front of the hotel doorway. He felt a warm breeze against his
face. He told the doorman, Luis, that he had met a woman on
Belle Isle who was going to pick him up in a few minutes. She
was going to take him dancing. The doorman nodded, rubbing
his chin with his hand. Anders said that she was friendly and
wanted to show him, a foreigner, things. The doorman shook his
head. "Yes, I agree," Luis said. "Dancing. Make sure that this is
what you do."

"What?"

"Dancing," Luis said, "yes. Go dancing. You know this
woman?"

"I just met her."

"Ah," Luis said, and stepped back to observe Anders, as if to
remember his face. "Dangerous fun." When her car appeared in
front of the hotel, she was wearing a light summer dress, and
when she smiled, she looked like the melancholy baby he had
heard about in an American song. As they pulled away from the
hotel, he looked back at Luis, who was watching them closely,
and then Anders realized that Luis was reading the numbers on
Lauren's license plate. To break the mood, he leaned over to kiss
her on the cheek. She smelled of cigarettes and something else —
soap or cut flowers.

She took him uptown to a club where a trio played soft rock
and some jazz. Some of this music was slow enough to dance to,
in the slow way he wanted to dance. Her hand in his felt bony
and muscular; physically, she was direct and immediate. He wondered, now, looking at her face, whether she might be an American Indian, and again he was frustrated because he couldn't tell

one race in this country from another. He knew it was improper to ask. When he sat at the table, holding hands with her and sipping from his drink, he began to feel as if he had known her for a long time and was related to her in some obscure way.

Suddenly he asked her, "Why are you so interested in me?"

"Interested?" She laughed, and her long black hair, no longer pinned up, shook in quick thick waves. "Well, all right. I have an interest. I like it that you're so foreign that you take cabs to the park. I like the way you look. You're kind of cute. And the other thing is, your soul is so raw and new, Anders, it's like an oyster."

"What?" He looked at her near him at the table. Their drinks were half finished. "My soul?"

"Yeah, your soul. I can almost see it."

"Where is it?"

She leaned forward, friendly and sexual and now slightly elegant. "You want me to show you?"

"Yes," Anders said. "Sure."

"It's in two places," she said. "One part is up here." She released his hand and put her thumb on his forehead. "And the other part is down here." She touched him in the middle of his stomach. "Right there. And they're connected."

"What are they like?" he asked, playing along.

"Yours? Raw and shiny, just like I said."

"And what about your soul?" he asked.

She looked at him. "My soul is radioactive," she said. "It's like plutonium. Don't say you weren't warned."

He thought that this was another American idiom he hadn't heard before, and he decided not to spoil things by asking her about it. In Sweden, people didn't talk much about the soul, at least not in conjunction with oysters or plutonium. It was probably some local metaphor he had never heard in Sweden.

IN THE DARK he couldn't make out much about her building, except that it was several floors high and at least fifty years old. Her living-room window looked out distantly at the river—once upstairs, he could see the lights of another passing freighter—and through the left side of the window he could see an electrical billboard. The name of the product was made out of hundreds of small incandescent bulbs, which went on and off from left to right. One of the letters was missing.

It's today's CHEVR LET!

All around her living-room walls were brightly framed water-colors, almost celebratory and Matisse-like, but in vague shapes. She went down the hallway, tapped on one of the doors, and said, "I'm home." Then she returned to the living room and kicked off her shoes. "My grandmother," she said. "She has her own room."

"Are these your pictures?" he asked. "Did you draw them?"

"Yes."

"I can't tell what they are. What are they?"

"They're abstract. You use wet paper to get that effect. They're abstract because God has gotten abstract. God used to have a form but now He's dissolving into pure light. That's what you see in those pictures. They're pictures of the trails that God leaves behind."

"Like the vapor trails," he smiled, "behind jets."

"Yes," she said. "Like that."

He went over to her in the dark and drew her to him and kissed her. Her breath was layered with smoke, apparently from ciga-rettes. Immediately he felt an unusual physical sensation inside his skin, like something heating up on a frypan.

She drew back. He heard another siren go by on the street outside. He wondered whether they should talk some more in the living room—share a few more verbal intimacies—to be really civilized about this and decided, no, it was not necessary, not when strangers make love, as they do, sometimes, in strange cities, away from home. They went into her bedroom and undressed each other. Her body, by the light of a dim bedside lamp, was as beautiful and as exotic as he hoped it would be, darker than his own skin in the dark room, native somehow to this continent. She had the flared shoulders and hips of a dancer. She bent down and snapped off the bedside light, and as he approached her, she was lit from behind by the billboard. Her skin felt vaguely electrical to him.

They stood in the middle of her bedroom, arms around each other, swaying, and he knew, in his arousal, that something odd was about to occur: he had no words for it in either his own language or in English.

They moved over and under each other, changing positions to stay in the breeze created by the window fan. They were both lively and attentive, and at first he thought it would be just the usual fun, this time with an almost anonymous American woman. He looked at her in the bed and saw her dark leg alongside his own, and he saw that same scar line running up her arm to her shoulder, where it disappeared.

"Where did you get that?" he asked.

"That?" She looked at it. "That was an accident that was done to me."

Half an hour later, resting with her, his hands on her back, he felt a wave of happiness; he felt it was a wave of color traveling through his body, surging from his forehead down to his stomach. It took him over again, and then a third time, with such force that he almost sat up.

"What is it?" she asked.

"I don't know. It is like . . . I felt a color moving through my body."

"Oh, that?" She smiled at him in the dark. "It's your soul, Anders. That's all. That's all it is. Never felt it before, huh?"

"I must be very drunk," he said.

She put her hand up into his hair. "Call it anything you want to. Didn't you feel it before? Our souls were curled together."

"You're crazy," he said. "You are a crazy woman."

"Oh yeah?" she whispered. "Is that what you think? Watch. Watch what happens now. You think this is all physical. Guess what. You're the crazy one. Watch. Watch."

She went to work on him, and at first it was pleasurable, but as she moved over him it became a succession of waves that had specific colorations, even when he turned her and thought he was taking charge. Soon he felt some substance, some glossy blue possession entangled in the air above him.

"I bet you're going to say that you're imagining all this," she said, her hand skidding across him.

"Who are you?" he said. "Who in the world are you?"

"I warned you," she whispered, her mouth directly over his ear. "I warned you. You people with your things, your rusty things, you suffer so bad when you come into where *we* live. Did they tell you we were all soulless here? Did they say that?"

He put his hands on her. "This is not love, but it—"

"Of course not," she said. "It's something else. Do you know the word? Do you know the word for something that opens your soul at once? Like that?" She snapped her fingers on the pillow. Her tongue was touching his ear. "Do you?" The words were almost inaudible.

"No."

"Addiction." She waited. "Do you understand?"

"Yes."

IN THE MIDDLE of the night he rose up and went to the window. He felt like a stump, amputated from the physical body of the woman. At the window he looked down, to the right of the billboard, and saw another apartment building with heavy decorations with human forms near the roof's edge, and on the third floor he saw a man at the window, as naked as he himself was but almost completely in shadow, gazing out at the street. There were so far away from each other that being unclothed didn't matter. It was vague and small and impersonal.

"Do you always stand at the window without clothes on?" she asked, from the bed.

"Not in Sweden," he said. He turned around. "This is odd," he said. "At night no one walks out on the streets. But there, over on that block, there's a man like me, at the window, and he is looking out, too. Do people stand everywhere at the windows here?"

"Come to bed."

"When I was in the army, the Swedish army," he said, still looking out, "they taught us to think that we could *decide* to do anything. They talked about the will. Your word 'willpower.' All Sweden believes this—choice, will, willpower. Maybe not so much now. I wonder if they talk about it here."

"You're funny," she said. She had moved up from behind him and embraced him.

IN THE MORNING he watched her as she dressed. His eyes hurt from sleeplessness. "I have to go," she said. "I'm already late." She was putting on a light blue skirt. As she did, she smiled. "You're a lovely lover," she said. "I like your body very much."

"What are we going to do?" he asked.

"We? There is no 'we,' Anders. There's you and then there's me. We're not a couple. I'm going to work. You're going back to your country soon. What are you planning to do?"

"May I stay here?"

"For an hour," she said, "and then you should go back to your hotel. I don't think you should stay. You don't live here."

"May I take you to dinner tonight?" he asked, trying not to watch her as he watched her. "What can we do tonight?"

"There's that 'we' again. Well, maybe. You can teach me a few words of Swedish. Why don't you hang around at your hotel and maybe I'll come by around six and get you, but don't call me if I don't come by, because if I don't, I don't."

"I can't call you," he said. "I don't know your last name."

"Oh, that's right," she said. "Well, listen. I'll probably come at six." She looked at him lying in the bed. "I don't believe this," she said.

"What?"

"You think you're in love, don't you?"

"No," he said. "Not exactly." He waited. "Oh, I don't know."

"I get the point," she said. "Well, you'd better get used to it. Welcome to our town. We're not always good at love but we are good at that." She bent to kiss him and then was gone. Happiness and agony simultaneously reached down and pressed against his chest. They, too, were like colors, but when you mixed the two together, you got something greenish-pink, excruciating.

He stood up, put on his trousers, and began looking into her dresser drawers. He expected to find trinkets and whatnot, but all she had were folded clothes, and, in the corner of the top drawer, a small turquoise heart for a charm bracelet. He put it into his pocket.

In the bathroom, he examined the labels on her medicines and facial creams before washing his face. He wanted evidence but didn't know for what. He looked, to himself, like a slightly different version of what he had once been. In the mirror his face had a puffy look and a passive expression, as if he had been assaulted during the night.

After he had dressed and entered the living room, he saw Lauren's grandmother sitting at a small dining-room table. She was eating a piece of toast and looking out of the window toward the river. The apartment, in daylight, had an aggressively scrubbed and mopped look. On the kitchen counter a small black-and-white television was blaring, but the old woman wasn't watching it. Her black hair was streaked with gray, and she wore a ragged pink bathrobe decorated with pictures of orchids. She was very frail. Her skin was as dark as her granddaughter's. Looking at her, Anders was once again unable to guess what race she was. She might be Arabic, or a Native American, or Hispanic, or black. Because he couldn't tell, he didn't care.

Without even looking at him, she motioned at him to sit down.

"Want anything?" she asked. She had a high, distant voice, as if it had come into the room over wires. "There are bananas over there." She made no gesture. "And grapefruit, I think, in the refrigerator."

"That's all right." He sat down on the other side of the table and folded his hands together, studying his fingers. The sound of traffic came up from the street outside.

"You're from somewhere," she said. "Scandinavia?"

"Yes," he said. "How can you tell?" Talking had become a terrible effort.

"Vowels," she said. "You sound like one of those Finns up north of here. When will you go back? To your country?"

"I don't know," he said. "Perhaps a few days. Perhaps not. My name is Anders." He held out his hand.

"Nice to meet you." She touched but did not shake his hand. "Why don't you know when you're going back?" She turned to look at him at last. It was a face on which curiosity still registered. She observed him as if he were an example of a certain kind of human being in whom she still had an interest.

"I don't know . . . I am not sure. Last night, I . . . ."

"You don't finish your sentences," the old woman said.

"I am trying to. I don't want to leave your granddaughter," he said. "She is"—he tried to think of the right adjective—"amazing to me."

"Yes, she is." The old woman peered at him. "You don't think you're in love, do you?"

"I don't know."

"Well, don't be. She won't ever be married, so there's no point in being in love with her. There's no point in being married *here*. I see them, you know."

"Who?"

"All the young men. Well, there aren't many. A few. Every so often. They come and sleep here with her and then in the morning they come out for breakfast with me and then they go away. We sit and talk. They're usually very pleasant. Men are, in the morning. They should be. She's a beautiful girl."

"Yes, she is."

"But there's no future in her, you know," the old woman said. "Sure you don't want a grapefruit? You should eat something."

"No, thank you. What do you mean, 'no future'?"

"Well, the young men usually understand that." The old woman looked at the television set, scowled, and shifted her eyes to the window. She rubbed her hands together. "You can't invest in her. You can't do that at all. She won't let you. I know. I know how she thinks."

"We have women like that in my country," Anders said. "They are—"

"Oh no you don't," the old woman said. "Sooner or later they want to get married, don't they?"

"I suppose most of them."

She glanced out the window toward the Detroit River and the city of Windsor on the opposite shore. Just when he thought that she had forgotten all about him, he felt her hand, dry as a winter leaf, taking hold of his own. Another siren went by outside. He felt a weight descending in his stomach. The touch of the old woman's hand made him feel worse than before, and he stood up quickly, looking around the room as if there were some object nearby he had to pick up and take away immediately. Her hand dropped away from his.

"No plans," she said. "Didn't she tell you?" the old woman asked. "It's what she believes." She shrugged. "It makes her happy."

"I am not sure I understand."

The old woman lifted her right hand and made a dismissive

wave in his direction. She pursed her mouth; he knew she had stopped speaking to him. He called a cab, and in half an hour he was back in his hotel room. In the shower he realized that he had forgotten to write down her address or phone number.

HE FELT itchy: he went out running, returned to his room, and took another shower. He did thirty push-ups and jogged in place. He groaned and shouted, knowing that no one would hear. How would he explain this to anyone? He was feeling passionate puzzlement. He went down to the hotel's dining room for lunch and ordered Dover sole and white wine but found himself unable to eat much of anything. He stared at his plate and at the other men and women consuming their meals calmly, and he was suddenly filled with wonder at ordinary life.

He couldn't stand to be by himself, and after lunch he had the doorman hail a cab. He gave the cabdriver a fifty and asked him to drive him around the city until all the money was used up.

"You want to see the nice parts?" the cabbie asked.

"No."

"What is it you want to see then?"

"The city."

"You tryin' to score, man? That it?"

Anders didn't know what he meant. He was certain that no sport was intended. He decided to play it safe. "No," he said.

The cabdriver shook his head and whistled. They drove east and then south; Anders watched the water-ball compass stuck to the front window. Along Jefferson Avenue they went past the shells of apartment buildings, and then, heading north, they passed block after block of vacated or boarded-up properties. One old building with Doric columns was draped with a banner.

PROGRESS! THE OLD MUST MAKE WAY
FOR THE NEW
Acme Wrecking Company

The banner was worn and tattered. Anders noticed broken beer bottles, sharp brown glass, on sidewalks and vacant lots, and the glass, in the sun, seemed perversely beautiful. Men were sleeping on sidewalks and in front stairwells; one man, wearing a hat, urinated against the corner of a burned-out building. He saw other men—there were very few women out here in the light of day—in groups gazing at him with cold slow deadly expressions. In his state of mind, he understood it all; he identified with it. All of it, the ruins and the remnants, made perfect sense.

AT SIX O'CLOCK she picked him up and took him to a Greek restaurant. All the way over, he watched her. He examined her with the puzzled curiosity of someone who wants to know how another person who looks rather attractive but also rather ordinary could have such power. Her physical features didn't explain anything.

"Did you miss me today?" she asked, half-jokingly.

"Yes," he said. He started to say more but didn't know how to begin. "It was hard to breathe," he said at last.

"I know," she said. "It's the air."

"No, it isn't. Not the air."

"Well, what then?"

He looked at her.

"Oh, come on, Anders. We're just two blind people who staggered into each other and we're about to stagger off in different directions. That's all."

Sentences struggled in his mind, then vanished before he could say them. He watched the pavement pass underneath the car.

In the restaurant, a crowded and lively place smelling of beer and roasted meat and cigars, they sat in a booth and ordered an antipasto plate. He leaned over and took her hands. "Tell me, please, who and what you are."

She seemed surprised that he had asked. "I've explained," she said. She waited, then started up again. "When I was younger I had an idea that I wanted to be a dancer. I had to give that up. My timing was off." She smiled. "Onstage, I looked like a memory of what had already happened. The other girls would do something and then *I'd* do it. I come in late on a lot of things. That's good for me. I've told you where I work. I live with my grandmother. I go with her into the parks in the fall and we watch for birds. And you know what else I believe." He gazed at the gold hoops of her earrings. "What else do you want to know?"

"I feel happy and terrible," he said. "Is it you? Did you do this?"

"I guess I did," she said, smiling faintly. "Tell me some words in Swedish."

"Which ones?"

"House."

"Hus."

"Pain."

"Smärta."

She leaned back. "Face."

"Ansikte."

"Light."

"Ljus."

"Never."

"Aldrig."

"I don't like it," she said. "I don't like the sound of those words at all. They're too cold. They're cold-weather words."

"Cold? Try another one."

"Soul."

"Själ."

"No, I don't like it." She raised her hand to the top of his head, grabbed a bit of his hair, and laughed. "Too bad."

"Do you do this to everyone?" he asked. "I feel such confusion."

He saw her stiffen. "You want to know too much. You're too

messed up. Too messed up with plans. You and your rust. All that isn't important. Not here. We don't do all that explaining. I've told you *everything* about me. We're just supposed to be enjoying ourselves. Nobody has to explain. That's freedom, Anders. Never telling why." She leaned over toward him so that her shoulders touched his, and with a sense of shock and desperation, he felt himself becoming aroused. She kissed him, and her lips tasted slightly of garlic. "Just say hi to the New World," she said.

"You feel like a drug to me," he said. "You feel experimental."

"We don't use that word that way," she said. Then she said, "Oh," as if she had understood something, or remembered another engagement. "Okay. I'll explain all this in a minute. Excuse me." She rose and disappeared behind a corner of the restaurant, and Anders looked out the window at a Catholic church the color of sandstone, on whose front steps a group of boys sat, eating popsicles. One of the boys got up and began to ask passersby for money; this went on until a policeman came and sent the boys away. Anders looked at his watch. Ten minutes had gone by since she had left. He looked up. He knew without thinking about it that she wasn't coming back.

He put a ten-dollar bill on the table and left the restaurant, jogging into the parking structure where she had left the car. Although he wasn't particularly surprised to see that it wasn't there, he sat down on the concrete and felt the floor of the structure shaking. He ran his hands through his hair, where she had grabbed at it. He waited as long as he could stand to do so, then returned to the hotel.

LUIS was back on duty. Anders told him what had happened.

"Ah," Luis said. "She is disappeared."

"Yes. Do you think I should call the police?"

"No," Luis said. "I do not think so. They have too many disappeared already."

"Too many disappeared?"

"Yes. All over this city. Many many disappeared. For how many times do you take this lady out?"

"Once. No, twice."

"And this time is the time she leave you?"

Anders nodded.

"I have done that," Luis said. "When I get sick of a woman, I too have disappeared. Maybe," he said suddenly, "she will reappear. Sometimes they do."

"I don't think she will." He sat down on the sidewalk in front of the hotel and cupped his chin in his hands.

"No, no," Luis said. "You cannot do that in front of the hotel. This looks very bad. Please stand up." He felt Luis reaching around his shoulders and pulling him to his feet. "What you are acting is impossible after one night," Luis said. "Be like everyone else. Have another night." He took off his doorman's cap and combed his hair with precision. "Many men and women also disappear from each other. It is one thing to do. You had a good time?"

Anders nodded.

"Have another good time," Luis suggested, "with someone else. Beer, pizza, go to bed. Women who have not disappeared will talk to you, I am sure."

"I think I'll call the police," Anders said.

"Myself, no, I would not do that."

He dialed a number he found in the telephone book for a local precinct station. As soon as the station officer understood what Anders was saying to him, he became angry, said it wasn't a police matter, and hung up on him. Anders sat for a moment in the phone booth, then looked up the Church of the Millennium in the directory. He wrote down its address. Someone there would know about her, and explain.

THE CAB let him out in front. It was like no other church he had ever seen before. Even the smallest places of worship in his own country had vaulted roofs, steeples, and stained glass. This building seemed to be someone's remodeled house. On either side of it, two lots down, were two skeletal homes, one of which had been burned and which now stood with charcoal windows and a charcoal portal where the front door had once been. The other house was boarded-up; in the evening wind, sheets of newspaper were stuck to its south wall. Across the street was an almost deserted playground. The saddles had been removed from the swing set, and the chains hung down from the upper bar and moved slightly in the wind. Four men stood together under a basketball hoop, talking together. One of the men bounced a basketball occasionally.

A signboard had been planted into the ground in front of the church, but so many letters had been removed from it that Anders couldn't make out what it was supposed to say.

> Ch r ch of   c Mill n i m
> Rev. H r old T.   oodst th, Pas or
> Everyo e   elco e!
> "Love on   other, lest ye f ll to   d t le for r le m!"

On the steps leading up to the front door, he turned around and saw, to the south, the lights of the office buildings of downtown Detroit suspended like enlarged stars in the darkness. After hearing what he thought was some sound in the bushes, he opened the front doors of the church and went inside.

Over a bare wood floor, folding chairs were lined up in five straight rows, facing toward a front chest intended as an altar, and everywhere there was a smell of incense, of ashy pine. Above the chest, and nailed to the far wall where a crucifix might be located in a Protestant church, was a polished brass circle with a nimbus of rays projecting out from its top. The rays were extended along the wall for a distance of four feet. One spotlight from a corner behind him lit up the brass circle, which in the gloom looked either like a deity-sun or some kind of explosion. The bare walls had been painted with flames: buildings of the city, some he had already seen, painted in flames, the earth in flames. There was an open Bible on the chest, and in one of the folding chairs a deck of playing cards. Otherwise, the room was completely empty. Glancing at a side door, he decided that he had never seen a church so small, or one that filled him with a greater sense of desolation. Behind him, near the door, was a bench. He had the feeling that the bench was filled with the disappeared. He sat down on it, and as he looked at the folding chairs it occurred to him that the disappeared were in fact here now, in front of him, sitting or standing or kneeling.

He composed himself and went back out onto the street, thinking that perhaps a cab would go by, but he saw neither cabs nor cars, not even pedestrians. After deciding that he had better begin walking toward the downtown area, he made his way down two blocks, past a boarded-up grocery store and a vacated apartment building, when he heard what he thought was the sound of footsteps behind him.

He felt the blow at the back of his head; it came to him not as a sensation of pain but as an instant crashing explosion of light in his brain, a bursting circle with a shooting aura irradiating from it. As he turned to fall, he felt hands touching his chest and his trousers; they moved with speed and almost with tenderness, until they found what they were looking for and took it away from him.

He lay on the sidewalk in a state somewhere between consciousness and unconsciousness, hearing the wind through the trees overhead and feeling some blood trickling out of the back of his scalp, until he felt the hands again, perhaps the same hands, lifting him up, putting him into something, taking him somewhere. Inside the darkness he now inhabited, he found that at some level he could still think: *Someone hit me and I've been robbed.*

At another, later, point, he understood that he could open his eyes; he had that kind of permission. He was sitting in a wheelchair in what was clearly a hospital emergency room. It felt as though someone were pushing him toward a planetary corridor. They asked him questions, which he answered in Swedish. "Det gör ont," he said, puzzled that they didn't understand him. "Var är jag?" he asked. They didn't know. English was what they wanted. He tried to give them some.

They X-rayed him and examined his cut; he would need four stitches, they said. He found that he could walk. They told him he was lucky, that he had not been badly hurt. A doctor, and then a nurse, and then another nurse, told him that he might have been killed—shot or knifed—and that victims of this type, strangers who wandered into the wrong parts of the city, were not unknown. He mentioned the disappeared. They were polite, but said that there was no such phrase in English. When he mentioned the name of his hotel, they said, once again, that he was lucky: it was only a few blocks away, walking distance. They smiled. You're a lucky man, they said, grinning oddly. They knew something but weren't saying it.

As the smaller debris of consciousness returned to him, he found himself sitting in a brightly lit room, like a waiting room, near the entryway for emergency medicine. From where he sat, he could see, through his fluent tidal headache, the patients arriving, directed to the Triage Desk, where their condition was judged.

They brought in a man on a gurney, who was hoarsely shouting. They rushed him through. He was bleeding, and they were holding him down as his feet kicked sideways.

They brought in someone else, a girl, who was stumbling, held up on both sides by friends. Anders heard something that sounded like Odie. Who was Odie? Her boyfriend? Odie, she screamed. Get me Odie.

Anders stood up, unable to watch any more. He shuffled through two doorways and found himself standing near an elevator. From a side window, he saw light from the sun rising. He hadn't realized that it was day. The sun made the inside of his head shriek. To escape the light, he stepped on the elevator and pressed the button for the fifth floor.

As the elevator rose, he felt his knees weakening. In order to clear his head, he began to count the other people on the elevator: seven. They seemed normal to him. The signs of this were coats and ties on the men, white frocks and a stethoscope on one of the women, and blouses and jeans on the other women. None of them looked like her. From now on, none of them ever would.

He felt that he must get home to Sweden quickly, before he became a very different person, unrecognizable even to himself.

At the fifth floor the doors opened and he stepped out. Close to the elevators was a nurses' station, and beyond it a long hallway leading to an alcove. He walked down this hallway, turned the corner, and heard small squalling sounds ahead. At the same time, he saw the windows in the hallway and understood that he had wandered onto the maternity floor. He made his way to the viewer's window and looked inside. He counted twenty-five newborns, each one in its own clear plastic crib. He stared down at the babies, hearing, through the glass, the cries of those who were awake.

He was about to turn around and go back to his hotel when one of the nurses saw him. She raised her eyebrows quizzically and spread her hands over the children. He shook his head to indicate no. Still she persisted. She pointed to a baby with white skin and a head of already-blond hair. He shook his head no once again. He would need to get back to the hotel, call his bank in Sweden, get money for the return trip. He touched his pants pocket and found that the wallet was still there. What had they taken? The nurse, smiling, nodded as if she understood, and motioned toward the newborns with darker skin, the Hispanics and light-skinned blacks and all the others, babies of a kind he never saw in Sweden.

Well, he thought, why not? Now that they had done this to him.

HE FELT himself nodding. Sure. That American word. His right arm rose. He pointed at a baby whose skin was the color of clay, the color of polished bronze, or flames. Now the nurse was wheeling the baby he had pointed to closer to the window. When it was directly in front of him, she left it there, returning to the back of the nursery. Standing on the other side of the glass, staring down at the sleeping infant, he tapped on the panel twice and waved, as he thought fathers should. The baby did not awaken. Anders put his hand in his pocket and touched the little turquoise heart, then pressed his forehead against the glass of the window and recovered himself. He stood for what seemed to him a long time, before taking the elevator down to the ground floor and stepping out onto the front sidewalk, and to the air, which smelled as it always had, of powerful combustible materials and their traces, fire and ash.

Saul and Patsy
Are Pregnant

~~~///

A SMELL of spilled gasoline: when Saul opened
his eyes, he was still strapped in behind his lap-
and-shoulder belt, but the car he sat in was upside
down and in a field of some sort. The Chevy's
headlights illuminated a sky of dirt, and, in the
distance, a tree growing downward from that
same sky. Perhaps he had awakened out of sleep
into another dream. "Patsy?" he said, turning
with difficulty toward his wife, strapped in on
the passenger side, her hair hanging down from
her scalp, but, from Saul's perspective, standing
up. She was still sleeping; she was always a sound
sleeper; she could sleep upside down and was
doing so now. The car's radio was playing Ray
Charles's "Unchain My Heart," and Saul said,
"You know, I've always liked that song." His
voice was thick from beer and cigarettes, and he
knew from the smell of the beer that this was no
dream because he had never been able to imagine
concrete details like that. No: he had fallen asleep
at the wheel, driven off the road, and rolled the
car. Here he was now. A thought passed through
him, in an unpleasant slow-motion way, that the
car was tilted and that the ignition was still on;

191

he switched it off and felt intelligent for three seconds, until the lap belt began to hurt him and he felt stupid again. No ignition, no Ray Charles. His mind, often anxiety-prone, was moving slowly down a dark narrow alleyway cluttered with alcohol, fatigue, and the first onset of shock. Probably the car would blow up, and the only satisfaction his mother would receive from this accident would come years from now, when she would tell people, when they were all through reminiscing about Saul, "I *told* him not to drink. I told him about drinking and driving. But he never listened to me. Never."

"Patsy." He reached out and gave her a little shake.

"What?"

"Wake up. I rolled the car. Patsy, we've got to get out of here."

"Why?"

"Because we have to. Patsy, we're not at home. We're in the car. And we're upside down. Come on, honey, wake up. Please. This is serious."

"I am awake." She blinked, twisted her head, then looked calm. Her opal earring glittered in the light of the dashboard. The earring made Saul think of stability and a possible future life, if only he would normalize himself. Patsy smiled. Saul thought that this smile had something to do with guardian angels who, judging from the evidence, flew invisibly around her head, beaming down benevolence. "Well," she said, turning to look at him carefully, "are you all right?"

"Yes, yes. I'm not hurt at all."

"Good. Well. Neither am I." She reached up for the ceiling. "This isn't fun. Did *you* do this, Saul?"

"Yes, I did. How do we get out of here?"

"Let's see," she said, speaking calmly, in her usual tone. "What I think you do is, you release your seat belt, stick your arms straight up, then lower yourself slowly so you don't break your neck. Then you crawl out the window, the higher one. That would be yours."

"Okay." He held his arm up, then unfastened the clasp and felt himself dropping onto the car's ceiling. He pulled himself toward the side window. When he was outside, he leaned over, back in, and extended his hand to Patsy to help her out.

As she was emerging through the window, she was smiling. "Haven't you ever rolled a car before, Saul? I have. Or one of my boyfriends did, years ago." She was breathing rapidly. She dragged herself out, dusted her jeans, and strolled a few feet beyond the car's tire tracks in the mud, as if nothing much had happened. "Beautiful night," she said. "Look at those stars."

"Jeez, Patsy," Saul said, jumping down close to where she stood, "this is no time for being cosmic." Then he gazed up. She was right: the sky was pillowed with stars. She took his hand.

"Are you really okay?" she asked. "My God, feel that. You're shaking like a leaf. You must be in shock." She wrapped her arms around him and held him for half a minute. "There," she said, "now that's better."

"We could have died," Saul said, his mouth dry.

"But we didn't."

"We *could* have."

"All right. Yes. I know. You can die in your sleep. You can die watching television." She watched him in the dark. "I wish I had been driving. It's so warm, a spring night, I think I would have been singing along to the radio. 'Unchain My Heart'—I would have been singing along to Ray Charles and we'd be home by now." She leaned over. "Smell the soil? It's loamy. You know, Saul, you should turn the car's headlights off."

"Patsy, the car is *wrecked!* Look at it."

"Don't be silly." She studied the car with equanimity, one hand raised to her face, the other hand cradling her elbow. Patsy's equanimity was otherworldly and constant. The combination of her beauty and her persistent unexplainable interest in Saul was the cause of his love for her; he loved her desperately and addictively. He had loved her this way before they were married, and it was still the same now. "Saul, that car is fine. We might be driving it tomorrow. The roof will have a dent, that's all. The car turned over slowly and softly. It's hardly hurt. What we have to do now is get to a house and call someone to help us. We could walk across this field, or we could just take the road back to Mad Dog's." Mad Dog was the host of the party they had come from. He was a high school gym teacher whose real name was Howard Bettermine. He looked, in fact, like a dog, but not a mad dog, as he thought, but a healthy and sober golden retriever.

"Patsy, I can't think. My brain has seized up."

"Well," she said, taking his hand, "I happen to like these stars, and that looks like a nice field, and I'd rather stay away from Highway 14 this time of night, what with the drunks on the road, and all." She gave him a tug on his sleeve, and he almost fell. "There you are," she said. "Come on."

AS SAUL walked across the field, hearing the slurp of his shoes in the spring mud, he saw the red blinking light of a radio tower in the distance, the only remotely friendly sight anywhere beneath the horizon. The fact that he was here at all was a sign, he thought, that his life was disordered, abandoned to chaos among Midwesterners, connoisseurs of violence and piety. He smelled manure, and somewhere behind him he thought he heard the predatory wingbeat of a bat or an owl.

Sick of cities, Saul had come to the Midwest two years before from Baltimore as a high school history teacher, believing that he was a missionary of some new kind, bringing education and the higher enlightenments to rural, benighted adolescents, but somehow the conversion had gone the other way, and now he was acting like them: getting drunk, falling asleep, rolling his car. It was the sort of accident Christians had. He felt obscurely that he had given up personal complexity and become simple. He was like those girls who worked in the drugstore arranging greeting cards. They were so straightforward that two seconds before they did anything, like give change, you could see every gesture coming. He was becoming like that. As a personality, Saul had once prided himself on being interesting, almost Byzantine, a challenge to any therapist. But he had lately joined the school bowling league and couldn't seem to concentrate on Schopenhauer on those days when, at odds and ashamed with himself, he took the battered Signet Classic down from the shelf and glowered at the incomprehensible lines he had highlighted with yellow magic marker in college. When he did understand, the philosopher no longer seemed profound, but merely a disappointed idealist with a bad prose style.

"Saul?"

"What?"

"I've been talking to you. Didn't you hear me?"

"Guess not. I was lost in thought." He stumbled against a bush. He couldn't see much, and he reached out for Patsy's hand. "I was thinking about girls in drugstores and Schopenhauer and the reasons why we ever came to this place."

"Oh. That. If you had been listening to me, you wouldn't have stumbled into that bush. That's what I was warning you about."

"Thanks. Where are we?"

"We're going down into this little gully, and when we get up on the other side, we'll be right near that farmhouse. What's the matter?"

He turned around and saw, across the field, the headlights of his car shining on the upturned dirt; he saw the Chevy's four tires facing the air; and he thought of his new jovial recklessness and of how he had almost killed himself and his wife. He said nothing because he was beginning to feel soul-sick, a state of spiritual dizziness. He was possessed by disequilibrium; he felt the urge to giggle, and was horrified by himself. He had a sudden marionette feeling.

"Saul! You're drifting off again. What is it this time?"

"Puppets."

"Puppets?"

"Yeah. You know: the way they don't have a center of gravity. They way they look . . ."

"Watch out for that stump."

He saw it in time to avoid it. "Patsy, how do you live in the world? This is a serious question."

"Stop it, Saul. You've been to a party. You're tired. Don't get metaphysical. It's two in the morning. You live in the world by knocking on the door of that farmhouse, that's what you do. You ring the doorbell."

They walked up past a shed whose flaking red door was hanging open, and they crossed the pitted driveway onto a small front yard with an evenly mowed lawn. A tire swing, pendulating slowly, hung down from a tree branch. Saul couldn't see much of the house in the dark, but as they crossed the driveway, kicking a few stones, they heard the bark of a dog from inside the house, a low bark from a big dog: a farm dog.

"Anti-Semites," Saul said.

"Just ring the bell."

After a moment, the porch light went on, yellow, probably a bug light, Saul thought; and then under the oddly colored glare a very young woman appeared, pale blond hair and skin, very pretty, but under the effect of the bulb, looking a bit jaundiced. With her fists she was rubbing her eyes with sleepiness. She wore a bathrobe decorated with huge blue flowers. Saul and Patsy explained themselves and their predicament—Saul was sure he had seen this young woman before—and she invited them in to use the phone. When they entered, the dog—old, with a gray muzzle—growled from under a living-room table but did not bother to get up. After Patsy and the woman, whose name was Anne, began talking, it developed that they had met before in the insurance office where Patsy worked as a secretary. They leaned toward each other. Their voices quickly rose in the transfiguration of friendliness as they disappeared into the kitchen. They seemed suddenly chipper and cheery to Saul, as if a new party had started. He had the impression that women enjoyed being friendly, whereas for men it was an effort; at least it was an effort for *him*. He heard Patsy dialing a number on a rotary phone, laughing and whispering as she did so.

He was left alone in the living room. Having nothing else to do, he looked around: high ceilings and elaborate wainscoting, lamps, table, rug, dog, calendar, the usual crucifix on the wall above the TV. There was something about the room that bothered him, and it took a moment before he knew what it was. It felt like a museum of earlier American feelings. Not a single ironic sentence had ever been spoken here. Everything in the room was sincere, everything except himself. In the midst of all this Midwestern earnestness, he was the one thing wrong. What was he doing here? What was he doing anywhere? He was accustomed to asking himself such questions.

"Mr. Bernstein?"

Saul turned around and saw the man of the house, who at first glance still seemed to be a boy, standing at the bottom of the stairs. He had his arms crossed, and he wore a sleepy but alert look on his face. He had on boxer shorts and a T-shirt, and Saul recognized, underneath the brown hair and the beard, a student from last year, Emory . . . something. Emory McPhee. That was it. A good-looking, solid kid. He had married this woman, Anne, last year, both of them barely eighteen years old, and moved out here. That was it. That was who they were. He had heard that Emory had become a housepainter.

"Emory," Saul said. The boy was stocky—he had played varsity football starting in his sophomore year—and he looked at Saul now with pleased curiosity. "Emory, my wife and I have had an accident, over there, on the other side of your field."

"What kind of accident, Mr. Bernstein?"

"We drove off the road." Saul waited, his hands in his pockets. Then he said the rest of it. "The car turned over on us."

"Wow," Emory said. "You're lucky you weren't hurt. That's amazing. Good thing it wasn't worse."

"Well, yes, but the car was going slow." Saul always sounded stupid to himself late at night. The boy's bland blue-eyed gaze stayed on him now, not moving, genial but inquisitorial, and Saul thought of all the people who had hated school, never liked even a minute of it, and had had a low-level suspicion of teachers for the rest of their lives. They voted down school bond issues. They didn't even like to buy pencils.

"How did you go off the road?"

"I fell asleep, Emory. We'd been to a party and I fell asleep at the wheel. Never happened to me before."

"Wow," Emory said again, but slowly this time, with no real surprise in his voice. He shrugged his shoulders, then bent down as if he were doing calisthenics. Saul knew that his own breath smelled of beer, so there was no point in going into that. "Do you want a cup of coffee? I'd offer you a beer, but we don't have it."

Saul tried to smile, an effort. "I don't think so, Emory, not tonight." He looked down at the floor, at his socks—he had taken off his muddy shoes—and saw an ashtray filled with cigarette butts. "But I would like a cigarette, if you could spare one."

"Sure." The boy reached down and offered the pack in Saul's direction. "Didn't know you smoked. Didn't know you had any vices at all."

They exchanged a look. "I'm like everybody else," Saul said. "Sometimes the right thing just gets loose from me and I don't do it." He picked up a book of matches. He would have to watch his sentences: that one hadn't made any sense. On the outside of the matchbook was an advertisement.

SECRETS
OF THE
UNIVERSE
***   see inside   ***

Saul put the matchbook into his pocket, after lighting up.

"Were you drunk?" the boy said suddenly.

"No, I don't think so."

"Teachers shouldn't drink," Emory said. "That's my belief."

"Well, maybe not."

Saul inhaled from the cigarette, and Emory came closer toward him and sat down on the floor. He gave off the smell of turpentine; he had flecks of white paint in his hair. He rubbed at his beard again. "Do you remember me from school?"

Saul leaned back. He tried to think. "Sure, of course I do. You sat in the back and you played with a ballpoint pen. You used to sketch the other kids in the class. Once when we were doing the First World War, you said it didn't make any sense no matter how much you read about it. I remember your report on the League of Nations. You stared out the window a lot. You sat near Anne in my class and you passed notes to her."

"I didn't think you'd remember that much." Emory whistled toward the dog, who thumped his tail and waddled over toward Emory's lap. "I wasn't very good. I thought it was a waste of time, no offense. I wanted to get married, that's all. I wanted to get married to Anne, and I wanted to be outside, not stuck inside, doing something, making a living, earning money. The thing is, I'm different now." He stood up, as if he were about to demonstrate how different he had become or had thought of something important to say.

"How are you different?"

"I'm real happy," Emory said, looking toward the kitchen. "I bet you don't believe that. I bet you think: here's this kid and his wife, out here, ignorant as a couple of plain pigs, and how could they be happy? But it's weird. You can't tell about anything." He was looking away from Saul. "Schools tell you that people like me aren't supposed to be happy or . . . what's that word you used in class all the time? 'Fulfilled'? We're not supposed to be that. But we're doing okay. But then I'm not trying to tell you anything."

"I know, Emory. I know that." Saul raised his hand to his scalp and touched his bald spot.

"Hell," Emory said, apparently building up steam, "you could work all your life to be as happy as Anne and me, and you might not do it. People . . . they try to be happy. They work at it. But it doesn't always take." He laughed. "I shouldn't be talking to you this way, Mr. Bernstein, and I wouldn't be, except it's the middle of the night, and I'm saying stuff. You know, I respected you. But now here you are, smelling of beer, and I remember the grades you gave me, all those D's, like you thought I'd never do anything in life except fail. But you can't hurt me now because I'm not in school anymore. So I apologize. See, I apologize for messing up in school and I forgive you for flunking me out."

Emory held out his hand, and Saul stood up and took it, thinking that he might be making a mistake.

"You shouldn't flunk people out of school," Emory said, "if you're going to get drunk and roll cars."

Saul held on to Emory's hand and tried to grip hard and diligently in return. "I didn't get drunk, Emory. I fell asleep. And you didn't flunk out. You dropped out."

Emory released his hand. "Well, I don't care," he said. "I was sleeping when you came to our door. I don't go to parties anymore because I have to get up and work. I sleep because I'm married and working. I can't see anything outside that."

Saul suddenly wanted Patsy back in this room, so that they could go. Who the hell did this boy think he was, anyway?

"Well, none of this is nothing," Emory said at last. "I don't blame you for anything at all. Maybe you did me a favor. I had to do something in my life, so I got my mom and dad to buy us this farm, which we're paying them back for every month, every dollar and cent, even though we aren't farming it. But we might. I'm reading up on horticulture." He pronounced the word carefully and proudly. "You want to sleep on the floor, you can, or on the sofa there. And there's a spare bed upstairs, you want it."

"Sorry about the bother," Saul said.

"No trouble."

"I appreciate this."

"Forget it." Emory patted the dog.

"But thanks."

"Sure."

The two men looked at each other for a moment, and Saul had one of his momentary envy-shocks: he looked at this man, this boy—he couldn't decide which he was—his hair standing up, and he thought: whatever else he is, this kid is real. Emory was living in the real; Saul felt himself floating up out of the unreal and rapidly sinking back into it, the lagoon of self-consciousness and irony.

In a kind of desperation, Saul looked up at the wall, where someone had hung a picture of a horse with a woman beside it, drawn in pencil, and framed in a cheap dime-store frame. The woman was probably Anne. She looked approximately like her. "Nice picture."

"I drew it."

"You have real talent, Emory," Saul said, insincerely examining the details. "You could be an artist."

"I *am* an artist," Emory said, staring at his old teacher. He picked at a scab on his calf. He turned his back to Saul. "I could draw from when I was a kid." A baby's cry came from upstairs. Emory looked at the ceiling, then exhaled.

"What kind of horse is that?" Saul asked, in what he vowed silently would be his final effort at politeness this evening. "Is that any kind of horse in particular?"

Emory was going back up the stairs. Then he faced Saul. "Every horse is some horse in particular, Mr. Bernstein. There aren't any horses in general. You can sleep there on the sofa if you want to. Good night."

"Good night."

Whatever happened to the God of the Old Testament, Saul wondered, looking at Emory's crucifix, the God that had chosen Israel above the other nations? Why had He allowed this scene to take place and why had He allowed Emory McPhee, this dropout, to make him feel like a putz? The Red Sea had not parted for Saul in a long time, in any sense; he felt he had about as much clout with God as, perhaps, a sparrow did. The whole evening |was a joke at Saul's expense. He heard God laughing, a sound like surf on rocks.

When Patsy and Anne came out of the kitchen, announcing that an all-night towing service was on its way and would probably have the car turned over and running in about half an hour, Saul smiled as if everything would be as fine as they claimed. Anne and Patsy were laughing. The flowers on Anne's bathrobe were laughing. God was, even now, laughing and enjoying the joke. Feeling like a zombie, and not laughing himself, but wearing the smile of the classically undead, Saul hooked his hand into Patsy's and went back outside. Some nights, he knew, had a way of not ending. This was one.

"How was Emory?" Patsy asked.

"Emory? Oh, Emory was fine," Saul told her.

ON THE DAYS following, Saul began to be obsessed with happiness, an unhealthy obsession, but he couldn't get rid of it. His feelings had always been the city of dreadful night. He was ball-and-chained to his emotions. On some days the obsession weighed him down so heavily that he could not get out of bed to go to work without groaning and reaching for his hair, as if to drag himself up bodily for the working day.

Prior to his accident and his meeting with Emory McPhee, Saul had managed to forget about happiness, a state that had once bothered him for its general inaccessibility. He loved Patsy; that he knew. Now he believed that compared to others he was actually and truly unhappy, especially since his mind insisted on thinking about the problem, poring over it, ragging him on and on. It was like the discontent of adolescence, the discontent with situations, but this was larger, the discontent with being itself, a psychic itch with nowhere to scratch. This was like Schopenhauer arriving at the door with a big suitcase, settling down for a long stay in the brain.

Patsy wasn't ordinary for many reasons but also because she loved Saul. Nevertheless, she was happy. Early in the summer he stole glances at her as she turned the pansies over in their pots, tamping them out, and planting them in the flower beds near the front walk. Blue sky, aggressive sun. She was barefoot, because she liked to go barefoot in the summer—her tomboy side—and she was squatting down in her shorts, wearing one of Saul's old flannel shirts flecked with dirt, and the sleeves rolled up to the elbows. Her brown hair fell backward down her shoulders. From the front window he watched her and studied her hands, those slender fingers doing their work. Helplessly, his eyes took in the clothed outlines of his wife. He was hers. That was that. She liked being a woman. She liked it in a way that, Saul now knew, he himself did not like being a man. There was the guilt, for one thing, for the manly hobbies of war and the thorough-going destruction of the earth. Patriarchy, carnage, rape, pleasurable bloodletting and bloodsport: Saul would admit a gender responsibility for all these, if anyone asked him, though no one ever did.

Patsy wiped her forehead with the back of her hand, saw Saul, and waved at him, turning her head slightly, tilting it, as she did whenever she caught sight of him. She smiled, a smile he had gladly given his life away for, a look of radiant intelligence. She was into the real, too; she didn't ponder it, she just planted flowers, if that was what she wanted to do. Beyond her was the driveway, and their Chevrolet with its bashed-in roof.

Saul turned from the window—it was Saturday morning—and tried to think for a moment of what he wanted to do. Taking a Detroit Tigers cap off the front-hall hat rack, he went outside and with great care put it, from behind and unannounced, on Patsy's head. "Save you from sunburn," he said, when she turned around and looked at him. "Save you from heatstroke."

"I want a motorcycle," Patsy said. "I've been thinking about it. We don't need another car, but I want a motorcycle. I always have. Women *can* ride motorcycles, Saul, don't deny it. Oh. And another thing." She dropped one hand into the dirt and balanced herself on it. "This morning I was trying to think of where the Cayuse Indians lived, and I couldn't remember, and we don't have an encyclopedia to check. We need that." She put her hand over her eyes, to shade them. "Saul, why are you looking like that? Are you in a state?"

"No, I'm not in a state."

"A motorcycle would do wonders for *both* of us, Saul. A small one, not one of those hogs. Do you like my petunias? Should I have some purple over there? Maybe this is too much red and white. What would you think of some dianthus right there?" She pointed with her trowel. "Or maybe some sweet william?"

"Sure, sure." He didn't know what either variety looked like. Flowers seemed so irrelevant to everything. He looked down at her bare feet.

"Where *did* the Cayuse Indians live, Saul?"

"Oregon, I think."

"What do you think about a motorcycle? For little trips into town."

"Sounds okay. They aren't exactly safe, you know. People get killed on motorcycles."

"Those people aren't careful. I'll be careful. I'll wear a helmet. I just want to do it. Imagine a girl—me—on one of those machines. Makes you feel good, doesn't it? A motorcycle girl in Michigan. The car's silly for small trips. Besides, I want to visit my friends in town."

It was true: Patsy already had many friends around Five Oaks. She belonged here, but she always seemed to belong anywhere. Now she stood up, dropping her trowel, and put her feet on Saul's shoes and leaned herself into him. The visor of her cap bumped into his forehead. But she embraced him for only a moment. "Want to help, Saul? Give me a hand putting the rest of these flowers in? And what do you say to some dianthus over there?"

"Not right now, Patsy. I don't think so."

"What's the matter?"

"I don't know."

"You *are* in a state."

"I guess I might be."

"What is it this time? Our recent brush with death? The McPhees?"

"What about the McPhees?" he asked. She had probably guessed.

"Well, they were so cute, the two of them. So sweet. And so young, too. And I know you, Saul, and I know what you thought. You thought: what have these two got that I don't have?"

She *had* guessed. She usually did. He stepped backward. "Yes," he said, "you're right. What *do* they have? And why don't I have it? I'm happy with *you,* but I—"

"You can't be like them because you can't, Saul. You fret. That's your hobby. It's how you stay occupied. You've heard about spots? About how a person can't change them? Well, I *like* your spots. I like how you're a professional worrier. And you always know about things like the Cayuse Indians. I'm not like that. And I don't want to be married to somebody like me. I'd put myself to sleep. But you're perfect. You're an early-warning system. You bark and growl at life. You're my dog. You do see that, don't you?"

"Yes." He nodded.

After he had kissed her, and returned to the house, he took the matchbook he had pocketed at the McPhees' up to his study. At his desk, with a pair of scissors, he cut off the flap of the matches, filled in his name and address, and wrote a check for six dollars to the Wisdom Foundation, located at post office box number in Cincinnati, Ohio. Just to make sure, he enclosed a letter.

Dear Sirs,

Enclosed please find a check for six dollars for your SECRETS OF
THE UNIVERSE. Also included is my name and address, written
on the back of this book of matches. You will also find them typed
at the bottom of this letter. Thank you. I look forward, very much,
to reading the secrets.

> Sincerely,
> Saul Bernstein

He examined the letter, wondering if the last sentence might
not be too ironic, too . . . something. But he decided to leave
it there. He took the letter, carefully stamped—he put commem-
orative stamps on all his important mail—out to the mailbox, and
lifted the little red flag.

He thought: I am no longer a serious person. My grandfather
read the Torah, my father read Spinoza and Heine and books on
immunology, and here I am, writing off for this.

ON HIS trips into town, Saul began to take the long route, past
the McPhees' house, slowing down when he was close to their
yard. Each time that he found himself within a mile of their farm,
he felt his stomach knotting up in anxiety and sick curiosity. He
felt himself twisting in the coils of something like envy, but not
envy, not exactly. Driving past, at evening, he occasionally saw
them out in the yard, Emory mowing or clipping, their baby
strapped to his back, Anne up on a ladder doing something to
the windows, or out in the garden like Patsy, planting. They
could have been anybody, except that, for Saul, they gave off a
disturbing aura of unreflective happiness.

The road was far enough away from their house and the
flaking shed so that they wouldn't see him; his car was just
another car. But on a particular Friday, in early June, after work,
he drove past their property and saw Emory in the front yard,

in the gold twilight, pushing his wife, who was sitting in the swing. Emory, the ex–football player, had on his face (through Saul's binoculars) a solemnly contented expression. The baby was in a stroller close by. His wife was in a white T-shirt and jeans, and Emory himself was wearing jeans but no shirt. She was probably proud of her breasts and he was probably proud of his shoulders. Anne held on to the ropes of the swing. Her hair flew up as she rose, and Saul, who took this all in in a few seconds, could hear her cries of delight from his car. Taking his surreptitious glances, he almost drove off the road again. Of course they were children, he knew that, and that wasn't it. They gave off a terrible glow. They had the blank glow of angels.

They lived smack in the middle of reality and never gave it a minute's thought. They'd never felt like actors. They'd never been sick with irony. The long tunnel of their thoughts had never swallowed them. They'd never had restless sleepless nights, the urgent wordless unexplainable wrestling matches with the shadowy bands of soul-thieves.

God damn it, Saul thought. Everybody gets to be happy except me. Saul heard Anne's cries. The sun was sweating all over his forehead. He felt faint, and Jewish, as usual. He turned on the radio. It happened to be tuned to a religious station and some choir was singing "When Jesus Wept."

"IT'S YOUR play, Saul."

"I know, I know."

"What's the matter? You got some bad letters?"

"The worst. The worst letters I've ever had."

"You always say that. You whine and complain. You're such a whiner, Saul, you even whine in bed. You were complaining that time just before you spelled out 'axiom' over that triple word score and got all those points last winter. You do this act when we play Scrabble and then you always beat me." Patsy was sitting cross-legged in her chair, as she liked to do, with a root beer bottle positioned against her instep, as she arranged and rear-ranged the letters on her slate.

Saul examined the board. The only word he could think of spelling out was "paint," but the word made him think of Emory McPhee. The hand of fate again, playing tricks on him. Glancing down at the words on the board, he thought he saw that same hand at work, spelling out some invisible story.

DEER
O
U
MOONBEAM
U   T   I
ROAR   LUST
KEY   D
Y

Saul always treated Scrabble boards as if they were fortune-telling equipment, with the order creating a narrative. Patsy had started with "moon," and he had added "beam" onto it. When she hung a "mild" from the moonbeam, he spiced it up with "lust," but she had replied to his interest in sex with "murky," hanging the word from that same moonbeam. "Mild" and "murky" came close to how he felt. His mother, Delia, had said so on the phone yesterday. "Saul, darling," she said, "you're sounding rather *dark* and *mysterious* lately. What's gotten into you?" He had not told her about the accident. She would have been alarmed and would have stayed alarmed for several months. She was a fierce mother, always had been. "I'm okay, Ma," he had said. "I'm just working some things through."

"You're leaving Five Oaks?" she asked hopefully.

"No, Ma," he had said. "This town suits me."

"All that mud, Saulie," she had said, dubious as always about the soil. "All those farms," she added vaguely. "You didn't have a *seder* this year, did you?"

"No, Ma. I told you we didn't."

"You didn't open the door for Elijah? When you were a little boy you loved to do that. When it came time in the service, you always ran for the front door and held it open and you—"

"Saul," Patsy said. "Wake up." She shook him. "You're wool-gathering."

"Just thinking about my mother," he said. He looked up at Patsy. "What are all those deer doing on our Scrabble board?" he asked. "Give me a swig of your root beer."

She handed it to him. He appreciated the golden color of the fine hairs on her arm in the lamplight. "I think I saw some, as a matter of fact," she said. "I thought I saw, what would you call it, a herd of deer, far in back, beyond our property line, a few nights ago. If you ever go back up to the roof, honey, give a look around. You might see them."

"Right, right." He couldn't put all five of his letters for "paint" on the Scrabble board. He removed the *t*. Pain. He held the four letters for pain in his hand, and he added them to the final *t* in "lust."

"Funny how 'pain' and 'lust' give you 'paint,' " Patsy said. "Sort of makes me think of the McPhees and the heady smell of turpentine."

They glanced at each other, and he tried to smile. A fly was buzzing around the bulb in the lamp. He was thinking of Patsy's new blue motorcycle out back, shiny and powerful and dangerous to ride. The salesman had said it could go from zero to fifty in less than six seconds. The hand of fate was ready to give him a good slapping around. It had announced itself. Saul felt a groan coming on. He looked at Patsy with helpless love.

"Oh, Saul," she said. She clambered into his lap. "You always get this way during these games. You always do." He saw her smiling in the reflection of his love for her. "You're so cute," she said, then kissed him a long time.

AT TEN MINUTES past three o'clock, he rose out of bed, half to get a glass of water and half to look out the back window. When he did, he saw them: just about where Patsy said they would be, far in the distance, beyond their property line, a herd of deer, silently passing. He ran downstairs in his underwear and went out through the unlocked back door as quietly as he could. He stood in the yard in the June night, the crickets sounding, the moon dimly outlined behind a thin cloud in the shape of a scimitar. In this gauzy light, the deer, about eight of them, distant animal forms, walked across his neighbor's field into a stand of woods. He found himself transfixed with the mystery and beauty of it. Hunting animals suddenly made no sense to him. He went back to bed. "I saw the deer," he said. he didn't know if Patsy was asleep. During the summer she wore Saul's T-shirts to bed, and that was all; her arms were crossed on her chest like a Crusader. "I saw the deer," he said again, and, awake or asleep, she nodded.

TWO DAYS later, the letter containing the secrets of the universe came from the Wisdom Foundation in Cincinnati. Saul sat down on the front stoop and tore the letter open. It was six pages long and had been printed out by a computer, with Saul's name inserted here and there.

Dear **Mr. Bernstein,**
Nothing is settled. Everything is still possible. Your thoughts are both yours and someone else's. Sometimes we say hello to the world and then goodbye, but that is not the end and we say hello again.

God is love, **Mr. Bernstein** , denying it only makes us unhappy. Riches are mere appearances. **Our thoughts are more real
than hammers and nails.** We can make others believe us, **Mr.
Bernstein**   , if the truth is in us. Buddha and Jesus the Christ and
Mohammed agreed about just about everything. Causing pain to
others only prolongs our own pain. A free and open heart is the best
thing. Live simply. Don't pretend to know something you don't
have a clue about. You may feel as if you are headed toward some
terrible fate, **Mr. Bernstein** , but that may not come to pass.
You can avoid it. **Throw your bad thoughts into the mental
wastebasket.** There is a right way and a wrong way to dispose of
bad thoughts. Everything about the universe worth knowing is
known. What is not known about the universe is not worth knowing. Follow these steps. Remember that trees will always be with
us, mice will always be with us, mosquitoes will always be with us.
Therefore, avoid mental cleanliness. Never start a sentence with the
words 'What if everybody . . .'

It went on for several more pages. Saul liked the letter. It
sounded like his other grandfather, Isaac, the pious atheist, an
exuberant man much given to laughter at appropriate and inappropriate moments, who offered advice as he passed out candy
bars and halvah to his grandchildren. This letter, from the Wisdom Foundation, was signed by someone named Giovanni
d'Amato.

Saul looked up. For a moment the terrifying banality of the
landscape seemed to dissolve into geometrical patterns of color
and light. Taken by surprise, he felt the habitual weight on his
heart lifting, as if by pulleys, or, better yet, birds of the spirit sent
by direct mail from Giovanni d'Amato. He decided to test this
happiness and got into the dented car.

He drove toward the McPhees'. The dust on the dirt road
whirled up behind him. He thought he would be able to stand
their middle-American happiness. Besides, Emory was probably
working. No: it was Saturday. They would both be home. He

would just drive by and that would be that. So what if they were happy, these dropouts from school? He was happy, too. He would test his temporary happiness against theirs.

The trees rushed past the car in a kind of chaotic blur.

He pressed down on the accelerator. A solitary cloud—wandering and thick with moisture—straying overhead but not blocking the sun, let down a minute's worth of vagrant rainbowed shower on Saul's car. The water droplets, growing larger, actually bounced on the car's hood. He turned on the wipers, causing the dust to streak in perfect protractor curves. The rain made Saul's car smell like a nursery of newborn vegetation. He felt the car drive over something. He hoped it wasn't an animal, one of those anonymous rodents like mice and chipmunks that squealed and died and disappeared.

Ahead and to the left was the McPhees'.

As usual, it looked like something out of an American genre painting, the kind of second-rate canvas hidden in the back of most museums near the elevators. Happiness lived in such houses, where people like Saul had never been permitted. In the bright standing sunshine its Midwestern Gothic acute angles pointed up straight toward heaven, a place where there had been a land rush for centuries and all the stakes had been claimed. Standing there in the bright theatrical sun—the rain had gone off on its way—the house seemed to know something, to be an answer ending with an exclamation point.

Saul crept past the front driveway. His window was open, and, except for the engine, there was no sound: no dog barking. And no sign, either, of Anne or Emory or their baby, at least out here. Nothing on the front porch, nothing in the yard. He *could* stop and say hello. That was permitted. He could thank them for their help two weeks ago. He hadn't done that. Emory's pickup was in the driveway, so they were at home; happy people don't go much of anywhere anyway, Saul thought, backing his car up and parking halfway in on the driveway.

When he reached the backyard, Saul saw a flash of white, on

legs, bounding at the far distances of the McPhees' field into the woods. From this distance it looked like nothing he knew, a trick of the eye. Turning, he saw Anne McPhee sitting in a lawn chair, reading the morning paper, a glass of lemonade nearby, their baby in the crib in the shade of the house, and Emory, some distance away, in a hammock, reading the sports section. Both of them held up their newspapers so that their view of him was blocked.

Quietly he crossed their back lawn, then stood in the middle, between them. Emory turned the pages of his paper, then put it down and closed his eyes. Anne went on reading. Saul stood quietly. Only the baby saw him. Saul reached down and picked out of the lawn a sprig of grass. Anna McPhee coughed. The baby was rattling one of its crib toys.

He waited for a minute, then walked back to his car. Anne and Emory had not seen him, and he felt like a prowler, a spy from God. He felt literally now what he had once felt metaphorically: that he was invisible.

When he was almost home, he remembered, or thought he remembered, that Anne McPhee had been sunning herself and had not been wearing a blouse or a bra. Or was he now imagining this? He couldn't be sure.

PATSY nudged him in the middle of the night. "I know what it is," she said.

"What?"

"What's bothering you."

He waited. "What? What is it?"

"You're like men. You're a man and you're like them. You want to be everything. You want to have endless endless potential. But then you grow up. And you're one thing. Your body is, anyway. It's trapped in *this* life. You have to say goodbye to the dreams of everything."

"Dreams of everything."

"Yes." She rolled over and made designs on his chest with her fingers. "Don't pretend that you don't understand. You want to be an astronaut and a Don Juan and Elvis and Einstein."

"No. I want to be Magic Johnson."

"Whatever. But you want to be all those people. You want to be a whole roomful of people, Saul. That's kid stuff." She let her head drop so that her hair brushed against him.

"What about you?"

"Me? I don't want to be anything else," she said sleepily, beginning to rub his back. "I don't have to be a great person. I just want to do a little of this and a little of that."

"What's wrong with ambitions?" he asked. "You could be great at something."

Her hand moved into his hair, tickling him. "Being great is too tiring, Saul, and it's boring. Look at the great ambition people. They're wrecking the earth, aren't they. They're leaving it in bits and scraps." She concentrated on him in the dark. "Saul," she said.

"Your diaphragm's not on."

"I know."

"But."

"So?"

"Well, what if?"

"What if? You'd be a father, that's what if." She had turned him so that she was right up against him, her breasts pressing him, challenging him.

"No," he said. He drew back. "Not yet. Let me figure this out on my own. There'd be no future."

"For the baby?"

"No. For me." He waited, trying to figure out how to say this. "I'd have to be one person forever. Does that make sense?"

"From you, it does." She pulled herself slightly away from him. They rearranged themselves.

THE FOLLOWING Saturday he drove into Five Oaks for a haircut. When his hair was so long that it made the back of his neck itch, he went to Harold, the barber, and had it trimmed back. Harold was a pale, slightly bland-looking Lutheran, a terrible barber with a nice disposition who was in the same bowling league with Saul and who sometime practiced basketball at the same times that Saul did. Many of the men in Five Oaks looked slightly peculiar and asymmetrical, thanks to Harold. The last time Saul had come in, Harold had been deep in a conversation with a woman who was accusing him of things; Saul couldn't tell exactly what Harold was being accused of, but it sounded like a lovers' quarrel, and Saul liked that. Anyone else's troubles diminished his.

By coincidence, the same woman was back again in the barbershop with her son, whose hair Harold was cutting when Saul rang the bell over the door as he entered. To pass the time and achieve a moment's invisibility, he picked up a newspaper from the next chair over and read the morning's headlines.

SHOTS FIRED AT HOLBEIN REACTOR
Iranian Terrorists Suspected

Shielded by his paper, Saul heard the woman whispering directions to Harold, and Harold's faint, exasperated "Louise, I can do this." Saul pretended to read the article; the shots, as it turned out, had been harmless. Even though there had been no damage, some sort of investigation was going on. Saul thought Iranians could do better than this.

There was more whispering, which Saul tried not to hear. After the woman had paid for her son's haircut and left, Saul sat himself down in Harold's chair.

"Hey, Saul," Harold said, covering him with the white cloth. "You always come in when she does. How do you do that?"

"Beats me. Her name Louise?"

"That's right. The usual trim, Saul?"

"The usual. Harold, this time try to keep it the same length on both sides, okay?"

"I try, Saul. It's just that your hair's so curly."

"Right, right." Saul saw his reflection in the mirror and closed his eyes. He felt like asking Harold, the Lutheran, a moral question. "Harold," he said, "do you ever wonder where your thoughts come from? I mean, do we own our thoughts, or do they come from somewhere else, or what? For example, you can't always control your thoughts or your impulses, can you? So, whose thoughts are those, anyway, the ones you can't control? And another thing. Are you happy? Be honest."

The scissors stopped clipping. "Gosh, Saul, are you okay? What drugs have you been taking lately?"

"No drugs. Just tell me: are your thoughts always yours? That's what I need to know."

The barber looked into the mirror opposite them. Saul saw Harold's plain features. "All right," Harold said. "I'll answer your question." Then, with what Saul took to be great sadness, the barber said, "I don't have many thoughts. And when I do, they're all mine."

"Okay," Sal said. "I'm sorry. I was just asking." He tried to slump down in his chair, but the barber said, "Sit up straight, Saul." Saul did.

DAYS LATER, Saul is asleep. He knows this. He knows he is asleep next to Patsy. He knows it is night, that cradle of dreams, but the earth's mad companion, the moon, is shining stainless-steel beams across the bed, and Saul is dreaming of being in a car that cannot stop rolling over, an endless flip of metal, and this time Patsy is not belted in, and something horrible must be happening to her, judging from the blur of her head. She is being hurt terribly thanks to the way he has driven the car, the mad way, the un-American way, and now she is walking across a bridge made of moonlight, and she falls. The door, Saul's door, is being kept open for Elijah, but Elijah does not come in. How will we recognize him? Saul's mind is not in Saul's head; it is above him, above his yarmulke, above his prayer shawl, his tallith. Patsy is hurt, she lies in a ditch. Deer and doubt mix with the murky roar of mild lust on the Scrabble board. And here, behind the barber chair, is Giovanni d'Amato, sage of Cincinnati, saying, "You shouldn't flunk people out of school if you're going to get drunk and roll cars." Saul, the child, is speaking to Saul the grown-up: "You'll never figure it out," and when Saul the adult asks, "What?" the child says, "Adulthood. Any of it." And then he says, "Saul, you're pregnant."

SAUL woke and looked over at Patsy, still sleeping. He groaned audibly with relief that she hadn't been hurt. What an annoying dream. He had never even owned a tallith. After putting on his shirt, jeans, and boots, he went downstairs, and, taking the keys off the kitchen table, stepped outside.

The motorcycle felt quiet and powerful underneath him as he accelerated down Whitefeather Road. He had driven a motorcycle briefly in college—until a small embarrassing accident—and the process all came back to him now. This one, Patsy's new machine, painted pink and blue, 250 cc's, was easy to shift, and the machine gave him the impression that he was floating, or better yet, was flowing down the archways of dark stunted Michigan trees. His eyes watered, and bugs hit him in the face as he speeded up. He felt the rear wheel slip on the dirt. He didn't know what he was doing out here and he didn't care.

He turned left onto Highway 14, and then County Road H, also dirt, and he downshifted, feeling the tight, close gears meshing, and he let the clutch out, slowing him down. On the road the cycle's headlight was like a cone, leading him forward, away from himself, toward something more inviting and dangerous. In the grip of spiritual longing, a person goes anywhere, traveling over the speed limit. The night was warm, but none of the summer stars was visible. Behind the clouds the stars were even now rushing away in the infinity of expanding space. Saul felt like an astral body himself. He too would rush away into emptiness. In the green light of the speedometer he saw that he was doing a respectable fifty. Up ahead the wintry white eyes of a possum glanced toward him before the animal scurried into the high grass near the road. Saul wanted to be lost but knew he could not be. He knew exactly where he was: fields, forest, fields. He knew each one, and he knew whom they belonged to, he had been here that long.

And of course he knew where he was going: he was headed toward the McPhees', that house of happiness, that castle of light, where everyone, man woman and child, would be sleeping soundly, the sleep of the happy and just and thoughtless. Saul felt blank, gripped by obsession, simultaneously vacant and full of shame.

He looked at his watch. It was past midnight. Their house would be dark.

But it was not. On the road beyond their driveway, Saul slowed down and then shut off the engine, holding on tightly to the handlebars as he stared, like the prowler he was, toward the second-floor windows, from which sounds emerged. From where he was spying, Saul could see Anne sitting in a rocking chair by the window with their baby. The baby was crying, screaming; Saul could hear it from the road. And, in the background, back and forth, Saul could see Emory McPhee pacing, the all-night walk of the helpless father. An infant with colic, a rocking mother, a pacing father, screams of infant misery, and now the two of them, Anne and Emory, beginning to shout at each other over what to do.

Saul turned his motorcycle around, pushed it down the road, then started the engine. He felt better. He could have gone to their front door and welcomed them as the official greeter of ordinary disharmony. I was always just as real as they were, Saul thought. I always was.

On the left the broken fences bordering the farmland quavered up and down and seemed to start bouncing, visually, as he accelerated. The lines on the telephone poles jumped nervously as he passed them until they had the rapid and nervous movements of pens on graph paper marking an erratic heartbeat. Rain—he hadn't known it was going to rain, no one had told him—began falling, getting into his eyes and falling with cold precision on the backs of his hands. He felt the cloth of his shirt getting soaked and sticking to his shoulders. The rain was persistent and serious. He felt the tires of Patsy's motorcycle slipping on the mud, nudging the rear end of the bike off, slightly, thoughtfully, toward the left side. Then the road joined up with the highway, where the traction improved, but the rain was falling more heavily now, soaking him so he could hardly see. He came to a bridge, slowed the bike, and huddled in its shelter for a moment, until the rain seemed to let up, and he set out again. Accelerate, clutch, shift. He wanted to get home to Patsy. He wanted to dry his hair and get into bed next to her. He couldn't think of anything else he wanted.

A few hundred feet from his own driveway, he looked through the rain, only a drizzle now, and he saw, looking back at him, their eyes lit by his headlamp, the deer he had seen before, closer now, crossing his yard. They stood there, on his property. But this time, there was another, a last deer, one he hadn't seen before, behind the others, slightly smaller, as if reduced somehow. It was an albino. In the darkness and rain it moved in a haze of whiteness. Seeing it, Saul thought: oh my God, I'm about to die. The deer had stopped, momentarily frozen in the light. The albino's eyes—it was a doe—were pink, and its fur was as white as linen. The animal flicked its tail, nervously hypnotized. Its terrible pink eyes, blank as neutron stars at the center, stared at him. Saul turned off the engine and the headlight. Now, in the dark, two brown deer bounded toward the west, but the albino stood still, staring in Saul's direction, a purposeful stare. He gripped the handlebars so hard that his forearms began to knot into a cramp. The animal was a sign of some kind, he was sure—only a fool would think otherwise—and he felt a moment of dread pass through his body as the deer now turned her eyes away from his and began to walk off into the night. He saw her disappear behind a maple tree in his backyard, but he couldn't follow her beyond that. He was trembling now. Shivering spasms began at his wet shoulders and passed down his chest toward his legs. The dread he had felt before was turning rapidly into pure spiritual fright, alternating waves of chill and heat rushing up and down his body. He remembered to get off the road. He pushed the motorcycle into the garage, kicking down its stand. He crossed the yard and reached the back door. The rain picked up again and sprayed into him as the wind carried it. In his mind's eye he saw the deer looking back at him. He had been judged, and the judgment was that he, Saul, was only and always himself, now and onward into infinity. His boots were wet. They stank of wet leather. Outside the back door, on the lawn, he took the boots off, then his wet shirt and his jeans. It occurred to him to stand there naked. With no clothes on he stood in the rain and the dark, and he fell to his knees. He wasn't praying. He didn't know what he was doing. Something was filling him up. It felt like the spirit, but the spirit of what, he didn't know. He lay down on the grass. One sob tore through him, and then it was over.

He felt like getting up and running out into the field in back of the house, but he knew he couldn't break through his self-consciousness enough to do that. In the rain, which no longer felt cold, he sensed that he was entering a condition that had nothing to do with happiness because it was so far beyond it. All he was sure about was that he was empty before and now was filled, filled with both fullness and emptiness. These emotions didn't quite make sense, but he didn't care. The emptiness was sweet; he could live with it. He hurried into the house and dried off his hair in the dark downstairs bathroom. Quickly he toweled himself down and then rushed up the stairs. There was a secret, after all. In fact there were probably a lot of secrets, but there was one he now knew.

He entered their bedroom. Rain fingernailed against the window glass. Patsy lay in bed in almost complete darkness, wearing one of Saul's T-shirts. Her arms were up above her head. He could see that she was watching him.

"Where were you?"

"I went out for a ride on your motorcycle. I couldn't sleep."

"Saul, it's raining. Why are you naked?"

"It's raining now. Not when I started."

"Why are you standing there? You don't have any clothes on."

"I saw something. I can't tell you. I think I'm not supposed to tell you what I saw. It was an animal. It was a private animal. Patsy, I took off my clothes and lay down on the lawn in the rain, and it didn't feel weird, it felt like just what I should do."

"Saul, what is this about?"

"I'm not sure."

"Try. Try to say."

"I think I'm pregnant."

"What does that mean?"

"I think it means that whoever I am, I'm not alone with myself."

"I don't understand that."

"I know."

"Come to bed, Saul. Get in under the sheet."

He climbed in and put his leg over hers.

"I can't quite get used to you," she said. "You're quite a mess of metaphors, Saul, you know that."

"Yes."

"A man being pregnant." She put her hand familiarly on his thigh. "I wonder what that means."

"It's a feeling, Patsy. It's a secret. Men have secrets, too."

"I never said they didn't. They love secrets. They have lodges and secret societies and stuff—the Fraternal Order of Moose."

"Can we make love now, right this minute? Because I love you. I love you like crazy."

"I love you, too, Saul. What if you make *me* pregnant? It

could happen. What if I get knocked up? Is it all right now?"

"Yeah. What's the problem?"

"What will we say, for example?"

"We'll say, 'Saul and Patsy are pregnant.' "

"Oh sure we will."

"Okay, we won't say it." He had thrown the sheet back and was kissing the backs of her knees.

"Are you crying? Your face is wet."

"Yes."

"But you're being so jokey."

"That's how I handle it."

"Why are you crying?"

"Because . . ." He wanted to get this right. "Because there are signs and wonders. What can I tell you? It's all a feeling. In the morning, I'll deny I said this."

She was kissing him now, but she stopped, as if thinking about his recent sentences. "You *want* to make me pregnant, too, don't you?"

"Yes."

"So you're not alone in this."

"That's right."

"One more little ambassador from the present to the future. That's what you want."

"Sort of." He moved up and took her fingers one by one into his mouth and bit them tenderly. Patsy had started to hum. She was humming "Unchain My Heart." Then she opened her mouth and sang quietly, "Unchain my heart, and set me free."

"I'll try, Patsy."

"Yes." They often talked while they made love. A moment later, she said, "This won't solve anything. There'll be tears. People—babies—you know how they cry."

"Yes." And even now Saul felt as though he heard someone wailing softly in the next room. Still he continued. Then he had a thought. "Patsy," he said, "the window. We should stand by the window."

"Why?"

"To try it." He disentangled himself from her, stood, and brought her over to the window. He opened it so that droplets of rain blew in over them. "Now," he said. There was a bit of lightning, and he lifted her to him. She held on, her arms clasped behind his neck. He felt as though a thousand eyes, but not human eyes, were looking in on them with tender indifference. They were and were not interested. They would and would not care. They would and would not love them. Finally they would turn away, as they tended to turn away from all human things, in time. Saul felt Patsy begin to tremble, a slight shivering along her back, a rising in tension before release. More rain came in, warm June rain on his arm. He felt Patsy's mouth on his curls, the ones recently cut by Harold; she was panting, and so was he, and for a split second, he understood it all. He understood everything, the secret of the universe. After an instant, he lost it. Having lost the secret, forgotten it, he felt the usual onset of the ordinary, of everything else, with Patsy around him, the two of them in their own familiar rhythms. He would not admit to anyone that he had known the secret of the universe for a split second. That part of his life was hidden away and would always be: the part that makes a person draw in the breath quickly, in surprise, and stare at the curtains in the morning, upon awakening.